THE BODY
IN THE
CASKET

The Body
in the
Casket

A FAITH FAIRCHILD MYSTERY

Katherine
Hall Page

WM

WILLIAM MORROW

An Imprint of HarperCollinsPublishers

HarperCollins books may be purchased for educational, business, or sales promotional use. For information, please email the Special Markets Department at SPsales@harpercollins.com.

FIRST EDITION

Title page spread photograph © by Ruud Morijn/Shutterstock, Inc.
Chapter opener art (masks) © by Shutterstock, Inc.

Library of Congress Cataloging-in-Publication Data

Names: Page, Katherine Hall, author.
Title: The body in the casket : a Faith Fairchild mystery / Katherine Hall Page.
Description: New York, NY : William Morrow, 2017. | Series: Faith Fairchild mysteries ; 24
Identifiers: LCCN 2017042258 (print) | LCCN 2017045133 (ebook) | ISBN 9780062439581 (ebook) | ISBN 9780062439567 (hardcover) | ISBN 9780062439574 (mass market) | ISBN 9780062688071 (large print)
Subjects: LCSH: Fairchild, Faith (Fictitious character)—Fiction. | Women in the food industry—Fiction. | Caterers and catering—Fiction. | Women detectives—Fiction. | BISAC: FICTION / Mystery & Detective / Women Sleuths. | GSAFD: Mystery fiction.
Classification: LCC PS3566.A334 (ebook) | LCC PS3566.A334 B652 2017 (print) | DDC 813/.54—dc23
LC record available at https://lccn.loc.gov/2017042258

ISBN 978-0-06-243956-7

17 18 19 20 21 LSC 10 9 8 7 6 5 4 3 2 1

FOR THE BRACKEN FAMILY:

Jeanne, Ray, Mollie—and Lisa
who left us much too soon but taught us Jeremiah
the Bullfrog's joyful wisdom by her example

Before you embark on a journey of revenge, dig two graves.

—CONFUCIUS (551–479 B.C.)

ACKNOWLEDGMENTS

Many thanks to the following: Dr. Robert DeMartino, Peter Filichia (theater critic, author, and host of the annual Theatre World Awards); at Greenburger: Faith Hamlin, Stefanie Diaz, and Ed Maxwell; at HarperCollins: Katherine Nintzel, Danielle Bartlett, Gena Lanzi, Shelly Perron, and Virginia Stanley.

The Body
in the
Casket

MAX DANE PRESENTS

A Birthday Party

Mine

Come As You Are—

Or Be Cast

ROWAN HOUSE
HAVENCREST, MASSACHUSETTS

January 29–31

Max Dane. It sounded like a made-up name, Faith thought when she first heard it. A stage name or the name of a character in a play. The thought turned out to be appropriate. But Maxwell Dane was the name on his birth certificate.

Faith learned his name was real over the course of that very long weekend. She learned other things, too. About him, his guests—and herself.

Would she have taken the job if she'd foreseen it all?

Probably not.

CHAPTER 1

"Have Faith in Your Kitchen," Faith Fairchild said, answering the phone at her catering firm. She'd been busy piping choux pastry for éclairs onto a baking sheet.

"Mrs. Fairchild?"

"Yes? This is Faith Fairchild. How may I help you?"

"Please hold for Max Dane." The voice had a plummy, slightly British tone, reminiscent of Jeeves, or *Downton Abbey*'s Carson. The only Max Dane Faith had heard of had been a famous Broadway musical producer, but she was pretty sure he'd died years ago. This must be another Max Dane.

She was put through quickly and a new voice said, "Hi. I know this is short notice, but I am very much hoping you are available to handle a house party I'm throwing for about a dozen guests at the end of the month. A Friday to Sunday. Not just dinner, but all the meals."

Faith had never catered anything like this. A Friday to Sunday sounded like something out of a British pre–World War II country house novel—kippers for breakfast, Fortnum & Mason–type hampers for the shoot, tea and scones, drinks and nibbles, then saddle of lamb or some other large haunch of meat for dinner with vintage clarets followed by port and Stilton—for the men only. She was intrigued.

"The first thing I need to know is where you live, Mr. Dane. Also, is this a firm date? We've had a mild winter so far, but January may still deliver a wallop like last year."

A Manhattan native, Faith's marriage more than twenty years ago to the Reverend Thomas Fairchild meant a radical change of address—from the Big Apple to the orchards of Aleford, a small suburb west of Boston. Faith had never become used to boiled dinners, First Parish's rock hard pews, and most of all, New England weather. By the end of the previous February there had been seventy-five inches of snow on the ground, and you couldn't see through the historic parsonage's ground-floor windows or open the front door. Teenage son Ben struggled valiantly to keep the back door clear, daily hewing a path to the garage. The resulting tunnel resembled a clip from *Nanook of the North*.

"I'm afraid the date is firm. The thirtieth is my birthday. A milestone one, my seventieth." Unlike his butler or whoever had called Faith to the phone, Max Dane's voice indicated he'd started life in one of the five boroughs. Faith was guessing the Bronx. He sounded a bit sheepish when he said "my birthday," as if throwing a party for himself was out of character. "And I live in Havencrest. It's not far from Aleford, but I'd want you to be available at the house the whole time. Live in."

Leaving her family for three days was not something Faith did often, especially since Sunday was a workday for Tom and all too occasionally Saturday was as well, as he "polished" his sermon. (His term, which she had noticed over the years, could mean writing the whole thing.)

Ben and Amy, two years younger, seemed old enough to be on their own, but Faith had found that contrary to expectations, kids needed parents around more in adolescence than when they were toddlers. Every day brought the equivalent of scraped knees, and they weren't the kind of hurts that could be soothed by *Pat the Bunny* and a chocolate chip cookie. She needed more time to think about taking the job. "I'm not sure I can leave my family—" was interrupted.

"I quite understand that this would be difficult," Dane said and then he named a figure so far above anything she had ever been offered that she actually covered her mouth to keep from gasping out loud.

"Look," he continued. "Why don't you come by and we'll talk in person? You can see the place and decide then. I don't use it myself, but the kitchen is well equipped—the rest of the house, too. I'll e-mail directions and you can shoot me some times that work. This week if possible. I want to send out the invites right away."

Well, it wouldn't hurt to talk, Faith thought. And she did like seeing other people's houses. She agreed, but before she hung up curiosity won out and she asked, "Are you related to the Max Dane who produced all those wonderful Broadway musicals?"

"Very closely. As in one and the same. See you soon."

Faith put the phone down and turned to Pix Miller, her closest friend and part-time Have Faith employee.

"That was someone wanting Have Faith to cater a weekend-long birthday celebration—for an astonishing amount of money." She named the figure in a breathless whisper. "His name is Max Dane. Have you ever heard of him?"

"Even I know who Max Dane is. Sam took me to New York the December after we were married and we saw one of his shows. It was magical—the whole weekend was. No kids yet. We were kids ourselves. We skated at Rockefeller Center by the tree and . . ."

Her friend didn't go in for sentimental journeys, and tempted as she was to note Pix and Sam skated on Aleford Pond then and now, Faith didn't want to stop the flow of memories. "Where did you stay? A suite at the Plaza?" Sam was a very successful lawyer.

Pix came down to earth. "We barely had money for the show

and pretheater dinner at 21. That was the big splurge. I honestly can't remember where we stayed and I should, because that's where—" She stopped abruptly and blushed, also unusual Pix behavior.

"Say no more. Nine months later along came Mark?"

"Something like that," Pix mumbled and then in her usual more assertive voice added, "you have to do this. Not because of the money, although the man must be loaded! Think of who might be there. And the house must be amazing. We don't have anything booked for then, and I can keep an eye on the kids."

The Millers lived next door to the parsonage, and their three children, now grown, had been the Fairchilds' babysitters. Pix played a more essential role: Faith's tutor in the unforeseen intricacies of child rearing as well as Aleford's often arcane mores. Faith's first social faux pas as a new bride—inviting guests for dinner at eight o'clock—had happily been avoided when her first invite, Pix, gently told Faith the town's inhabitants would be thinking bed soon at that hour, not a main course.

Faith had started her catering business in the city that never slept before she was married and was busy all year long. Here January was always a slow month for business. The holidays were over and things didn't start to pick up until Valentine's Day—and even then scheduling events was risky. It all came down to the weather.

Pix was at the computer. Years ago she'd agreed to work at Have Faith keeping the books, the calendar, inventory—anything that did not involve any actual food preparation.

"We have a couple of receptions at the Ganley Museum and the MLK breakfast the standing clergy host."

The first time Faith heard the term "standing clergy," which was the town's men and women of any cloth, she pictured an upright, somberly garbed group in rows like ninepins. And she hadn't been far off.

"That's pretty much it," Pix added, "except for a few luncheons and Amelia's baby shower—I think she babysat for you a couple of times when she was in high school."

"I remember she was very reliable," Faith said.

"Hard to believe she's the same age as Samantha and having her second!" Pix sounded wistful. She was the type of woman born to wear a I SPOIL MY GRANDCHILDREN tee shirt. Faith wouldn't be surprised if there were a drawer somewhere in the Millers' house filled with tiny sweaters and booties knit by Pix, "just to be ready." Mark Miller, the oldest, was married, but he and his wife did not seem to be in a rush to start a family.

Samantha, the middle Miller, had a long-term beau, Caleb. They were living together in trendy Park Slope, Brooklyn, and Sam, an old-fashioned paterfamilias, had to be restrained from asking Caleb his intentions each time the young couple came to Aleford. Pix was leaning that way herself, she'd told Faith recently, noting that young couples these days were so intent on careers they didn't hear the clock ticking.

Faith had forgotten that Amelia—who apparently had paid attention to time—was Samantha's age and quickly changed the subject to what was uppermost in her mind—the Dane job. "Where is Havencrest?" she asked. "I thought I knew all the neighboring towns."

"It's not really a town so much as an enclave between Weston and Dover. I don't think it even has a zip code. I've never been there, but Mother has. You can ask her about it. The houses all date to the late nineteenth and early twentieth centuries. I believe there's a gatehouse at the entrance. It's an early equivalent of the midcentury modern planned communities like Moon Hill in Lexington. Havencrest wasn't a bunch of architects like that one though. Just very rich Boston Brahmin families who wanted privacy and plenty of space. I wonder how Max Dane ended up there? From what Mother has said, the houses don't change hands, just generations."

"I think I'll check my e-mail and see if there's anything from him yet," Faith said. "And maybe drop by to see Ursula on my way home." Stopping to visit with Ursula Lyman Rowe, Pix's mother, was no chore. The octogenarian was one of Faith's favorite people. She turned back to the éclairs, which were part of a special order, and added a few more to bring to her friend.

"I know you'll take the job," Pix said. "I'm predicting the weekend of a lifetime!"

Driving over to Ursula's house, Faith thought about Max Dane's birthday party. She was approaching a milestone birthday herself, although many years away from seventy, and had been feeling blue. She liked to think of herself as a person to whom age didn't matter. That with family, friends, good health, and the many advantages she'd had in life, she should simply count her lucky stars, not years. Yet time seemed to be passing more quickly lately and she found herself wincing as she scrolled the drop-down year-of-birth menu online when filling out forms. The only person she felt free to commiserate with was her sister, Hope, a year younger and virtually in the same boat. They had a pact to tell each other when it was time for a discreet vacation to do something about their suitcases—not the carry-on kind, but under the eyes—one of the Sibley women's less welcome inherited gifts.

It was more than appearance, though. Rather weltschmerz, mild depression, the "is this what the rest of my life will be?" -ness. Hope, a financial lawyer in New York City, as was her husband, Quentin, had even described herself as being in a "rut." With a doorman prewar three-bedroom, two and a half baths, eat-in kitchen, view of the Park on the Upper East Side and a house in the Hamptons, it was a pretty comfy rut, but Faith knew what she meant. "I'm thinking of taking flying lessons, getting a pilot's license," Hope had said the last time they'd talked. Faith had suggested that Hope should reread Erica Jong's *Fear of Flying* for fun instead. Maybe go for a less extreme hobby, although not the one in the book.

She pulled up to Ursula's house. There was a car in the driveway, which Faith assumed belonged to the student who was living there now, or maybe the home health aide who came several times a week. Concern about Ursula's being on her own in the large Victorian house had been solved by moving her bedroom to the first-floor library and converting a small bath off the kitchen into one that was handicapped accessible. The student was around at night to give Ursula her dinner and argue about who would do the dishes. During vacations, Pix happily filled in. She'd wanted her mother to move into her house—"Plenty of room now that all the kids are gone"—but Ursula had refused, pointing out that they had avoided mother/daughter conflicts ever since a few rocky shoals when Pix was fourteen and she wasn't about to chance it now.

Faith rang the bell and was surprised when an elderly gentleman answered. "Hello," she said. "I'm Faith Fairchild. Is Ursula home?"

"Faith? Is that you? Come into the living room. We're just having drinks," Ursula said.

"I'm Austin Stebbins," the man said, putting out his hand.

Faith shook it. He had a strong grip, and as he led the way from the hall, Faith noticed his straight spine, full head of thick silver hair, and well-cut navy chalk stripe suit. She knew the name of Ursula's lawyer, so this wasn't a visit from him, yet Mr. Stebbins had that sort of air about him. Family retainer air.

"Don't get up," she said, going to kiss Ursula who was starting to stand. "I just wanted to drop off these éclairs. I'll put them away in the kitchen."

"You spoil me. Thank goodness. Get yourself a glass and have some sherry with us."

Faith thought she would. It was only five o'clock and she'd cooked chili yesterday for tonight's dinner. All that remained was to heat it up, grate some cheese, and make a salad.

When she returned from the kitchen, Austin and Ursula were sitting next to each other on the pretty rosewood couch that had been Ursula's grandmother's. The two leapt apart like guilty teenagers, although so far as Faith could tell they had only had heads close together in conversation. Curiouser and curiouser.

"Austin is an old friend," Ursula said.

"Not all that old," he said with a smile. "But we do go way back. I have been living away from Boston, my hometown, for most of my adult life and now happily find myself contemplating a permanent return. And considering the Stebbins plot is in Mount Auburn Cemetery, it may well be forever." There was that smile again. He had a Kirk or Michael Douglas cleft in his chin that deepened each time.

About to gently prod for more information, Faith felt her phone vibrate in her pocket. "Sorry," she said, checking the caller. "It's Tom." She added for Austin's benefit, "My husband."

Ursula waved permission. "Go ahead, take it."

"Hi, honey," Faith said to Tom, "I'm at Ursula's."

"Could you get home as soon as possible? There's a Planning Board meeting at six and Ben's having a meltdown."

Ben was not her meltdown child. Faith quickly said good-bye to Ursula and her guest. Questions about Mr. Stebbins would have to wait for another time. As would the ones regarding Havencrest.

When Faith got home, Tom was at the door, his overcoat on. "Gotta run. Have no idea why the chairperson called a special meeting. Ben's in his room. Won't talk, but raced in, looked like he was about to cry, and slammed his bedroom door shut. Told me to go away." He gave his wife a quick kiss and was gone before Faith could ask if he'd eaten anything. He probably had, although it wasn't the chili. That was still in the fridge, she saw, taking it out and setting it on the counter. The nature of the job meant that the men of the cloth she knew—husband, father, and grandfather—

had all been able hunter/gatherers, grabbing sustenance on the fly. Interrupted meals were a way of life. The crumbs on the breadboard and a mustard-covered knife in the sink meant Tom had made a sandwich.

Amy was at a play rehearsal—Thornton Wilder's *Our Town*. She'd landed the part of Emily's mother, Mrs. Webb, as much for her height as her skills as a thespian, Faith suspected. Both her children were going to be even taller than their parents before they were done growing. Faith grazed five foot eight, and Tom was six foot one.

Something must have happened at school to set Ben off, but what? They'd had a few issues around his college choices, but that was over before Christmas, and now it was just a waiting game. He was a good student with decent scores, a better-than-average soccer player, state finals track star plus enough extracurricular activities including a regular volunteer commitment at the Boston Food Bank to make him an attractive candidate.

She took out a wedge of Monterey Jack. Maybe she should grate the cheese now to give him time to calm down. She sighed. Who was she kidding? She was the one who wanted some time. Whatever it was, it was big. Amy was sunshine and tears. Ben steady as a rock.

No more avoiding the problem. She went upstairs to try to find out what crowbar had been used on her beloved boulder.

"Ben?" She tapped on his door. When there was no answer, she said, "Please let me in. Dad said you were upset about something."

Still no answer. She tried the knob. The door was locked. "Honey, come down and have something to eat while we talk." Food, the panacea for most ills.

She waited. Dead silence. She waited a minute more. "Okay, when you're ready. I'll be in the kitchen."

She was turning to go back down the hall when the door was flung open so hard it hit the wall with a loud bang. Ben's face was bright red and streaked with tears, instantly transporting Faith back many years into his childhood. She had to stop herself from reaching to cradle him in her arms.

"She needs some space!" He spat out the words.

No need to ask whom he was talking about.

Mandy Hitchcock.

Years ago at the urgings of the Millers and Ursula, the Fairchilds had rented a cottage on Sanpere Island in Penobscot Bay, Maine. Ursula's Bostonian grandparents had built a large summerhouse there, The Pines, back when the trip meant travel first by train, then coastal steamer. Dubious about freezing cold water and rocky beaches, Faith had given in to their and her outdoorsy husband's urgings. She figured one summer wouldn't kill her and then they could hit her kind of beach—one preferably on Long Island, or even the South of France. Instead, the Fairchilds ended up buying land and building their own house—not on the scale of The Pines—and Faith had succumbed to the beauty and peace of the island. Her kids adored it, too. Two summers ago Ben had met Mandy at The Laughing Gull Lodge, where both were working. Ben fell for the girl hard, and last summer she'd stopped treating him like a younger friend—she was almost two years older—and they became a couple.

Mandy was bright, resilient, and very pretty. Faith had come to love her, too, especially for the way the girl had coped with tragic events resulting from an extremely dysfunctional family that first summer, a situation that had intensified Ben's affection for Mandy. But Faith and Tom worried about the strength of Ben's attachment at such a young age, although they knew plenty of people—the Millers for example—who had met their mates as teens and lived happily ever after.

Mandy had graduated from the island high school and was

now in the middle of her first year at Bates College in Lewiston, Maine. She'd taken a gap year to work and save money, although she had received substantial financial help from Bates as well as a scholarship from a silent benefactor on Sanpere.

The college wars that had raged in the Fairchild household starting last spring had to do with Ben's absolute insistence on applying only to Maine schools, with Bates his first choice. He'd finally agreed to a few others on the Common App, including Tom's alma mater, Brown. From the start, though, he was adamant that the only place of higher learning he'd attend would be in the Pine Tree state.

What Faith, and Tom, had feared—that Mandy would meet someone else with a suffering Ben all too close by—had apparently happened. "I need some space" was akin to "We need to talk" and "Let's take some time apart" as kisses of doom for a relationship. Faith felt a certain amount of relief that it had happened now and not during Ben's freshman year somewhere near Mandy's doorstep.

"Come downstairs and we'll talk while I make supper," Faith coaxed.

The look her son gave her pierced her heart. "There's no use talking, Mom. She's gone."

He closed the door and she heard the lock click.

"Good chili," Amy said. The two of them were eating in the kitchen, the male Fairchilds both absent. Faith had left a tray outside Ben's door, calling out that it was there, but she expected it would stay untouched. Tom had phoned to say in a markedly strained voice that she shouldn't wait up for him. She'd leave dinner out for him, too—and *that* would get eaten even at midnight.

"Maybe she really does just need a little space and then they'll get back together," Amy said, ever the optimist. Faith had told her all she knew.

"It certainly could happen." Faith was not an optimist but cherished the quality in her daughter. "I have flan for dessert. Do you want some now?"

"Maybe later," Amy answered. "I'm going to check Mandy's Facebook page. Her profile picture is a selfie she and Ben took last summer out on Barred Island."

"I'll clean up, you go check." Faith made a point of not friending her children or her children's friends. There was such a thing as TMI.

Amy was back too soon. "No new posts, but she's changed the photo. Just one of her. Although I think Ben took it." Amy's face brightened. Still the optimist.

After her daughter left to do her homework, Faith retrieved the full tray from the upstairs hall and went to her own computer to check her e-mail. Max Dane had sent several dates and times to meet, all in the next couple of days. He'd added again that he wanted the invitations to go out immediately and wondered if she could commit to the job right away. "I've been told the kitchen is all any chef could want," he wrote. "And I should have mentioned that your fee is for your services. Sky's the limit on what you'll have to spend on the food." An unlimited budget! Even her wealthiest clients had never offered that.

Faith leaned back in her chair and stretched. With all the drama going on in the house—she was sure Tom's unexpected Planning Board meeting boded ill—the notion of a few days away from hearth, home, and even kin was extremely attractive. Maybe this rare opportunity would jolt her out of her own personal doldrums. She decided to call her sister.

"Hi, is this a good time?" she asked when Hope answered. "You're not helping Quent with his homework or other mommy chores?"

"Sweetheart, that's why God invented afterschool help. By the time I get home, it's all done. Dinner, too. He and his father are watching some sort of sports thing."

The Sibley family had not been particularly sportif, yet both daughters married men who were passionate about everything from basketball to tiddlywinks. Fortunately, as their children grew up, they shared these paternal interests, allowing the two sisters to relinquish their places before the TV and occasionally the playing field with relief.

Faith quickly filled Hope in on what she was now thinking of as The Mandy Projectile, launched and sure to pick up speed.

"It's no use saying that someday he won't even remember her name, because he won't believe you—and maybe it won't be true," Hope said.

"Don't tell me you're still secretly pining for Andy," Faith teased.

Hope sighed. "We were good together weren't we?"

"As the only kids I ever knew who had subscriptions to the *Wall Street Journal* in elementary school, yes, you were a perfect match."

"Until that surfer girl from L.A. moved into his building, and suddenly he was all about following his perfect wave, or more like her perfect curves."

Faith laughed. "It still hurts doesn't it all these years later? Poor Ben."

"Poor you," Hope said. "If it were Amy, and it will be, you'd get to hand her Kleenex and she'd let it all out. Ben will be the Spartan standing without complaint while the fox he's got under his tunic gnaws at his entrails."

"Thanks, sis. Now I'll have to think about this image every time I look at him. If he ever comes out of his room again, that is. But I called to ask your advice about something else."

After hearing about Max Dane's party, including the fee offered, Hope said, "You're probably expecting me to tell you to take the money and run, as in straight for the job, but I'm telling you to take it for the hell of it. Of course money is nice, but, Fay"—Hope was the only person to use this nickname, one Faith had never liked, but she had also never figured out how to tell that to her favorite and only sibling—"Max Dane! He's a legend. The house is bound to be incredible and the guests even more so. What's stopping you?"

It was almost word for word what Pix had said.

"Nothing now. I have to check with Tom. He's at a Planning Board meeting tonight, but I'm sure he'll tell me to do it, too."

"Dane's obviously heard about your expertise. He could have hired a Boston firm or even flown in a chef from New York or anywhere. Say Paris."

"Maybe he was at one of the events I catered before I moved," Faith said. When she did meet with him, she'd ask him how he'd heard about Have Faith.

"Fay!" Hope shouted into the phone. "I just remembered. Call Aunt Chat. I'm almost certain he was a client. I mean one or more of his shows."

Charity Sibley was their father's older sister, the youngest of the three Sibley girls named, as had been their female forbearers and those who followed: "Faith," "Hope," and "Charity." Faith's parents had stopped short. Chat had started out in public relations straight from college, writing press releases and making coffee (in the bad old days for women). By the time she'd retired a few years ago she had one of the most prestigious and successful firms based in Manhattan and specialized in show business.

The sisters talked a bit more. Faith hung up longing for her native land, as she always did after contact with anyone there. She missed being able to go outside anytime of day or night and find food from any part of the globe, as well as things like books, haircuts, films, music, you name it. The food choice in Aleford was Country Pizza—and Harry did make a great pie—but it closed at seven thirty, sometimes even seven. There was a convenience store in nearby Concord rumored to be open until eight, but Faith had not been able to find it the few times she'd discovered they were out of milk after the Shop'n Save closed.

Resolving to call her aunt in the morning, she went back to her computer and e-mailed Max Dane: "Send out your invitations. Will meet with you Monday morning at 10:00. Sincerely, Faith Fairchild." Monday was four days from now.

She felt as if she had crossed some sort of Rubicon. Life was becoming more interesting. Dreary January was suddenly taking on a whole new aspect. The feeling was reinforced when his reply came back immediately: "Couldn't be more pleased. Sent the invites out this afternoon after talking to you. Max."

According to anyone from Massachusetts it was Tip O'Neill who said, "All politics is local," when he ran for office in 1935. As Faith waited up for her own Thomas, the words popped into her head. Faith had soon come to believe in the phrase—and also believed it could be dangerous. When Sam Miller served on the Aleford school committee, he'd received several anonymous, ominous threats when he reorganized the school bus schedule. A friend on the Board of Selectmen found a slashed plastic rat on her doorstep after calling for a leash ordinance. Planning Board was the worst in Faith's opinion, and anyone foolish enough to dip a toe into the maelstrom of property permits was just asking for trouble. Of course, her husband was the first to volunteer to fill a vacant seat. The previous incumbent had not left a forwarding address. "I feel a responsibility to the town," Tom said. "It has been very good to us." Faith was not sure exactly how the town had been good to them specifically, but she couldn't help but be proud of her spouse. If anything, *he* was the one who was good. Too good. He was a Fairchild to the core. Fairchilds, responsible citizens, had always been involved in local politics, the first stepping onto if not Plymouth Rock, then one nearby, with campaign buttons at the ready.

It was after ten o'clock when Tom came into the kitchen looking weary and angry, his face, as always, an open book. She gave him a hasty kiss, put the chili in the microwave, and poured him a Sam Adams Winter Lager. Then she waited while he ate and drank, enjoying the quiet of the kitchen this late at night. The new LED lighting the Vestry had allowed Faith to install—at her own expense—was casting soft shadows on the goldenrod-colored walls, which she had also received permission to paint. Herself.

"What was so pressing?" she asked. "Someone planted a tree on the wrong side of the property line?"

"I wish," Tom said. "Seems a developer has purchased the old Grayson House and is submitting plans to raze it for a strip mall."

Faith was aghast. "But it's in the Historic District. You can see it from our backyard and the church!"

Tom nodded. "We can see it, but it's not part of the District. The house was used as a kind of nursing home from the nineteen forties until not that long ago and there was a zoning change to allow it, removing it from the District. Any more of this chili?"

The next morning Faith was waiting by the front door for Ben as he came downstairs in his jacket, carrying his knapsack ready to leave for school. "Here." She put a glass of juice in his hand, and when he drained it quickly switched it for a warm breakfast sandwich—her version of the fast-food staple: poached egg, sliced tomato, and sharp cheddar on a homemade ciabatta roll.

Ben had dark circles under his eyes, and she was sure he hadn't slept much. She knew enough not to try to hug him and he left without a word. Amy came tearing down the stairs afterward. She'd already eaten the steel cut oatmeal with fruit that Faith made overnight in a small slow cooker most winter school days. She did hug her mother and called out, "Bye, Dad" over her shoulder.

Tom was sitting over his third cup of coffee, surrounded by copies of the town's previous zoning decisions and ordinances that he had stayed up late printing out from the board's online site—a state requirement for transparency still regarded as Big Government intrusion by several Alefordians. He too had circles under his eyes.

"Let me make you an omelet or other eggs," Faith said. "I have some of that good applewood bacon too."

He shook his head. "No time, but thanks. I'll take these to work and look at them when I can. Sam made copies, too. He's coming over after we both get home to talk the whole mess over."

The proposed strip mall was not the kind with a massage parlor and dollar store, Faith had learned very late last night, but a two-story building with offices for small businesses below, apartments above. "All very legit," according to the developer. "A real asset for the community."

Tom was hoping to get him on the issue of parking. One of the things he and the board had to resolve was how many spaces had to be allotted for this kind of use. There was a good-size lot in place behind Grayson House from its previous incarnation. Faith kept her mouth shut, but she was pretty sure the developer had already determined it would meet any requirement. Her mother was a real estate lawyer in Manhattan, and Faith had had a ringside seat at real estate bouts, whereas Tom's family business, Fairchild Realty, on Boston's South Shore, had employed much kinder, gentler fisticuffs.

As he left she put the extra breakfast sandwich in his hand. Before Faith finished loading the dishwasher, Pix walked in and sat down in Tom's still-warm chair at the large round table.

"Coffee?" Faith said automatically. This was one of the things she had learned from her friend. In New England, you didn't say "Hello" first, you offered coffee, then you said hello.

"Love some."

Tom hadn't eaten any of the corn muffins Faith had put out with the strawberry jam she'd made last summer in Maine. For a normally hungry guy, it was not a good sign. She hoped he'd noticed the sandwich.

She handed Pix a mug of coffee with one Splenda, no milk,

and pushed the muffin plate in her direction. Pix, a normally hungry gal, didn't take one. It was not a good sign.

"Do you believe in bad news coming in threes?" Pix asked.

Pix was the least superstitious person Faith knew.

"Absolutely not." Faith stood up. She had the feeling she was going to need some more coffee herself.

"Samantha called last night." Pix put down the mug and held up one finger. "She's lost her job." She put up another finger. "She's broken up with Caleb." A third went up. "She's left the apartment—the lease is in Caleb's name." The fingers came down and Pix folded them into a fist. "Oh, and she's moving back home. Could you warm up one of these muffins for me?"

Pix stayed for several muffins and fresh coffee. "I love being with Samantha, but it's been wonderful to go back to just Sam and me. Danny left only a few weeks ago. I can walk around in my pj's again."

Considering Pix's lingerie was opaque L.L.Bean flannel in the winter and almost as thick cotton in the summer—not exactly Victoria's Secret, more Queen Victoria—Faith found this newfound freedom a bit hard to envision. But it was true that the nest was only recently empty. Sam had finally decided it would be cheaper to help his twenty-three-year-old son with rent money for the Somerville apartment Dan was now sharing with college buddies than continue to keep him fed out in Aleford. Dan had a job with an IT firm that was up, but still coming, along with a livable salary. Mental health—Sam's—had entered into the decision as well.

"I'm sure Samantha will want to be out on her own as soon as possible," Faith reassured her friend. "Plus Samantha likes to cook." Pix classed the chore below ditch digging, relying heavily on boxes in her pantry with HELPER on them. When on her own for dinner, she ate cornflakes—a habit Faith found extremely hard to believe.

"She'll do her wash." Pix perked up at the thought, but then her face fell. "She sounded like her little-girl self last night. Between sobs she kept saying she couldn't wait to be in her old room. You've read all the statistics about the numbers of millennials still living at home and how hard it is for them to find jobs, even someone with Samantha's credentials."

Faith had read the dispiriting numbers, too, and while part of her was agonizing over Ben's departure for college—somewhere— she also hoped gone would be gone. That he'd be able to find a fulfilling job and live independently when he graduated. One could dream . . .

Driving to work she detoured through Ursula's neighborhood. There was time for a quick visit. Faith's assistant Niki Constantine would be baking the brownies and lemon squares for the afternoon Friends of the Library tea they were catering. Faith herself would put the sandwiches together later—traditional cucumber and watercress ones, less traditional curried chicken salad, and thinly sliced roast beef with horseradish aioli. They'd made shortbread cookies and petit fours yesterday.

There was no snow on the ground, but it was a cold gray winter day, a day when spring seemed very, very far off. Prepared to swing into the driveway, Faith straightened the wheels and kept driving. The same car, which she now knew belonged to Austin Stebbins, seemed to be in exactly the same place as yesterday. Was he a houseguest?

Or something more?

Faith didn't get a chance to call her aunt until Friday afternoon. Tom had enlisted her help in going over the zoning regulations and coming up with plausible objections. Objections other than NIMBY.

"Hi, Aunt Chat, it's Faith."

"Remarkable!"

Faith knew she was one of her aunt's favorites, but this was a new high.

"Those ESP people could be right. It's remarkable timing. I was looking up your number to call you."

Her aunt sounded happy, so it wasn't to call with bad news. But despite her name Chat never called to pass the time of day. She always had a reason. Faith could get to hers once she found out what Chat wanted.

Her aunt came straight to the point. "I'm coming to Cambridge on the nineteenth for two days. Some sort of pioneering women entrepreneurs conference at the B school—Harvard's nod toward political correctness, and reality I must say. I'm speaking and they're putting me up at the Charles Hotel plus an appropriate fat fee, so I can take you and Tom someplace special. You choose. And I'd love to come out and see the children."

Dinner with Chat would be a treat, but Faith wasn't so sure about an Aleford visit given that one of the "children," when seen at all, was looking more like Banquo's ghost than a hale and hearty teen and was about as verbal.

They talked about possible restaurants and times—"the first night is a dreary banquet, so the twentieth"—and then Faith mentioned why she had called.

"Max Dane! Living in a Boston suburb! Hard to believe. Yes, I knew him well; but perhaps best not to mention my name. We had the account for his last show, and I do mean last. I think he blames me for the flop heard round the world. I'll tell you all about it when I see you. Take the job, of course, but my darling niece, do be careful. He's, well, he's not a very nice man."

Armed with extremely detailed instructions, Faith felt a sense of relief as she drove toward her meeting with Max Dane at Rowan

House. It had been one of those weekends. Just as she was beginning to think Ben was coming to terms with Mandy's decision, he
came tearing into the living room Saturday night shrieking, "She's
unfriended me!" Amy was at his heels. "Me too! And Daisy.
Probably all the Maine friends we have in common." While her
decibels were lower, her emotions were running as high as her
brother's.

"You know what this means, right?" Ben had said, slumping
down on the couch. Faith did know what it meant. Mandy was
with someone new and posting things that she didn't want Ben to
see or hear about from mutual friends. On the one hand it was in
the girl's favor that she was protecting him from feeling hurt; on
the other, Mandy should have realized that what he would imagine was probably far worse.

"Guess she'll marry him. He's probably a senior. We'll read
about it in *The Island Crier*," Ben had said bitterly. Faith tried a
few platitudes and then went to make cocoa for the kids, pouring
herself a large glass of Merlot.

Sunday wasn't much better. Ben spent most of the day checking
out application deadlines for places like the University of Alaska in
the hope he could still apply for the fall.

Now, after pulling over twice to check Max Dane's instructions—he'd mentioned not to bother with her GPS, it wouldn't
show Havencrest—Faith began to think the location had more in
common with the Bermuda Triangle than MetroWest Boston.

At last she saw the turn he'd described, marked by a huge
granite boulder with HAVENCREST incised in Gothic letters. Several labyrinthine turns later she came to the "gatehouse": turreted
stone, a high wall extending on either side as far as the eye could
see, interrupted by an elaborate and very secure looking iron gate
across the drive. Dane had written that it was electronically operated. She got out of the car and found the intercom button where
he'd said it would be, cleverly disguised as one of the ornamental
gryphon's eyes. She pressed it firmly. Instantly a voice—the one

who had told her to hold for Max Dane—issued instructions: "Get back in your car, please, and when the gate is completely open, proceed. Do not try to enter before then." There was a click as he hung up, or took his finger from a button in the house somewhere ahead.

It was all very Lewis Carroll or Ian Fleming or a car wash. Faith kept at a standstill until the entrance gaped wide and came to a stop.

Out of curiosity she looked at her odometer once through and then checked again as she parked under the porte cochere at the front of the house. The drive was a mile and a half long and passed a natural-looking landscape that could only be the result of a great deal of time and money. Banks of rhododendrons that must be spectacular in the spring; dense birch groves; towering oaks and pines. A landscape that had to have been in place for many, many years. She remembered what Pix had said, that the houses were handed down from generation to generation. Somehow she doubted this was the case with Max Dane, and it wasn't just his New York accent. Brahmin families were known to disown members who went into show business or married someone in it. Fine to kick up one's heels as a Harvard undergraduate back in the days of Ann Corio at the Old Howard in Scollay Square, but one turned to Boston's Blue Book for a blue-blooded mate.

As it came into view Faith immediately guessed the house was the work of the architect H. H. Richardson or one of his students. The facade combined Romanesque-type stonework archways with Morris-like Arts and Crafts dark shingles. It all blended into the hills behind it as if sprung from them by some kind of medieval—or Tolkien—magic.

An attractive man who appeared to be in his fifties opened the car door and ushered her up the front steps and across a wide veranda and into a vast foyer. He was wearing a pale yellow V-neck sweater that looked like cashmere; the shirt underneath was cornflower blue. His tan chinos had knife creases. Not formal butler attire, but he seemed to be playing that role.

"My name is Ian Morrison. We spoke on the phone. Please come in. Mr. Dane is waiting in the library."

He ushered her into a foyer as large as a ballroom. The floor glowed with a number of Persian carpets that picked up the warm golden oak woodwork and rose-colored walls. There was no clutter, just a few pieces of Asian blue-and-white porcelain. A fireplace ample enough to roast a large pig or small ox took up most of one wall. Several landscapes hung on the others, including an enormous piece that occupied pride of place across from the entrance that Faith was sure was by Frederic Church. Not one of his Hudson River scenes, but one of the Andes series. The only other painting of equal size was to the left of the fireplace. It was a portrait, by John Singer Sargent or a close adherent, of a young woman wearing an elaborate white gown. Possibly the artist had hoped his detailed rendition of her jeweled choker and smooth white shoulders would distract the viewer from her rather homely face and its sober expression.

Ian Morrison crossed the room and opened a door, gesturing Faith to follow him through. "May I bring you something to drink? Coffee, tea?"

"Or champagne?" Max Dane strode into their path, his hand outstretched. "Such a pleasure to meet you, Mrs. Fairchild."

"And I you," Faith said, smiling and shaking his hand. She turned to Ian. "I'd love a cup of tea, any kind but Earl Grey if you have it. No sugar or milk."

"Same for me, but add my usual, " Max said. Ian nodded and quietly disappeared through the door.

The library was what Faith would have expected from what she had seen so far. Floor-to-ceiling bookcases, another fireplace—this one surrounded by Roycroft tiles—and an expanse of arched windows looking out toward a bluestone-covered veranda, accessed by French doors. The naturalistic landscape Faith had noted driving in continued beyond the veranda: ledges and boulders had been left in place and no formal flowerbeds interrupted the fields' now-pale stubble, but come spring they would be covered with a variety of grasses and other plantings as well. Dane was following her gaze. "All we do is mow on this side and let nature take its course. Daisies come first then things like goldenrod. Back in the day gardeners planted hundreds of daffodil bulbs, but they have mostly fallen prey to the squirrels, voles, and other creatures. I like it this way better."

There was a moment of silence. Faith found herself looking at Dane, sizing him up. The impresario was tall, but not heavy. Like Ian Morrison, he was dressed casually, a tan suede vest over a subtle tartan shirt and gray wool pants. He was a redhead, although age had sprinkled salt with a liberal hand. He kept his hair short, whether because there wasn't enough now to lend itself to a longer style or because like the field, he just liked it that way better.

She sensed he was sizing her up, too.

"Please take a seat. Ian won't be long and afterward I'll give you the tour."

Faith smiled. "I'm looking forward to it. Your house is beautiful."

He nodded. Something other than where he lived seemed to be on his mind. Something else was on Faith's, too, and she decided to come out with it.

"I've been wondering how you heard about me. I started out with the same name in Manhattan over twenty years ago. Maybe you were at an event I catered there?"

"Possibly. But, Mrs. Fairchild, while I am sure you are superb as a caterer, I am hiring you for what I understand is your other expertise. Your, shall we say, sleuthing ability?"

Startled, Faith said, "My sleuthing? But why?"

"One of my guests wants to kill me."

CHAPTER 2

"How do you know?" Faith asked, her mind rapidly running over a number of possible indications. Anonymous poison pen letter, blocked ALL CAPS text; equivalent of horse head in his bed; gift package of chocolates redolent of bitter almonds?

"I think I'll save the answer to that for the end of the house tour." Max Dane did not seem at all perturbed, although the way he'd spoken made it clear he was very sure of the threat. "Oh, and it was Ian who found you. He keeps an ear close to the ground around here."

As if on cue, the man, who was beginning to seem much more than a factotum in the Dane household, arrived with the tea and left. It was not an elaborate service. Two cups and the absence of any comestibles made it clear the intent was not to linger. Faith sipped quickly. Whatever Dane had in his cup was either not as hot as Faith's tea or he had an asbestos mouth. A few gulps and he set the cup on the tray.

"If you are finished with your tea, shall we start?"

Faith stood up. Much as she wanted to see the whole house and take time looking at what she was sure were many exquisite details and furnishings, she wanted to get to the revelation at the end fast.

Max stood up as well and went to a tapestry bellpull hanging next to the fireplace. He tugged on it and Ian appeared almost at once. He couldn't have gone too far. The tray had barely been delivered.

"I'm going to be busy with Mrs. Fairchild for a while. Would you mind picking up the mail? I'm eager to see if we've had any replies." He turned to Faith. "I have a post office box in Weston. Rowan House—I disliked the original name and chose this one— isn't on any delivery route."

Rowan House? Rowan was a tree she knew, although horticulture was not Faith's forte. Thanks to Harry Potter she *did* know that the Rowan tree was good for wands and recalled something about people planting them in earlier times as a protection against witches. Pix, an avid gardener, would fill in the blanks.

Max led the way back through the foyer and into a large room with almost floor-to-ceiling windows overlooking the sloping front lawn. It was comfortably furnished with Arts and Crafts–style furniture, some of which Faith recognized as the work of Thomas Moser, a nationally known Maine furniture maker.

"I don't know how familiar you are with late-nineteenth-century American architecture, but the house was designed by Henry Hobson Richardson, or I should say he added onto and remodeled what was a smaller Federal-style summer home. Sadly, he did not live to see his work completed, but his firm finished it and continued to update it for many years. Frederick Law Olmsted . . ."

"Central Park." Faith beamed, happy to recall what had been her favorite childhood haunt.

"Yes." Max Dane smiled as well. "Anyway, Olmsted designed the landscape, working with Richardson. This room, called the winter parlor, is in the addition, which more than tripled the size of the original house. The summer parlor is smaller and at the far end of the rooms on the other side of the foyer. Besides the size, the difference between the two is that the summer parlor opens onto a veranda, a cool place to sit in the afternoon. It has a small pantry space with a sink, originally for the preparation of afternoon tea. I added a microwave and generally use it for the cocktail hour."

He gestured toward a door to the left of the fireplace. "The main dining room is through here." Faith followed him into an almost baronial dining room. The table could easily sit twelve and she was sure there were additional leaves. She followed Dane again down the hall into a smaller, more intimate dining area suitable for breakfasts and lunch. Passing it, they reached the kitchen, which stretched across the back of the house.

"The house is not on any historic register, so I was able to completely demolish the old kitchen and put this larger one in. I used some of the original cabinetry and trim to match the feel of the rest of the house, but as you can see, you won't have trouble preparing meals while trying to cope with outdated appliances."

It was Faith's dream kitchen and one she knew she would never have unless a major reversal of fortune, and lifestyle, placed her in a similar setting. A Wolf stove—double gas burners with grill and griddle, double electric convection ovens below. She knew the model well—going to the company Web site, and other kitchen-related ones, was what she called "culinary porn."

"I don't entertain much," Dane was saying, "but planned for any eventuality, hence the two dishwashers. There is an industrial freezer and another refrigerator off the butler's pantry. Go ahead, open the cabinets so you'll know what you have."

It was a kid-in-a-candy-shop moment. All Faith would need to bring were her knives and chef's clothing. The glass-fronted original cabinets revealed several china services, both for everyday and more elaborate sets she suspected were original to the house. The butler's pantry contained enough glassware for a small hotel and shelves of serving dishes. She wanted to play with the decorative reproduction taps at the marble sink, but this was not the time.

"It's perfect. Truly one of the most beautiful and functional kitchens I've ever seen," she said.

He smiled, a broad smile. It was the most emotion he had shown so far—all his remarks had been delivered with a cool, almost detached expression.

Max gestured to the row of windows on the back wall of the kitchen. Looking out, Faith could see a very large patio, devoid of summer furniture at the moment, that was enclosed by a low stone wall. Several structures, some closer to the house than others, were just visible beyond it.

"There are several outbuildings besides the barn, which you can't see from this angle. I converted it into a garage and the apartment where Ian lives. What you are looking at beyond is the original stone icehouse and formerly the head gardener's quarters. Storage use."

She'd been watching his face and now concentrated on his voice. That, and some of his vocabulary, were the only clues so far as to Max Dane's theatrical past. No framed posters or Tony awards on display. He could well have been an actor himself. There was a studied quality to his conversation, as if he were reciting lines. There was also something in the way he moved. Men his age and height were usually stooped in varying degrees. Max was as straight as a ramrod and walked in a rather precise manner. Again theatrical, as if hitting his mark on a stage.

"There is room for you in one of the other buildings, but if you are agreeable I'd like you here in the main house. There is a rather nice housekeeper's suite."

He opened a door to the left of the one to the pantry and Faith followed him through to the suite. If this was for the help, Faith thought, what could the other bedrooms be like?

The suite was filled with sun this morning. Both the bedroom and sitting room were beautifully furnished in the same Arts and

Crafts style as the other rooms she'd seen so far. The artwork was not period artwork, as she'd noted in the rest of the house, but they weren't grandmother's botanical prints either, ubiquitous in guest rooms of the day. Faith recognized an original of one of Wayne Thiebaud's oil paintings of cakes—appropriate for the suite's occupant—and some bright abstract monoprints suggestive of the landscape outside.

The bathroom was, as the cliché so accurately put it, "to die for." Faith was starting to hope this would be the first of many gigs at Rowan House. She hurried after Max to a back staircase, the servants' access, up to the second floor. "There are ten bedrooms plus the master, all en suite. I've invited ten guests, so we should be fine. I'm pretty sure I'm not going to get any refusals. Two of them used to be married to each other and may still be legally, but word has it that they like to sleep alone—or not with each other, anyway."

The hall ended at the top of the wide staircase that Faith had admired when she walked in the front door. In the sun, the oak treads and ornately carved banister gleamed gold.

"As you see, the landing is large enough for drinks. I thought we'd gather in front of the fireplace"—he pointed to a small one in the corner surrounded by Minton tiles—"when people arrive Friday. Then dinner in the summer parlor. Buffet breakfast in the dining room. There are plenty of warming dishes for the sideboard and you can pop in to see if there are any special requests. Knowing this group, there will be. Possibly even breakfast in bed, but I will discourage that."

From his tone, Faith certainly would not want to be the individual demanding a tray. Her expression must have revealed her thoughts, because Max added in a more genial voice, "The point is for all of us chums to be together again."

As she trailed after him up the stairs to the third floor, Faith couldn't help but think, Chums together? One a possible killer?

"This was the servants' quarters and I don't use it much. I don't have live-in help. Ian has been wearing many essential hats for many years and sees to my needs more than adequately. He is, as I said, in his own digs. The grounds are maintained by a crew from Waltham starting in the early spring. I also call them if I need snow removal."

Faith continued to follow, reflecting that the bond between the two men now seemed to be much closer than employer and employee. She wondered whether Ian had been in the theater as well.

Max opened a door at the end of the narrow hall, no polished golden oak or period details up here. "This was my room."

Faith peered into a windowless, airless space barely large enough for the narrow iron bedstead with a thin mattress covered in blue and white ticking. A small table with a lamp was squeezed next to it. The roof sloped so sharply it would be a challenge for an adult to stand up.

"Your room?" she asked.

"Oh yes," he said, closing the door firmly. "I used to be permitted a week every year when I was a child to visit my grandparents."

His accent, melodious as it was, did not indicate a New England upbringing, or roots. Once again, Faith placed him in one of the boroughs—the Bronx or Brooklyn. He was quick to pick up on her quizzical look.

"It's a long story. Perhaps another time. Now we cross over to the other side of the house, the original Federal wing, where my quarters are."

Descending the staircase, he didn't stop at the second floor where his rooms presumably were, but continued on down, turning left when they reached the grand entrance foyer.

"No need to explore any farther except to show you the summer parlor."

He picked up his pace and Faith quickened hers to keep up. On this side of the foyer, the house was a rabbit warren. Rooms opened to more rooms in succession, some large, some small, a few lined with bookcases and window seats. The bookcases were filled—not with books by the yard from a decorator, but with an assortment of sizes, hard/soft covers, and subjects. A telescope on a tripod stood in front of a bay window. A profusion of Oriental carpets covered most of the floors.

They arrived at a room that did not lead to another door but to a large arch carved with acanthus leaves. Max waved Faith through and with a flourish of his hand directed her attention to the fireplace at the far end of the room. "Ta-da!"

The substantial andirons had been pulled forward. At the moment they were not holding logs.

They held a coffin.

As a finale, it was definitely final.

"At least they cared enough to send the very best," Max said as he and Faith walked toward the ornate mahogany casket. The lid was open and the interior was lined with tufted white velvet. "It is a recent arrival," he added.

Faith had seen a great many similar final resting places—it went with ecclesiastical territory—so was able to agree that what was in front of them was top of the line, adding, "As a message, not very subtle. How was it delivered?"

"When Ian went out for his morning run last Tuesday there was an enormous packing case at the front door, the content before you. I'm a night owl—usually awake until one at least—and he's an early bird. He discovered it around six, so it must have been placed there in the wee hours. I'm a sound sleeper and heard nothing in the night, nor did Ian back where he is."

"How would the delivery have gotten through the gate?" Faith asked.

"Ian and I have puzzled over that. It couldn't. We have a surveillance camera and there's nothing on it for that time except the usual passing wildlife. But someone could have brought it through the woods and over the field. Perhaps using some sort of cart. The coffin is empty, or almost, so not as heavy as one in normal use."

"No identifying marks on the crate?"

"Unfortunately, the donor did not include a return address for my thanks. We did some cyber sleuthing—you can buy this model online from any number of vendors. Also it's a model that has been available for years, which may suggest forethought."

"A nasty thing to do, but why assume the giver has murderous intent?" Faith found herself speaking lines, too. She doubted she had ever said anything like "murderous intent" before.

"Ah, you see, it was not completely empty. Here's your first real clue." Max reached into the casket and pulled out a *Playbill* with its familiar black logo on bright yellow. Just the sight of it gave Faith the feeling of excitement she got when an usher handed her one of the theatrical programs. Followed, once seated, by reading about the performance and looking at ads for restaurants and luxury items she couldn't afford—always fun.

She took the *Playbill* from Max's outstretched hand. The front pictured actors dressed as angels and devils, although the costumes were unconventional—a suggestion of wings, halos, pointed tails fashioned from coat hanger-type wire. The title confirmed the roles: "Max Dane Presents" *Heaven or Hell: The Musical.*

"All the guests I've invited after I received this, shall we say, 'calling card,' had a role in the production. Ian has made a list of names for you with the roles each played." He paused. "It was my last musical production and I'm afraid it was not a success. The individuals on the list quite possibly blame me. No, make that they definitely do."

Faith looked at the date on the *Playbill*. "But this was twenty years ago!"

Dane shook a finger at her. "I hope I have not been deceived in your abilities. As the bard put it, 'If you wrong us, shall we not revenge?' Twenty years is but a blink of the eye, my dear. Now perhaps we could talk a bit about my birthday dinner. I thought we could close the lid and use this for a raw bar and mounds of caviar. Foie gras, too. Everything in excess." The smile he gave her was more Lucifer than Peter at the Pearly Gates, and Faith was reminded of her Aunt Chat's warning—"he's not a very nice man."

Adrian St. John reached for his paper knife. He'd picked it up in Morocco years ago and was fond of the intricate metalwork on the hilt. It looked like a dagger, and he imagined ones like it had been put to uses other than slitting an envelope.

He had found the letter on his desk with a small pile of not so interesting post his secretary had left for him. Rare to get what was called "snail mail" these days. The stamp indicated it was from someone in the States. His name and address had been written by a calligrapher or someone elderly enough to have been taught penmanship rather than how to keyboard.

A swift motion with the sharp knife put paid to the frisson of suspense he'd been enjoying and he pulled out a stiff card. It was an invitation. A slow smile spread across his face and he walked over to one of the large bay windows. The gardens were not as lush as they would be come spring and summer, but he found the varying shades of green displayed by the nondeciduous trees and bushes quite beautiful. That he was a resident in Eaton Square in the heart of Mayfair tickled him immensely. Not bad for a boy from Blackpool. He looked down at the invitation again. He would be sure to name-drop—Vivian Leigh, Rex Harrison, and Sean Connery had all lived in one of Eaton Square's houses, as well as many non-theatrical luminaries. It was London's most elite address, save for Buckingham and Kensington palaces—and some would dispute that, placing it higher.

There were three other enclosures besides the invitation. He pulled them out, pausing to admire his slender hands—no signs of liver spots and the only ring a signet one with his nom de plume initials. A very inside joke.

He sat back down at his desk, purchased at one of Christie's auctions—it had belonged to Graham Greene—and spread the sheets of paper out. There was a first-class round-trip ticket from London Heathrow to Boston, a note with information regarding a livery service that would fetch him when supplied with his flight information, and finally another stiff card. A pithy RSVP card: __Will Attend or __Will Not Attend. There was a return envelope with British postage.

Oh yes, Adrian St. John, pronounced "Sinjin," would attend. He'd been waiting for a very long time.

As Faith drove away from Rowan House, she looked out at the meadow, the tall grasses slightly bent in the morning sun. When she'd driven in, the sharp points had still been covered with light frost, stiff like sabers. She glanced back at the house in the rearview mirror. Now that she knew how many rooms it contained—and what they contained—it loomed even larger than when she had first approached.

After his dramatic finish, Max had led Faith back to the kitchen, where Ian was waiting. "Ian will take it from here. A pleasure to meet you, Mrs. Fairchild."

"Please, call me Faith," she'd said.

"And please call me 'Mr. Dane,'" he'd replied, his smile not quite taking the sting from his words as he left the room.

Ian had partially made up for it. "Now, Faith, may I? And you must call me Ian; we have a few things to go over. I don't want to keep you, as I am sure you are a very busy lady. First off, we thought it would be fun to feature some food at the birthday dinner referencing heaven or hell."

"Deviled Eggs, Lobster Pasta Fra Diavolo, Angel Food Cake? I think I can come up with some ideas." (See dinner party recipes, pages 233–238.)

"Exactly, but we'll need to have other offerings as well. If you could send us a few possible menus with suggestions for the rest of the meals, we can get the food part squared away. Here is the contract. If you will be so kind as to sign and date it, we're all set for now."

Faith had been taken aback and said, "I'm afraid this is not the way I normally do business. I supply the contract with cost estimates and Mr. Dane or you sign it."

He'd given her the kind of smile she reserved for parishioners and others who required polite refusals, as in "No, I cannot cater your daughter's wedding for cost."

"I think you'll find this straightforward. It merely indicates that you will cater the meals designated, arriving Friday morning and leaving Sunday evening. I will act to serve at meals and lend a hand cleaning up. Since there will be at most ten guests plus Max and myself, it shouldn't be too difficult. You will not be expected to do any other household tasks. The cleaners will have done their work ahead, setting up all the guest rooms, and I will act to supply the guests' needs for more towels etcetera should they arise. And here is the deposit. As you place your food orders, we will issue further checks, but this one is, well, a nonrefundable one on our part. If for some reason the job is canceled, you keep the full amount."

The check had been attached to the contract. He removed the paper clip and handed it to her. Faith looked at the amount—and signed. Nothing so far had been normal about the job; so in for a penny, in for a pound. Many pounds.

She was at the bottom of the long drive. The gates swung open slowly and she waited until the way was clear before driving through. Although she felt as if she had been at Rowan House for a very long time, it had only been a little over an hour. She'd go see Ursula and find out more about Havencrest—maybe Max Dane, too. The gates closed noiselessly behind her.

Austin Stebbins's car was not in Ursula's driveway. Earlier Faith had pulled over and called Ursula to make sure it was a convenient time for a visit. She might have required a change in her living arrangements, but Ursula was by no means housebound. Besides volunteering at the library and going to Aleford's recreation center for yoga several times a week, she also regularly strolled to meet friends for lunch at the venerable Minuteman Café with an unchanging menu that featured sandwiches like "The Gobbler," their own roast turkey with cranberry sauce, stuffing, and mayo on plain old homemade white bread—no chichi focaccia or the like.

She must have been watching for her out the window because she opened the front door before Faith could ring the bell. "What a delightful surprise," Ursula said. "Come and sit down."

Faith immediately noticed that Ursula was wearing a soft royal blue wool dress not from Orvis or Talbots, but someplace with a bit more pizzazz. Both Ursula and Pix were unvarying in their devotion to the two purveyors' tried-and-true offerings, although Faith had occasionally been able to get Pix into Eileen Fisher when the outlet store had opened in Burlington. Ursula was also wearing her best jewelry—the double strand of pearls Faith knew had been a gift from her late husband, Arnold, on a significant anniversary. The outfit and the fact that Ursula did not offer coffee indicated she was on her way out somewhere special—or waiting for *someone* special?

There was no need to speculate. Ursula, like Pix, was genetically programmed to be straightforward. Faith herself had marveled at the trait, while not totally adopting it. There were times when needs must . . .

"Austin, whom you met the other day, is picking me up in half an hour for lunch."

"How nice. Where are you going?" Ursula was too dressed up for the Café, so it was probably the Colonial Inn over in Concord. Mother and daughter were devoted to its chicken potpie.

"We're going to a place called L'Espalier in town. Austin thinks I'll enjoy it."

"Town" meant Boston, Faith had learned early on. "Town" as

in the only possible one. As for L'Espalier, it was one of Boston's most expensive restaurants with a fabulous nontraditional French menu. It would make quite a change for Ursula, who normally ate at one of her clubs—Chilton or St. Botolph—when she wasn't going to a museum and eating there.

"Afterward he has an appointment with a Realtor and would like me to come along. He's lived away for so long that he's not familiar with the area the way he once was. He's planning to rent until he knows where he wants to be. For now he's staying here. Even with the student, this house is much too big and there's room for any number of guests. Silly to pay for a hotel."

Was there a flash of something like rebellion in the look Ursula gave her? As if daring Faith to say something? What Faith wanted to say—but didn't—was "Does Pix know all this?"

Much as Faith wanted to pursue this line of conversation—how and when did Ursula meet Austin?—she was aware she didn't have much time before the possible swain arrived to carry Mrs. Rowe off. She needed to ask Ursula about Havencrest.

"I've accepted a weekend catering job the end of the month at a house in Havencrest. I'd never even heard the name. Pix said you would know more about it than she did."

"Goodness, I haven't thought about Havencrest in ages," Ursula said. "It's the kind of place that only seems real if you are actually there and I haven't been for many, many years. What is the name of the house? They all have names."

"It's called 'Rowan House,' but the current owner changed it. I don't know what it was called before."

"Changed it! I'm sure that wasn't popular. It's a funny sort of enclave—the opposite end of the spectrum from a holler I suppose. From what I remember a group of Boston businessmen decided the city wasn't a good place to raise a family, so they joined together and purchased the acreage in the late nineteenth and on into the early twentieth centuries. One of them named the community Havencrest, since it was going to be a haven. Not the two-acre zoning some towns adopted in the nineteen fifties that we all thought was large. More like forty and fifty acres, each a kind of private park."

"But it's part of Weston?"

"Yes. They pay taxes to the town—hefty ones. Used to have private contractors for services and probably still do. They consider themselves a separate entity. Arnold had a client who insisted on meeting at his house. Wouldn't come into the office. Too demeaning. Arnold said he always felt relieved when he made it onto route one seventeen without being turned into a toad. The place gave him the creeps! Still he was always very happy to indulge the man—a large account."

"The man I'm working for is Max Dane. He was the director and producer of some famous Broadway musicals. Is the name familiar? Pix said the houses don't change hands, just generations."

Ursula shook her head. "She's right. It was always said that the only way a person leaves Havencrest is in a casket."

Faith gave a start, but Ursula didn't notice and was continuing to speak. "The name 'Max Dane' is familiar, but that must be because of his career. Although I'm afraid we never got to New York City much." Ursula gave the three words the same intonation that Tom did—as if speaking of somewhere faraway and exotic—Ulan Bator or Kilimanjaro. "I've never heard of a Max Dane, or any Danes, at Havencrest."

"But you have been there? To one of the houses?"

"Yes, quite often growing up and once in a blue moon for some function with Arnold when I was older. But mostly when I was a girl. It was close enough to Aleford, so many Havencrest daughters went to the Cabot School here as day students, the way I did when we moved from Town. I was good friends with one of them, Helen Frost, and I'd occasionally be invited to spend a Saturday afternoon at her house. I thought it was great fun, since their chauffeur would pick me up and bring me back."

Faith recalled the tale Ursula had told her some years earlier about how her family came to Aleford from Beacon Hill after Ursula's father lost almost everything in the aftermath of the Crash. The Aleford house had been left to Ursula's mother by an aunt and was a refuge for the family.

"The Frosts gave a big party for Helen's sixteenth birthday. Japanese lanterns strung in the trees, lobster, and all sorts of good things to eat that most of us had never had. Helen always wore such beautiful clothes. Her mother went to Paris for hers and would bring back sketches of appropriate frocks for their dressmaker to make for Helen. I'm afraid I was terribly envious."

Faith gave her a smile. "Well, you are wearing a beautiful dress today and it looks couture to me." Ursula acknowledged the compliment with a nod.

"Helen desperately wanted to go to college. Wellesley—where dear Samantha went. Helen's father didn't believe in education beyond high school for women. She was being groomed for a suitable marriage. Not to a titled Englishman like so many American heiresses—Havencrest people thought that would be a step down—but a Harvard boy, not too wild, with good bloodlines, a house in town, and a cottage in Newport or Bar Harbor."

"Cottage," Faith knew, referred to something the size of a resort.

"I needed to work after high school, so with my Katie Gibbs typing and shorthand diploma, I got a secretarial job. Arnold and I were married when I was nineteen. Helen and Havencrest became part of my past, although I recall hearing from another classmate once that there had been some sort of trouble." Ursula sighed. "But I don't remember any details. I'm afraid this is happening to me more and more."

Ursula had seemed so cheerful when Faith first came in and there was a cloud across her face now. "Nonsense," Faith said quickly, feeling responsible. "You remember more than I do. I found that I had put a pot holder in the freezer for some reason the other day. It was meant to remind me of something, but I have no idea what."

This produced a smile. "Thank you, dear. The truth is that,

like Arnold, I never felt comfortable at Havencrest. Despite the house, which was a Richardson one by the way. You know, Henry Hobson Richardson, the architect who designed Trinity Church in Copley Square and so many other wonderful places?"

There must have been more than one Havencrest house designed by the firm, Faith thought swiftly, aware that Ursula had stood up. There wasn't a hint of a cloud in her expression now. "I hear a car in the drive. It must be Austin. Let him in, will you? I need to freshen up." She raised a hand to her hair, like Pix's thick and short with soft waves produced by nature. Pix's hair was chestnut, which Ursula's may have been once. Now it was pure white, almost platinum.

"You look lovely," Faith said. "But go along and I'll let him in."

As she went to the front door, she was glad that Ursula had something new in her life. Glad, yes, but was she also feeling a little wary? Ursula was certainly old enough to look after herself. Wasn't she?

The catering kitchen smelled delicious. Niki had been making various soup stocks. Have Faith was still supplying the food for the Ganley Museum's small café, and this time of year people wanted soup, not salad. Faith immediately felt herself relax on her home turf. Since Rowan House, and even Ursula's, she'd been feeling a bit as if she were in someone else's movie.

She put the manila envelope Ian had given her containing a copy of the contract, another *Heaven or Hell Playbill,* and the list of invited guests on her desk. She'd have time to go over the names and hit the Internet for the start of her sleuthing once she'd talked to Niki about the café menus for the week. The museum was closed on Mondays. Tricia Phelan, who had started as a server years ago and then become an intern, had now taken over this part of Faith's business, but she had Sundays and Mondays off.

"Smoked chicken and wild rice? Scandinavian yellow pea soup is always popular, a change from split pea?" Niki's voice broke through her thoughts. "And how did it go at the famous Mr. Dane's?"

Faith found herself giving Niki a slightly edited account of the visit. She omitted the finale. Like Tom, Niki had misgivings about those activities that could conceivably put Faith in danger. Catering a weekend where a killer was an expected guest and a casket was the pièce de résistance definitely qualified as such. Faith steered the subject back to soup.

"We haven't had the Portuguese chourico with kale and white bean soup in a while. Maybe a different nationality each day for fun? Hungarian mushroom and call the chicken Asian tea-smoked. Add some Chinese five spice? We just need one more for Saturday."

"Look no further than the Greek girl in front of you. Avgolemono!"

"I could go for a bowl of it right now," Faith said. Avgolemono soup was on her list of foods for solace—rich chicken stock gently mixed with egg, lemon, and rice.

Niki and she got to work on the menus and worked out a timetable for all three of them for the week. Niki had become known for her baked goods, especially her cheesecakes. During these slow weeks, this was the one area where business didn't slack off—they always had plenty of special orders for all of the flavors, but especially Niki's new creation, a s'mores cheesecake with dark chocolate, marshmallows, and graham crackers. Faith helped with the cakes that needed to be ready tomorrow, then left Niki to it and turned her entire attention to Max Dane's guests.

Ian Morrison had exceptional penmanship, almost like calligraphy. The list was a work of art.

James Nelson •••••••• *Original director*

Adrian St. John ••••• *Writer* •••••••••••••••••• *London*

Philip Baker •••••••• Composer•••••••••••• Los Angeles

Betty Sinclair •••••••• Lyricist ••••••••••• New York City

Tony Ames •••••••••• Choreographer ••••• New York City

Jack Gold ••••••••••• Set designer ••••••• New York City

Eve Anderson •••••••• Actor •••••••• Holmes, New York

Alexis Reed •••••••••• Actor •••••••••••••• Los Angeles

Travis Trent••••••••••• Actor •••••••••••• Atlantic City

Bella Martelli •••••• Costume designer ••••••• Brooklyn

East Coast and West Coast with one overseas. Or perhaps another location. There was no place named after James Nelson—and what did "original director" mean? She sent off a quick e-mail to Ian asking if the omission had been an oversight. She doubted it, but perhaps they had tracked Mr. Nelson down by now. It would save Faith having to do so. Her plan was to learn as much as possible about these ten people before the weekend. Forewarned is always forearmed . . .

Tapping the invitation card against the window frame, Jack Gold looked out at Fourteenth Street. He'd lived in the East Village, specifically Alphabet City, ever since he arrived in New York thirty-three years ago. The last year of his teens and the last year for Indiana. He'd lived in all sorts of apartments with all sorts of roommates, but now he was alone and in a studio, more accurately a "shoe box." If he stretched out both arms he could almost touch the two walls.

But he was tall, and his reach was a good long one. It wasn't bad and it was cheap for Manhattan, a find on Craigslist—a little over a thousand a month, and who needed an elevator or a doorman? He'd created a sleeping loft with seating below. Jack had learned carpentry skills from his grandfather. Definitely not his father.

His nineteen-year-old Hoosier self didn't know anything about stagecraft, but he started with jobs he'd picked up at club concerts. Maybe he'd missed the 1970s Golden Age of Punk, but there was still plenty of music. CBGB and Club 57. He hung around the new art galleries that were springing up all over and absorbed Jeff Koons, Keith Haring, and Kiki Smith like a sponge. Someone told him he should be doing set design and he thought, Why not? A summer theater gig in the Berkshires and a fabricated résumé that included membership in his high school drama club—as if they would have had him. He was never sure if the reason kids bullied him was because he was a Jew or they suspected his sexual preference. He knew why his father regularly took a belt to him until Jack was taller and bigger. It had nothing to do with religion.

Jack thought about his mother and felt the familiar tightening around his heart. If she'd lived would things have been different or would his father have gone after her, too? He was nine when she lost her battle with cancer and didn't remember a time when she wasn't sick. Her parents just assumed they'd be raising Jack. He still remembered the scene after the funeral, his father shouting, "He's mine and I need him for chores." His father had seemed triumphant that he'd won, even if he didn't want the prize.

His grandmother had died when he was in his early teens, and a week after the funeral his grandfather had taken him to the local bank and opened up a savings account for him. He told Jack not to mention it to his father and made sure Jack could withdraw money himself. After he died two years later, Jack went to the bank. There was almost five thousand dollars in the account.

He left town straight from the high school after graduation ceremonies—his father hadn't come—took the money out and got on a bus.

He'd escaped and never looked back.

Before too long he didn't need to pad his experience as one gig led to another. Jack Gold was in demand. At least back then.

The sight of some slips of paper that had fallen from the envelope broke his reverie. He picked up a round-trip plane ticket to Boston from the floor.

It was more than a plane ticket. It was his ticket to the future. He'd been waiting for years. Pulling his phone from his pocket, he clicked a number on his Favorites list. It answered immediately and Jack started talking. He put it on speaker. His hearing wasn't what it used to be. Years of high decibels.

"Max is giving himself a birthday party."

"Yeah, I got one, too, Jack."

"Going?"

"Maybe. You?"

"Oh yes. And who are you kidding? You know you're going and I know why."

There was a loud chuckle. "Right. I'm in town. Meet for drinks? Tomorrow?"

"Works for me. Manitoba's? Avenue B. You know it? Four thirty?"

"I'll be busy until close to then. Come up here and we'll decide where. Ciao."

Jack ended the call and put the phone back in his pocket. He picked up the invitation and went back to the window. Soft sleet had started to fall, turning the streets and sidewalks into glistening surfaces beneath the backdrop of his beloved city. He never got tired of the scene. No play could equal what went on every day here in front of his eyes.

Niki said good-bye and Faith heard herself responding, but she kept her eyes fixed on the list. When the door closed she said the names softly aloud. Ten of them. Some common; others not. And one was apparently out for blood.

CHAPTER 3

While Faith had given up thinking of herself as an exile from
Manhattan—though not all that long ago—she still read her
hometown paper, the *New York Times,* from the front page to the
last with a scrutiny befitting a diamond cutter. Tom read the *Boston Globe* with less intensity, but closely enough that he could tell
her anything she might need to know. Over the years, she had
found it wasn't much, although she listened to his reports on the
vagaries of Massachusetts politics with appreciative disinterest.

The kids had gone off to school—Ben still looked as if he had
lost his best friend, and in fact he had—Tom was at work, and
Faith didn't need to be at the catering kitchen for an hour. She'd
had plenty of coffee, so although the weather outside did not call
for it, she poured herself a large glass of *agua fresca,* "fresh water"
in Spanish. In the summer she made it with strawberries, melons,
and other fruits. In the winter she made it with a simple sugar
syrup—not too sweet—lime and mint.

Her method for reading the paper, and she liked the print version, had been honed over the years. Making sure there wasn't an
article on the back she wanted to read, she clipped the crossword
puzzle to do before she went to sleep. Next she read the news

summary, turned back to the front page, and then, since today was Wednesday, went to the Food section. After that the New York Metropolitan news before International and National. Today her eye was immediately caught by the headline: APPARENT SUICIDE AT 14TH STREET STATION. She quickly skimmed the short article:

> Onlookers at the East Village's 14th Street station watched in horror as a man jumped in front of the oncoming 6 train heading uptown yesterday around 4 pm. One of the crowd noted that the individual, who had been standing in front of one of the pillars, seemed agitated. Police disclosed that a wallet found on the body identified the man as Jack Goldberg, age fifty-two. The landlord at the address listed on a driver's license said he knew the deceased as Jack Gold and that he had been involved with the theater as a set designer, also commenting, "Nice guy, paid his rent on time." There are no known next of kin.

Abandoning the rest of the paper, Faith went to her laptop, which was on the kitchen counter. She'd been looking up heaven or hell–related recipes. She opened today's *New York Post* and read the same story, albeit couched in much more dramatic language: "anguished" to describe the crowd on the subway platform and an interview with the train's "considerably shaken" driver, who said, "If they want to do it, they do. He was my second."

She then Googled both Jack Gold and Jack Goldberg, adding "set designer." Nothing for Jack Goldberg, but Jack Gold appeared immediately in the *Times* and *Post* articles. All the other hits were for shows he'd worked on.

Monday after Niki left, Faith had stayed on, reading the brief *Playbill* bios—some with photos—for each of Dane's guests. The online mentions confirmed what she recalled. Gold had been the set designer for a number of long-running award-winning shows, mostly musicals. His work was highlighted in a few reviews, which painted a picture of someone who was both creative and painstaking. Much was made of how well the sets were constructed—"an artist and a craftsman." There was little to nothing about his personal life anywhere. And she couldn't find any indication that he'd been connected to a show of any kind after *Heaven or Hell*. She had a growing list of questions she wanted to ask Aunt Chat when she saw her next week and added this. If Jack Gold had been with touring shows for which he had already designed the sets, where would she find mentions?

There were an enormous number of Jack Golds and Jack Goldbergs on Facebook, but when she checked the New York profiles, none fit. She went to Switchboard. No landline. These were becoming rare, especially in places like Manhattan, a city of cell towers. Switchboard did list an address and gave his age as fifty-two, as the papers had noted. Google Earth revealed he'd lived close to the subway station where he had met his death. She knew the neighborhood. It was modest—so far and probably not for much longer, given the current state of New York's luxury apartment building boom. Gentrification didn't come close. It was stratification with a very, very small percent on top.

Would Gold have had the wherewithal for an expensive casket? And how would he have delivered it to Max Dane's doorstep? Both questions were moot now.

As Faith tapped at the keys, one thought remained uppermost in her mind. Jack Gold was most certainly dead. She could cross him off the party's guest list—and the list of suspects, too?

Tom's predecessor at First Parish had been well liked, but there had not been much weeping or wailing—if New Englanders ever did indulge in such—when he left to write a history of celibacy. He was, as Faith had inferred upon hearing this, unmarried. Despite the kitchen's 1950s linoleum and appliances, as well as the taupe, faded walls in every room, he had made no changes to the parsonage save one she learned—a Canadian hemlock hedge along the driveway that ran between the Millers' house next door and the parsonage. By the time Faith arrived, the hedge had grown tall enough to screen off a Minotaur and certainly the neighbors. Soon, however, Tom and Sam cut an opening, reinforcing it with an attractive curved trellis as a shortcut—particularly for their wives, who had been sporting scratched forearms—to each other's houses.

Heading toward the garage to go to work, Faith saw Pix come through the hedge and stopped to wait for her.

"Samantha got home late last night," Pix called.

Faith waited until her friend was closer before asking, "How is she? Losing your job and your boyfriend the same day. Way too much for her to have to go through." She expected Pix to commiserate and was surprised when instead a very flushed Pix said angrily, "Don't feel sorry for her. She certainly doesn't seem to feel sorry for herself. Says she's fine. Has never been happier." She shook her head. "Wellesley, Wharton, London School of Economics, for goodness sake."

The litany was one Faith had heard before, but it was usually recited with pride. She wasn't sure where Pix was going with it now. "But that makes it harder to understand why they let her go. And don't you think she's just putting on a good front? She must be hurting inside."

"Then she should get an Academy Award. Maybe she'll talk to you—or Tom. All she is telling us is that she's taking a break, maybe a long one."

"Doing what? Has she said?"

"Oh yes, she's at a job interview now and I have no doubt she'll get it."

This was more like it, Faith thought. Smart, attractive, hardworking—what firm would not want to hire Samantha Miller? "Where?"

"The Starbucks at the corner of Charles and Beacon in town.

She's applying to be a barista, probably on the strength of the fancy espresso machine we gave her for Christmas last year, although I can't imagine they want any credentials other than a willingness to show up." Pix was grim-faced, but Faith could also see her friend's eyes were moist. "Oh, and one more thing—I know you have to get to work—the breakup. Caleb didn't dump her; she dumped him."

Before Faith could say anything, Pix walked back through the opening in the hemlocks, muttering, "Wellesley, Wharton, London School of Economics."

Faith got it now.

Eve Anderson peered at her face in the mirror. She'd surrounded it with high-wattage dressing room lights. Hollywood lights they were called and they were totally passé. Like herself? She made a slight moue at her reflection. The rest of the house was straight from the pages of Architectural Digest, but over the objections of her decorator she'd insisted on the lighting in here. She'd never been one to walk away from the truth—or from telling it, even when people didn't want to listen.

She put both hands on either side of her neck under the jawbone and pulled back. Necks always gave away a woman's age. She'd need to do something again soon. Sixty may well be the new fifty or even forty, but it didn't come without work. A lot of work.

Her voice was holding up. She'd never been a smoker, and the booze, well that had only been recently and she could stop tomorrow if she wanted. Today even.

The invitation had arrived last week. She was waiting to RSVP. Let Max sweat. She'd sweated for him plenty of times. But she'd go. Oh yes. Twenty years give or take, since that opening night. Twenty years without another. Just shit cameos in B movies. Commercials. When her agent had called with the most recent offer he'd laughed and told her that when he suggested her, the casting director had said, "Isn't she dead?"

She unscrewed the top from one of the jars on the dressing table—Chanel's Sublimage—and gently stroked some over her face and neck. Not a drugstore brand by any means, not Clé de Peau Syn-actif either—a thousand dollars for under an ounce and a half. She smiled. Not broadly. Let the pores absorb the cream smoothly. But she smiled. She'd be able to buy any brand she wanted before long. Dead? Not by a long shot.

"A guy who works for Max Dane called," Niki said. "Sounded English. Ian something. Asked you to call back 'at your convenience.' You have to take me out there. Couldn't you fit me in the housekeeper's suite? I'd be like the scullery maid."

"I wish you could come, but it's not that big a job, and Ian was pretty firm that he'd do everything. Serve, clean up. But I'll get you there the day before when I bring some of the food out in the van," Faith offered, but if Niki saw the casket, things could get dicey. Plus Faith knew the reason only her services were required was so she alone could concentrate on unmasking the merry, or deadly, prankster who had sent it. She could ask Dane if she could show a friend the house, particularly the kitchen, in the spring when the party was long over. Now she needed to return Ian's call. She was pretty sure she knew why.

"Rowan House." Ian answered after three rings. Not too eager. Not too rude.

"It's Faith Fairchild returning your call."

"Ah, yes. Well, there has been a slight change to the guest list."

It was what Faith had expected.

"Yes?"

"Jack Gold will not be with us."

Ever, Faith said to herself.

"In his stead, Mr. Dane has invited a Charles Frost. He lives in Boston and New York. I'll send you an updated list."

"What was his role in *Heaven or Hell*?"

"A small walk-on. His name appeared as an understudy. Also,

there's no immediate rush, but we would like to see the menus, especially for the birthday dinner."

"I can send some of our set menus for all the meals and you can choose what you like or I can propose several. The birthday dinner is almost done. I want to do more testing on a recipe that is new to me, a German dish called *Himmel und Erde*."

"Heaven and Earth," Ian said immediately. "Appropriate."

"Also I will need to know if there are any food allergies. Or specific vegetarian or vegan requests."

"No need to concern yourself. Neither of us has any and we can modify a dish or substitute for one should the need arise." His tone had become brusque. Faith might be catering, but neither Dane nor Ian would be accommodating the guests' real or preferred food preferences.

She was about to hang up when she realized she still hadn't received information on James Nelson, save "original director" after his name. And it was a common one. She hadn't had any luck finding him online and the *Playbill* bio only listed *Heaven or Hell* as a credit. "Have you found out where James Nelson is living?" she asked.

There was a long pause and she was beginning to think he had hung up when at last he answered, "We're on it. I'll let you know."

"So I should assume he's coming?"

"You should definitely assume he will be there. Good-bye."

As Faith hung up she wondered whether the last name of the new guest, Charles Frost, was connected to the Helen Frost Ursula had mentioned. The classmate who had lived with her family at Havencrest. Who was it that said there were no coincidences?

She hadn't thought she had asked the question aloud, but Niki piped up, "That would be Turtle in *Kung Fu Panda*. What's coincidental?"

"Nothing really. Just a random thought. But are you sure it isn't someone else? Like Einstein, Freud, or Mae West?"

"How can you doubt me, unenlightened one? 'There are no

coincidences in this world.' That's the direct quote. I have more too from the *Panda*. How about 'There are no accidents'?"

"How about helping me test the recipe I mentioned? The heaven part are apples and the earth are potatoes."

"I hope there are more ingredients. Sounds a big stodgy, but sure, let's give it a whirl."

Chip Frost edged his way out of bed. It wasn't that he was afraid of disturbing the other occupant—and who was she?—but if he moved too fast he'd toss his cookies before he could get to the can.

He just made it and embraced the cool porcelain throne with relief. It hadn't been cookies, but shots—a lot of shots. And then the lady—Rochelle? Rachel? something like that—wanted champagne. A lot of champagne. "Chip, old boy," he muttered aloud, "you know better than to mix drinks like that." Maybe bourbon and scotch, but definitely not champagne with hard liquor. And had he eaten yesterday?

He threw up again and passed out on the tile floor.

"Hey, Romeo! Wake up! I need to pee and where's my money?" She kicked him. It wasn't a gentle kick.

He sat up carefully. "No need to get rough. The place is all yours." The room was spinning, but not too bad. He grabbed the rim of the toilet and pushed himself to a standing position.

"It stinks in here! Jeez." She flushed the toilet. "Now scram. A lady needs her privacy."

"But you're no lady" was on the tip of his tongue. He recalled the kick and kept his mouth shut.

When he heard the shower running, he got dressed quickly, making sure his wallet was in his pocket, and also retrieved the cash he kept hidden. This one seemed smarter than most and he wouldn't put it past her to rip the place apart to find the dough. And he couldn't take the chance.

Unemployment was about to run out and he had pretty much run out of people to hit up. His immediate family had been happy to keep him afloat—and away—for years. But now Mother, Father—the people who cared about their God almighty name—were gone.

Something would turn up though. It always had.

The elevator was at his floor. A good sign. When he stepped out into the lobby, one of the doormen handed him his mail. Another offered him an umbrella. It was starting to rain. "Good morning, Mr. Frost. Have a good day." They spoke so close to one another, it could have been a chorus.

"You too, guys. You too."

He made sure to go to a coffee shop a good distance from the apartment, sat in a back booth just to make sure, and ordered a toasted plain bagel with lite cream cheese—he was over forty now, had to keep the waistline trim. They knew him here and the waitress handed him a cup of black coffee as soon as he sat down. He drained it quickly and she was at his side with a refill.

The small pile of mail contained plenty of bills, as expected, fund appeals—which was ludicrous—and a square envelope addressed with great finesse, like the writing on wedding invitations. The paper was superior as well. He'd done a stint in the stationery department at Tiffany and could tell. He turned the envelope over. Engraved return address. "Rowan House Havencrest." Well, well.

His bagel arrived and he took a large bite. He didn't have to open the envelope to know who sent it. Rowan House. Havencrest. "Chip, old boy," he said to himself, "looks like the time has come."

He decided to treat himself to a Danish. "Warm it, will you? Piping hot."

Faith loved Friday nights, especially if Tom had finished his sermon. Not having to get the kids up and off to school the next morning and in her slow season few or no catering jobs meant it was possible for the Fairchilds to go out themselves. Ben and Amy were in that blissful sitter-free period. Plus they both usually had plans with friends, as tonight. Faith toyed with the idea of a dinner à deux—lighting candles and opening a good bottle of wine now that the kids were out the door. She had leftovers from to-day's luncheon, a fancy plated one at the museum for potential do-nors. Smoked trout pâté with frisée salad followed by roasted duck breast on a bed of root vegetables with pommes Anna. Dessert had been mocha panna cottas. Or they could go to a movie—a rare treat when it came to both scheduling and finding something they wanted to see. She was leaning toward staying home and went into the living room to make sure there was a fire laid. They could eat in front of it with a snifter of brandy afterward and then after that . . .

Hearing the back door open, she went to greet Tom. Each Fairchild had a different step and different ways of opening the door, depending on mood. Tom's footfall was softer than usual and the door didn't bang shut. A good day?

"Honey, I'm in here," she called. "I need your fire-making skills. The kids are out, so I thought we could stay in."

Faith had not been a Girl Scout or Campfire Girl and any fires she tried to start burned brilliantly for about five minutes before dying. Tom, on the other hand, not only had been an Eagle Scout, but also had that particular male gene that endows an ability to take two twigs and create a bonfire in no time.

Tom came through the door from the kitchen with a glass of wine in each hand. "Thought we could get a head start," he said and came over to give Faith a very promising kiss.

"Hmmm. Unless you're very hungry, we could postpone din-ner for a while."

"Oh, I'm hungry all right," he said, heading for the stairs.

Following her husband, Faith gave a passing thought to what might have put him in such a cheerful, and amorous, mood, let-ting it very much pass.

Downstairs an hour or so later, Faith was starting to fill Tom in on the Samantha situation when she realized he wasn't paying attention.

"Aside from terrific quality time together, you seem very happy about something, sweetheart," she said.

"I am," Tom said. "Late this afternoon I got a call from another member of the Planning Board. We finally have a town counsel and one he expects will be able to prevent the strip mall from coming in. Blake Sommersby, new to town—our good luck—specializes in the Commonwealth's laws governing Historic Districts, as well as those that cover razing existing structures of possible value for a town's legacy."

"That's great! Wish someone like that had been in place when they tore down Penn Station." For Faith *local* meant the Big Apple still, especially when it came to the destruction of landmarks.

Since Aleford was a small town and the town's lawyer, or counsel, was appointed not elected, the salary was pretty minimal. The position had always been filled by someone who essentially wanted to volunteer. The previous counsel had retired from both his firm in downtown Boston and the Aleford post, moving to Florida with his wife when she declared she wasn't spending another winter up north. She'd been born and grew up in North Carolina. "I've done my time," she said at the farewell dinner friends gave for the couple, catered by Have Faith with food anticipated rather than what she was leaving behind, as requested—"I don't want to see a single baked bean on my plate." The town counsel post had been empty for months and Faith didn't envy the new appointee the backlog of issues, such as who pays for the removal of a tree that has fallen over the property line and the always controversial right-of-way feuds.

"Another reason I'm smiling—besides the obvious—is that Sam called this morning. He's been out of town. You probably know that, what with the tin cans and string telephone I believe you and Pix have. Anyway, he's lending a hand. Not, as he pointed out, completely out of the goodness of his heart, but because the new building impacts them even more than the church and us. He thinks there may be an ordinance about excavating so close to the cemetery, or as it was called then, 'the burial ground.'"

"You mean there could be bodies underneath the Grayson House property?"

"It's possible. Before the early sixteen hundreds, the date on the earliest stones we have, Sam thinks it could have been a Native American site. In any case, there were always those—paupers, miscreants—who would have been buried outside the walls."

"Also not all the original walls remain," Faith said, "so there could have been further ones extending the graveyard into the spot the developer wants to build on."

Tom nodded. "Now what's going on with Samantha?"

Selective hearing syndrome had been at work. Usually Tom was a terrific listener—went with the job—but Faith had already told him about this. That Samantha had lost her job and boyfriend possibly only a few hours apart. She told him again, adding that the young woman was now working at Starbucks.

"Well, Pix must be glad she's home. And knowing Samantha she'll get bored making lattes and be back on the fast track soon."

Deciding not to go into the whole Pix unexcited about the return to the nest despite laundry and cooking help, Faith said, "It's pretty puzzling. She hasn't shared why she was pink slipped, although she did tell her mother that she was the one who broke up with Caleb."

Ben had come in almost noiselessly. Overhearing the last remark, he blurted out, "Samantha dumped Caleb? What is wrong with these women!!!"

Tom and Faith exchanged glances. It was going to be a long haul.

"Take a break, kids," Tony Ames said. "Hydrate! And we'll take it from the top again in a few."

They weren't the best troupe of dancers he'd worked with; they weren't the worst. And by opening night they'd bring that special pizzazz from being onstage, which always gives energy to the opening number—the number that makes or breaks a show. Granted, the audience the first night would be mostly friends and relatives, but he thought the show had legs. A decent book and even better director. Sure it was off-off-Broadway, but hadn't A Chorus Line started off-off, too? Not that he thought this could be a megahit, another legend, but there was always a chance. And he was doing what he loved as opposed to the dry spells when he wasn't choreographing. Making the rent teaching adult ed swing dance classes in Jersey and yet another community theater production of Grease in Connecticut.

He'd stuffed the mail in his messenger bag and went to his seat to check what had come in. The bag's leather had softened over the last twenty-five years—shit, a quarter of a century! It had been his first splurge when he'd been hired for Dream Girls, starting his career as a hoofer before moving into choreography. Luck, a fluke, whatever. He'd barely stepped off the train from Albany, still hearing his mother's words of encouragement. She'd paid for the ticket and insisted it be one-way. "I'll come see you!" And she had. Every one of the shows he'd been a part of except for the last big gig. Her death had hit him hard, but there was that silver lining. She hadn't been at the opening—and closing—night. The night of the long knives in effect.

He pulled out what had been in his mailbox—a couple of days' worth—and rifled through it. Mostly circulars.

At first he thought the envelope was one of those fund appeals made to look fancy so you'd be sure to open it, thinking it might be a real invitation. But he could tell the calligraphy had been done by hand. Then he saw the return address on the back flap. He took his Swiss Army knife out of his pocket and used it as a paper knife. Tearing it open seemed inappropriate.

He scanned the words quickly. So Max was giving himself a

party. "Come as you are—or be cast." He'd come, oh yes, he'd most
certainly come—and as he was. No need to be cast. He knew what
his part would be. And he could have torn the envelope open.

Faith was loading the car with household trash and recyclables
for a dump run. The official name was the "transfer station," but
Faith had never heard anyone use it. Normally this was Tom's job
and one he happily assumed. The Aleford dump was a convivial
place, and he'd come home to report on whom he'd caught up
with and, during an election, who was there campaigning with
coffee and Munchkins. Besides the sightings, which Faith always
enjoyed, he also, however, invariably brought home one or more
finds from the Swap Table. These Faith did not enjoy. She'd have
to wait awhile before boxing up the perfectly good mugs, baskets,
utensils, and once a whole bag of candle stubs for Goodwill. If she
took them back to the dump, they'd miraculously appear at the
parsonage again.

Today, though, the dump task was hers. The night before,
Tom had gotten a call from the chair of the Planning Board, hoping he was free this morning to meet the new town counsel. It was
the only time they could all get together. Faith sent an assortment
of muffins from the freezer. The town hall had an abundance of
coffeemakers, but there wouldn't be any food.

It continued to be an unnatural winter. The forsythia was
starting to bud out and the air had a curious quality. No nip in it,
but not springlike either. It made wardrobe choices difficult. No
L.L.Bean down coat that made her look like the Michelin Man,
but her UNIQLO stuff jacket wasn't warm enough.

Faith turned to musing over the odd path her life had taken
that required trips to dumps in both places she lived—Sanpere and
Aleford—and was thinking nostalgically about the rumble of the
large garbage trucks on Manhattan streets when she heard someone call her name.

It was Samantha Miller. Faith hadn't seen her since the young woman had moved back home and went over to the opening in the hedge to give her a hug.

"Hi!" Samantha said. "I have a favor to ask. Could I borrow a bike? Mom seems to have given all ours to some sort of PTO fund-raiser."

Despite the fact that Pix's kids were old enough to have kids of their own, Pix was still involved with things like the PTO and even the Girl Scout cookie drive. There had been a sale of gently used athletic equipment last fall, Faith recalled. Tom had picked up some perfectly good hockey skates for all of them, even his nonskater wife. Faith hoped some organization would have another sale next year. Maybe in nearby Concord out of sight.

"Of course. Take your pick. It's certainly warm enough for a nice long ride."

"It is, but I need one for transportation. Dad's at some sort of meeting and Mom took the other car to go shopping in town with Granny. Apparently my grandmother wanted to go to Saks of all places."

While Faith was searching for some sort of comment—Saks was definitely not Ursula's usual clothier and her granddaughter did not seem to know about why Granny might want a new kind of wardrobe—Samantha began walking toward the garage. Instead Faith said, "Transportation? I'm on my way to the dump and could drop you where you need to go."

"Thank you, but I'm headed the opposite direction—the Shop'n Save." Samantha held up a backpack. "There's no real food in the house and I'm making Dad's favorite lasagna for dinner. The way you taught me—with béchamel sauce as well as tomato. I want to make a big salad, too, with sliced fennel if they have it."

Faith saw an opportunity. She could help Samantha out, good deed number one, and try to find out what had happened both with the job and boyfriend for Pix, good deed number two. Plus she was dying to know what had happened herself.

"I'm going to the market after the dump, so if you don't mind stopping there first, we could do our shopping together. And maybe go out to Verrill Farm. I need squash, plus they have the best selection of local cheeses."

Samantha beamed. "Great! I can do a big marketing. Would you believe Mom doesn't have olive oil?"

Faith would. She opened the passenger-side door for the girl, the words "Come into my parlor said the spider to the fly" springing unbidden to mind.

"And one more for the road," Travis Trent sang, hitting the keys with a flourish and flashing a smile at the customer who had requested it. Of course he had requested it. He'd had many more than one for the road. Travis just hoped the shots the guy had been doing while Travis was performing hadn't pushed him past his ability to stumble back to the tip jar and leave more than the measly two bucks he had stuck in earlier.

"Ladies and gentlemen, any more requests? You know you are a lovely audience . . ." Travis segued into the Beatles number, and as usual it worked; first one Boomer, then two more came up asking for the golden oldies of their youth. The 1960s. Good times. He played that one as well.

It was almost two when he called it quits and headed for his apartment. The dueling piano act in the bar near the Boardwalk was still going strong, but Travis knew that he wouldn't make much more, if anything, for what was left of the night. Before he left, he'd sat at the bar for his one-drink limit. Joe always had a whiskey sour waiting for him. Sipping the sweet liquid with its kick brought blessed silence, a kind of bubble after the evening's unvarying requests. Christ, didn't anybody know any other tunes? It was an age thing, he supposed. Time had stopped at the prom for most of the bar's customers.

Well, Bernie, he said to himself—he hadn't been "Bernard" for over forty years, "Travis Trent" a better stage name—no point in moving on. With Social Security not far down the line so long as the stupid politicians in Washington didn't totally screw it up. He should have invested. There was a time when he was making pretty decent money. But so long as his voice held out—hell, look at Tony Bennett—with this gig or one like it and the Social Security he could maybe even afford an apartment and not just a room. Not come in at the start of happy hour and make a dinner out of the greasy chicken wings and mozzarella sticks they put out. He'd been to the buffets at the casinos where they had prime rib, real food, too often lately. You'd think there would be more staff turnover, and why did they even care? So he wasn't hitting the tables. Never had. Bernie didn't believe in luck.

The glass was drained. He ate the cherry and caught a glimpse of himself in the mirror behind the bar. He patted his hair. Still had it. You were a good-looking bastard back in the day, Bernie, he told himself. Still not too bad if you didn't look close.

He put on his jacket. Weather was so warm he almost didn't need one, although the wind off the ocean could surprise you. He'd been in Atlantic City for Sandy, now that was wind.

The boardinghouse was a short walk away. He'd picked it for that reason. An old guy was an easy mark for the kind of scum out on the streets this time of night. He left his tips with the boss, too. Totaled it up and made sure it was added to his paycheck. Kept just enough for essentials. And on payday, the check went into the bank.

His landlady had left the light on in the downstairs hall and he was expected to turn it off when he came in. Put the chain up on the front door, too. The mail was in neatly labeled boxes on a table. His was almost always empty and he'd stopped checking early on. Who was going to write to him? Not because nobody used snail mail. He didn't get mail on a computer either. Didn't have a computer. Had to have a phone though. Had a TracFone, pay as you go. Could be his motto.

When he reached for the light switch, he saw an envelope in his box.

It was addressed to him all right. He turned it over. "Rowan

House Havencrest." Hmmm. He flicked the switch. Clutching the envelope, he climbed the stairs in the dim light from the upstairs hall, put his key in the lock, and went into his room. He sat on the bed, switched on the lamp next to it, and ripped the flap open, revealing what was inside. Besides the invitation there was a first-class round-trip airline ticket to Boston from Newark and instructions about a car service. There was also a money order for five hundred dollars and a note clipped onto it: "Treat yourself to a new outfit." It wasn't Max's handwriting. Wasn't his on the address either. It might have been twenty years, but Bernie would still recognize it.

Max Dane's birthday. Something to celebrate? Bernie would go and find something else to celebrate.

Faith was getting nowhere with Samantha. They went to Verrill Farm before the market and Faith treated her to coffee and a scone, one Faith had to admit was up there with hers and Niki's. Samantha was eager to chat about her Starbucks job. How fun the training was and how they'd said she was a natural. Her regular hours would start Monday and wasn't it neat that she could commute by train, a five-minute walk from the house? "I'm doing my best to keep my carbon footprints clean," she said. "And no worries about what to wear. Good-bye power suits!"

"Won't you miss the city?" Faith finally asked point-blank.

"Not a bit. I'm a Beantown babe," Samantha said jauntily. "Won't miss a single thing or a single person."

Well, Faith thought, that partly answered the Caleb question. She'd thought the couple had been good together. He'd even passed the all-important Sanpere test, the one where he was invited to the island and didn't ask "What do you find to do here?"

At the Shop'n Save, they each grabbed a cart and entered the market. Samantha stopped at aisle one and said, "I'll meet you at the checkout. Fifteen minutes enough time? Or do you need more?"

Since Faith only needed milk and was going to have to invent a list, she agreed.

"Oh, and Faith," Samantha said. "I know what you have been trying to do, but please tell my mother I'm not talking about the former job or former boyfriend, even to you. Not now or ever. I'm fine. Just fine and very happy." She gave Faith a quick hug to take away any sting her words might have had. Faith hugged her back, and feeling slightly shamefaced, decided to get the ingredients for the Heaven and Earth, *Himmel und Erde,* dish. (See recipe, page 235.) She thought how much she would have resented someone prying the way Faith had been attempting and resolved to steer clear of Samantha's work, love, and anything-else life unless Ms. Miller spoke first.

Faith had prepared the German dish with Niki, and it had been good but needed fine-tuning. She ran down the list: potatoes, some tart apples, onions, garlic, a lemon, and the spices—thyme and maybe nutmeg. Essentially it was mashed potatoes and cooked apples mixed together. She'd get her family's opinion. It would make a Saturday night comfort food addition to some good sausages, or she might cook the pork loin she had in the freezer if everyone was going to be home for dinner.

Driving back to the parsonage and the Millers' house, Faith kept the conversation on the weather veering only to the personal in regard to her own family.

"Has anyone mentioned that Mandy has told Ben she needs some space for a while? Texted him and has also unfriended both him and Amy."

"Oh no! I haven't heard. Poor Ben. He must be crazed. I don't think I've ever known anyone so in love, and devoted. I'll drop by later if he's home. He might want to talk to someone other than a parent."

Remembering Ben's bitter comment upon hearing that Samantha had dumped Caleb, Faith said, "Since he's not talking about it to either parent, you would be correct, but maybe hold off a bit."

Samantha nodded. "Men are not exactly the best communicators. Let me know if you think I should try though."

They pulled into the Millers' drive. Samantha had many more bags than Faith, and Pix came out to help them unload the car.

"What is going on with my mother? She bought what she called 'le cocktail,' plus two more outfits that she called 'everyday' and I'd call dressy. And shoes."

The Miller women, at least two of them, were doing very well in the secret-keeping department, Faith reflected. She couldn't think of an appropriate way to mention Ursula's friend Austin— obviously the reason for a wardrobe update.

"Thanks for the ride, Faith. Going to start my lasagna," Samantha said as she carried the last bag into the house.

Pix turned eagerly to Faith, but before she could say anything, Faith said, "Nada." The shrug both women gave simultaneously would have been comical if it hadn't also been accompanied by heavy sighs.

Entering the parsonage kitchen, Faith wasn't surprised to see Sam Miller at her kitchen table with Tom.

"Need some help, honey?" Tom asked.

"It's just this one bag, thanks." Both men had grinders from Country Pizza. Harry made good pies, but Tom often opted, as now, for the steak and cheese loaded with grilled onions and peppers. Sam appeared to have the same, and they each had a bottle of Heineken. From all appearances, the meeting had gone well.

"So, what's the town counsel like? Are our worries over?"

"Don't want to jinx anything," Sam, ever the judicious lawyer, said, "but we were very impressed. Blake presented a number of strategies and definitely knows the Commonwealth's arcane laws governing Historic Districts. I knew a lot was town by town, but there's plenty that are statewide, too. And since it all goes back a long way, there are many precedents."

Tom took a swig of his beer. "I don't believe in jinxes, so I can say that I think we're going to win this. It's not going to be a walk in the park, but Blake knows how to walk the walk for sure."

Faith laughed to herself. Tom was a cheap date, always had been. Half a bottle of beer and his voice had softened plus his metaphors increased in number and absurdity.

"Well, great. If this Blake is so conversant with these laws, it means the other side has to pay its lawyer or lawyers to match. And because ours is virtually pro bono, we can drag this out."

Sam nodded his approval. "Exactly. It's all about money as far as the developer is concerned."

"Yup," Tom said, and took a large bite of his grinder. "What do they call these in New York?" he asked Faith. "Something weird. Hoagies?"

"That's Philly, and 'grinder' isn't weird? Anyway, the correct term as far as I'm concerned is a 'hero.'"

Sam finished his beer, pushing back his chair. "And that's exactly what Blake is going to be. Our hero—Wonder Woman, I hope."

"Wait a minute," Faith said. "Blake's not a man?"

"Nope," her husband said. Both men were smiling, and Faith had the feeling it wasn't because the sandwiches had been unusually tasty.

Sam confirmed her thought. "And she's a knockout."

Chapter 4

"Letter for you, Jimmy." If Wendell Haskell was surprised he didn't show it. The man in front of him had never to his knowledge as postmaster on the island received a personal letter—especially not one with such fancy lettering on the front. "Figured it must be you, being as there are no other men named 'James' out here."

James Nelson smiled. "You'd make a good detective, although maybe this wasn't a hard one to figure out."

Wendell handed the letter over the counter. "What else can I get you? Weather's been so warm, some of the fishermen have been scalloping. And the wife baked this morning. Bread and blueberry muffins from berries she had in the freezer."

It made life easy that all his needs could be met by this one tiny general store, James thought. Even when the island was cut off from the mainland by bad weather, Wendell and his wife, Judy, kept everybody supplied. Each summer she put up more vegetables than the Jolly Green Giant and baked every day.

"A couple of muffins would go down a treat. Did my beans come in? I'm almost out." He indulged himself by grinding a strong dark *roast that he ordered from a place on Sanpere Island that roasted the beans themselves and put them on the mail boat fresh.*

"Not today. Maybe tomorrow." Wendell put the muffins in a bag.

James paid him, told him to thank Judy, and strode out into the weak January sunshine. He looked at the return address on the envelope and crumbled the letter into a ball. But he didn't toss it. He stuck it in his pocket and walked to his small cabin five miles across the island on the wilder side that directly faced the open ocean. He ate one of the muffins as the dirt road gave way to the path through the woods he'd worn over the years. The smell of the pines went well with the taste of the blueberries and he felt content.

After he got home and stoked the woodstove, he opened the envelope. Max had tracked him down. He was sure others had tried, but of course it would be Max who found him. He stared at the plane ticket, Bangor to Boston, and read that a car service would meet him. Attention to detail, that was Max. Every last detail. Well, James was pretty good at every last detail, too. Time would tell.

He grabbed a garment bag with the PAUL STUART *logo from the small closet that sufficed for his needs and unzipped it. He checked the contents, smiling. Camouflage.*

The MLK breakfast had gone well. Besides marking the day and honoring Dr. King, Faith knew that Dr. Charles V. Willie, the speaker from nearby Concord, had been a big draw. Dr. Willie was retired from a long, prestigious career in academia. He had been a classmate of King's at Morehouse and a close friend. It had been electrifying hearing the man, now almost ninety, talk about his friend and the struggle for civil rights—one that was still far from over.

Faith spent all her free moments over the weekend looking up Max's guests on the Internet. Late Saturday, she'd had an e-mail from Ian informing her that James Nelson lived on a small island in Penobscot Bay, Maine. Knowing the area well from her time at Sanpere, Faith immediately recognized the name of Nelson's island—Haute Mers Isle. The name was another legacy of Champlain's voyaging—a corruption of the French for "high seas." One side of the island had waters so treacherous even the fishermen avoided it. Only a handful of rusticators had discovered the small island in the late nineteenth century. It wasn't a Mount Desert with Bar Harbor, now overrun by mammoth cruise ships. As on Sanpere, the descendants of the original rusticators still arrived each summer to do what the families had always done—sail, swim in the frigid water, collect and press ferns, pick blueberries. The last Faith heard the year-round population was seventy-three and declining. James Nelson was off the grid.

She'd call her friends Rosalie and Steve Robbins, who caretaked out there, to see what they knew about him. With a community that small, there would be few secrets. Except for those in the past?

Despite the Internet's reputation for providing revelations of all natures, Faith hadn't discovered much more about the guests than what had been in the *Playbill* bios. Almost all of the head shots she'd been able to find looked out of date. There were a few brief references to what several had gone on to do—notably the choreographer Tony Ames, actress Eve Anderson, and Jack Gold, the set designer. Except Jack wasn't on the list anymore . . .

The last breakfast attendees had departed. Packing up with her staff, Faith was gratified to see that there was some food left over, but not too much. Nothing left meant they hadn't prepared enough, and the opposite that they had calculated wrong. After the van was loaded, she sent everyone home and set off for the kitchen with Niki to finish the cleanup.

"Isn't this the week your aunt Chat has that conference?" Niki said. "Will she be able to come out here?"

Faith shook her head. The two women had met on a number of occasions over the years and liked each other. Cut from the same cloth—a bright and very durable one. "I'm afraid not.

It is the week though. She's taking the train up today and her conference goes until Wednesday afternoon. But she has to go straight back early Thursday. Tom and I are meeting her for dinner Wednesday night. She's attending a banquet tomorrow night where she's getting an award—female business trailblazer, from what I've been able to tell—she's vague on any details. You know she would never brag. I'd like to be in the audience and afterward at the banquet, but she said she'd rather have a visit without rubber chicken."

"Where is it?"

"It's at the B School, so that means Harvard food services, which can be okay."

"Aren't they on strike?"

"Settled, which is a good thing. Chat would have had to nibble granola bars or something. She wouldn't have eaten strikebreaker food."

They arrived at the kitchen and it didn't take long before they had loaded the dishwashers and finished the rest of the cleanup.

"I've got to make a few cheesecakes," Niki said. "I swear my mother strong-arms people in Watertown Square into ordering them." In addition to making cheesecakes for Have Faith, she had, with Faith's approval, set up a small business making them to order.

"Go ahead. Amelia's shower isn't until Friday night, so we have plenty of time. There are only some sandwich platter orders and a few other things before that plus the Ganley café."

Faith sat down at her desk. Her weekend's work had convinced her that it was somewhat pointless to Google and Facebook Max's list. She'd be able to judge the guests herself soon enough, using her eyes and especially her ears. As the help, she would be invisible. The *pas devant les domestiques,* the "not in front of the servants," of past eras had disappeared with ubiquitous aspidistras. One of the first things she'd noticed when she'd started catering was that people said anything and everything as if she were a potted plant herself.

It was time to go back out to Rowan House. After all, Max Dane had created the list. He'd had a reason, or more than one, to suspect each person. It was time for him to share them with Faith. The party itself was only a little over a week away.

She shut down her computer. There was one significant thing she'd learned over the weekend during her searches. Max Dane hadn't produced or directed anything since *Heaven or Hell*. He'd been only fifty with a string of successes the envy of the Great White Way. What had happened to make him stop so abruptly? She was sure that particular part of his past was a prologue.

"Did you get one?"

"Get what? So far the Academy hasn't called with my nomination."

"Don't be coy, it doesn't suit you."

"But cute does. You always said I was cute."

"I said you were a lot of things."

"And 'bitch' never suited you, Betty. So, yes, I got the invite for Max's bash. Plane ticket, the works."

"Then you're going?"

"Of course I'm going. Have you ever known me to turn down a freebie? And this one is a first-class cross-country plane ticket. Might hang out with you afterward in the city for a while even if the weather is lousy. Nobody ever wrote 'Winter in New York,' even 'Autumn' was stretching it."

"What makes you think I have room—and want you?"

"You'll make room—and you always wanted me."

"I think it was vice versa," Betty Sinclair said dryly. When she'd started out as half of the Baker and Sinclair duo that became famous for a string of hit musicals—she was the words, Phil was the music—she had thought he was cute. Cute enough to marry.

"The question is: Do we come as we are or be cast?" Phil asked.

"Hmmm. Better be cast, since Lord knows what we are."

"Hey, how about loving husband and wife?"

"Buddy boy, I haven't laid eyes on you in over ten years. And that was after a quick drink in L.A. when we ran into each other in the lobby of the Beverly Hills Hotel. For all I know you're wearing a rug and using Depends now."

"Please, you were the cradle snatcher when we met."

"Three years younger! And you were no kid; you knew your way around." Her voice took on a harsh tone. "Before and after if memory serves."

"She meant nothing. I told you then and I'm telling you now."

"Think she'll be there? And the others?"

"Oh yes. In Bette's immortal words, 'Fasten your seat belts, it's going to be a bumpy night'—or weekend in this case."

For someone in particular, he thought to himself as he said good-bye and ended the call. He was sick to death of being known as a has-been, composing jingles at fifty-five. He was in the prime of life—or would be even more soon.

On the other side of the country, Betty Sinclair shut her phone, too. She turned to the young man stretched out on her couch. "You may have to find another place to stay soon, sweetheart. Mother has things to do."

"You're not old enough to be my mother," he said.

"But you're old enough to be my son. Now, when I say scoot, you scoot."

"But not yet?"

"No, not yet."

She was feeling happier than she had in ages. There was nothing like a good plan—or lyric. She started to hum one of her hits as she moved over to the couch.

When Tom announced that he wouldn't be able to make dinner on Wednesday night with Chat because there was a special Planning Board meeting with the new town counsel, Faith had mixed emotions. Her husband was no stoopnagle—a useful quirky word introduced to her by the Millers and unknown in the Manhattan neighborhood of her youth. Tom would most certainly be suspicious when Faith started pumping her aunt for information about Max Dane at dinner. The leap to the fact that Dane was not just another client would take seconds. Seconds more to his adamant request that she bow out of the job, envisioning not a curtain call, but curtains for his wife.

On the other hand, Faith wasn't happy that it was this particular meeting causing the cancellation. There seemed to be an increasing number of them. She'd have to attend the next one—much as she disliked sitting on the hard chairs in town hall for things like this, unable to do anything to pass the time except make up menus in her head. She wanted to have a look at Ms. Blake Sommersby. Tom might be a man of the cloth, but he was also a man. While Faith had no doubt that Tom had stuck to his vows—forsaking all others—and would continue to do so, she wanted to get a sense of what Blake was like.

Blake wasn't married and didn't have kids. Sam had supplied a few details before going home on Saturday. She had moved from Cambridge, the westward direction another unusual choice for a singleton. Suburban Aleford was a married or partnered town.

While expressing regret that he was missing a visit with Charity Sibley—she and Tom were in a mutual admiration club—Tom had seemed a tad too eager about the upcoming meeting. Let it go, Faith told herself, adding, for now, as she called the Harvest, one of her favorite Cambridge restaurants, and near Chat's hotel, to change the reservation from three to two. Besides the food, most locally sourced, it was one of sadly few restaurants where you could actually have a conversation at the table without competing with music or the noise of fellow diners wedged in to create more covers.

As she waited for her aunt, who had texted to say she would be a few minutes late, Faith was happy with her choice. The Harvest's winter menu was a tempting one. She decided to indulge herself with a glass of prosecco. Miles away her family was ably fending for itself. She'd left a hearty beef stew with carrots, parsnips, and caramelized onions simmering, a package of egg noodles on the counter. Both her kids knew their way around the kitchen.

She loved being with her family, but it was a treat to be anonymous. To not have to look at Ben's still woebegone face, listen to Amy's school chatter, or enthuse with Tom about a certain lawyer.

Her drink arrived and she took a sip, leaning against the banquette. The restaurant was filled with the usual People's Republic of Cambridge crowd. Some elderly, aging gracefully, and possibly customers for the whole forty years the restaurant had been in existence. She spotted several vintage Marimekkos. Then groups of academics, a visiting speaker taken out after a colloquium. You could always tell who it had been; palpable on those faces was relief that the talk was over and he or she hadn't muffed it. And yes, several Harris Tweed sports jackets with suede patches. A few tables of younger people, perhaps celebrating a special occasion. The Harvest wasn't cheap. Hip groups in black. Looking at them, she could have been in Manhattan.

She saw Chat come in and rose to greet her. Faith was always startled to see Chat in old family photographs, since her aunt always looked the same to her, which of course wasn't possible. But the young Charity Sibley had carried much the same weight—an armful—and was tall like all the Sibleys. Her hair was still mostly dark brown and pulled back in an approximation of a French twist. A few strands had escaped, as usual. She was wearing a pants suit, adopted years before Hillary created the trend, and when she enveloped her niece in a tight hug, smelled of her favorite scent, Arpége. The old slogan "Promise her anything, but give her Arpége" didn't apply to Chat, although she might have come up with it. Chat got more than promises—firm results, which was, Faith thought, why she had been honored by Harvard.

"Darling, so sorry. They would keep asking questions and the

students are such dears. So young they look as if they're dress-
ing up for Halloween as adults. But not to be fooled—they will
morph into very successful sharks. Now what are we drinking?
Prosecco?" She motioned to the server, who came immediately.
"Let's have a bottle. It goes with everything. Especially oysters.
Do you have them tonight?"

Hearing that they did, Chat ordered a dozen for them to start
on right away. While they waited, the two talked about family,
the B School event, books they were reading, politics, and whether
Chat should cut her hair—a constant topic and one that always
ended with her decision to leave it as it was. After the oysters, they
ordered their main courses. Faith loved venison, and this version,
juniper roasted served with red wine braised cabbage, very Nor-
dic, sounded perfect. Chat ordered butter-poached halibut with
hen of the woods mushrooms.

When the main courses arrived, there was a brief silence as
they savored the truly excellent preparations and then Chat said,
"Okay, Max Dane. I assume you took the job. What do you want
to know—and why?"

Faith gave her the expurgated version, emphasizing the spectacular house and admitting to being excited about creating a
Heaven or Hell banquet for those involved in the production. "You
said the firm did the PR for it. Why wasn't it a success?"

Chat seemed to be weighing her words carefully, taking her
time. "I brought copies of some of our promo materials, also the
synopsis, and whatever else I could lay my hands on. Max blamed
the agency for what was such a big flop; even Joe Allen's didn't put
the poster on the wall."

Joe Allen was a legendary restaurant on West Forty-sixth
Street, an easy stroll from Broadway theaters, known for the theatrical posters of major flops that lined its walls and good, old-
fashioned comfort food—especially their hamburgers, steaks, and
banana cream pie.

"Max also blamed pretty much everyone involved with the

show—let me see the guest list. I'm betting it includes the major actors, the composer and lyricist, set designer, and so forth. Everybody except Max himself. You have to remember that before *Heaven or Hell*, he'd had nothing but successes. His previous show immediately prior to it had had a three-year run. He closed it to make way for the new one. I can't remember the exact number of years, but there was a Max Dane show on Broadway each year pretty much since Hector was a pup."

Faith nodded. She'd read similar phrases—perhaps a bit less colorful—online when she Googled him. "He must have really believed in *Heaven or Hell*."

"It *should* have been a hit," Chat continued. "Maybe not a smash, but a decent run, then a few years on the road. The tryout in Boston was encouraging, and if Max had agreed to make some changes and not rushed it to Broadway—started it off-Broadway— I'm pretty sure things would have been different. His director quit, or I should say Max made it impossible for him to continue, at that point."

"James Nelson?"

"Yes. I wonder what happened to him? It was his first show and I'd heard he had a gift for getting good performances from the actors—especially since a few were surprising casts. Notably the female star, Eve Anderson, who at forty-something was playing a woman in her twenties. Her understudy was an ingénue, Alexis Reed, who really should have had the lead. Alexis changed her name to Alexis Abbot and ended up in L.A. on a sitcom you can still catch on TV Land."

Chat had an amazing memory, so Faith wasn't surprised at the details. It went with the business and partially explained her success.

"I'll read the synopsis, but tell me a little about it. The title is pretty unusual."

"The whole musical was, but that was a time when Broadway was taking risks with musicals. Like *Hamilton* now. *Rent* continued to be the hot ticket from the previous year and the revival of *Chicago* was a runaway. That opened just before *Heaven or Hell*. I know when he read the book Max was thinking *Rent* and even *Chorus Line*—a spare set, offbeat music, and a special kind of intimate connection between actors and audience."

"Oh, then it wasn't an original musical, but adapted?"

Chat smiled. "Sorry. 'The Book' refers to the script, the story, and it was original. Like the director, the writer Adrian St. John was a newbie. He'd never had one of his plays produced before, let alone on Broadway. He disappeared back to Britain when the show closed. Enchanting accent and looked like a young Olivier. I don't know how Max found him, but he had a nose for talent." She gave a sigh. "The play could have worked with minor tweaking and maybe the change in cast. Eve Anderson didn't nail her star turn. Her eleven o'clock number. That's the song that comes late in the show and the star is almost always alone onstage reflecting, to him- or herself. It gives the audience a moment to sit back before the last pull-out-all-the-stops ending number. I can't remember the tune or the lyrics, but it was very poignant. Or would have been if a younger actor played it. She's fallen in love and has to decide where to go for eternity."

"Phew—not one of your everyday dilemmas," Faith said. "Did Max have some kind of relationship with Eve Anderson? Haven't directors been known to cast significant others even when wrong for the part?"

"All the time. But not Max. He never let a little thing like love, or lust, get in the way of his success. He did have significant others, as you so quaintly put it, was married three or four times, each briefer than the last. In any case, he wasn't interested in Eve. If anyone, it was Alexis. No, unless Eve was blackmailing him— and Max isn't the type to give into something like that either—I have no idea how she ended up with the role. James Nelson may have been responsible. I can't remember who the casting director was, but no matter who was involved, Max would have had the last word."

Faith filed the notion of blackmail away, along with possible dynamics between Max and the two women.

Chat had speared a few mushrooms to get the last little bit of brown butter sauce from her plate and put her fork down. "The set was amazing, split in half and alternating between re-creations of Dante's flaming pit and biblical visions from the Book of Revelations. There was much reliance on fog and wind machines, colored silk scrims in both pastels and brilliant colors. The stationary set was a series of staircases running up to balconies on each side. Sounds hokey, but it worked. All the reviews praised the set designer. And the show had a terrific opening number. That's what makes or breaks a musical. If you don't grab the audience then, you never will. It almost made up for the weak star turn, since it was reprised at the end." She hummed a few bars and then sang softly:

"Heaven or Hell
Who can tell?
Below or above
What the devil is love?"

"I've heard that lyric," Faith said.

"It was a hit for a while. And even later. A bunch of people recorded it. Made money for Phil Baker and Betty Sinclair, who wrote it. And some for Max, too. There was probably a clause in the copyright giving him a percentage."

"So the musical revolves around choosing the pearly gates over red hot pitchforks?"

Chat grinned. "Nice summation. The premise was that God and Satan, or Lucifer as he's called in the show, have a bet. Lucifer's idea, of course. Each will select a handful from those dwelling above or below and switch them for an agreed-upon time. When it's over, the chosen get to decide: Heaven or hell? Stay or leave? It doesn't sound like a musical. You know the old chestnut about the movie mogul's prediction for *Oklahoma!*—'No girls, no jokes, no chance'—but like I said, *Heaven or Hell* worked. Sure it was about a moral dilemma, but mainly it was about love."

"Tom would be so interested in this! God and Lucifer laying odds," Faith said. "But a sucker bet, no? Who would agree to hell?"

"Never underestimate the power of heart's desire, sweetie. Max described the show to me as *Carousel* meets *The Crucible*. A good description. Remember I saw it in rehearsal to develop the PR campaign. We did a great poster, very Gustave Doré with a touch of Maxfield Parrish. I was also there opening night. Had not a clue that Max would pull the plug."

"Anything else you can remember about the cast and crew?"

"I've—happily—been away from that world since I sold up and retired, but I do know there were rumors of a jinx on anyone who had been involved with the show. Theater folk are very superstitious, and the taint of such a colossal flop doesn't go away easily."

"So you think maybe someone said 'Good luck' instead of 'Break a leg' or referred to *Macbeth*?"

Chat laughed. "Doubt it. They were all pros. But there could have been someone with a grudge against Max—and there were plenty back then, jealous of his success and for other reasons."

"But other than being jealous, what kinds of grudges?" Faith asked.

"I told you he wasn't a nice man and he was ruthless when it came to getting what he wanted. That included women, as well as the backing for his shows. When it came to it, Max always believed the end justified the means." Chat looked a bit worried. "Sure you want to do this job? One of the guests may well slip arsenic in Max's portion of something you prepare."

Faith tried not to react. "I'll keep an eye out for skull-and-crossbones bottles marked 'poison,'" she said with an attempt at levity. "Now I want a poisonous dessert, as in devilishly bad for me, and I hope you do, too, so I can taste it." Chat was good at sharing, just like everyone else Faith knew and loved. Nonsharers belonged in Dante's inferno.

Chat ordered the Taza chocolate hazelnut torte, and Faith decided she had to try the Harvest's birch beer float—described as house-made birch beer with black pepper ice cream, quince, and cinnamon anise tuiles. She was always on the lookout for unusual preparations to offer her clients, and this sounded like a good possibility. The first taste convinced her—the sweetness of the beer was offset by the pepper and anise.

After dessert, in no hurry to get home, Faith ordered espresso; Chat had a brandy. Both women were loath to end the evening. "I wish we lived closer," Faith said. "I miss you."

"I miss you, too. Come see me soon. You know I have plenty of room and the kids love the horses."

Charity Sibley had shocked her friends and family by moving to a large sprawling house in Mendham, New Jersey, with a stable on six acres. She bred miniature horses, another shock. Who knew it was her dream? But it wasn't the horses as much as crossing the river to Jersey that stunned everyone. However, once they'd braved the trip and managed to find their ways back to Manhattan again, she always had plenty of company, including the Fairchilds, although Faith relied heavily on her Waze app.

"Maybe during the February school vacation," Faith said. They started to talk about plans when Faith realized they were among the last in the restaurant, and knowing how much the staffs' feet were aching she asked for the check, which her aunt grabbed.

"I said, 'my treat,' missy."

"Okay, but let me leave the tip."

While they waited for the server to return, Faith remembered she had one more question about Max Dane. "The jinx must have fallen on him as well. I haven't been able to find any show he was involved with as producer or director after *Heaven or Hell.* Do you know of anything?"

"Right after *H or H* folded, Max brought back one of his biggest successes from the seventies. Revivals were, and are, popular if it's the right match for the times."

"But this wasn't?"

"It was at first. Now run along home and tell that husband of yours that he'd better not stand me up again!" The smile gave Chat's words their true meaning.

"I'll tell him." They walked out to the sidewalk and Faith hugged her aunt good-bye.

I'll tell him, she repeated to herself. Good to have Chat to myself, but this better have been a one-time thing . . .

Pix arrived at the catering kitchen shortly after Faith the next morning.

"Niki will be here soon to make the cupcakes for the shower cupcake tree. Amelia doesn't know what she's having—or isn't saying, right?" Faith said once Pix had hung up her jacket and was pouring them both coffees.

"She has a little boy and no, you're right. Either they want to be surprised or aren't saying. In my day whatever came down the shoot was what you got and happy for it."

"We didn't want to know," Faith said. "It was a kind of leave-it-to-the-Almighty thing with Tom, and I just wanted the whole thing to be over. A puppy would have been fine at that point."

Pix laughed. She well remembered both of Faith's pregnancies, which gave a lie to both the term "morning" sickness and the promise that it would pass after fourteen weeks. She put Faith's mug down next to her. "I have firm instructions from Samantha that neither of us are to mention Caleb, her old job, her new job, or in fact anything about her whatsoever at the shower."

"But she's going to be there isn't she? Amelia was one of her best friends in high school."

"She'll be there and she'll say as little or as much as she wants. Her words."

"Oh dear. I hadn't thought about mentioning anything about her and now I'll be thinking of it the whole time."

"No you won't. You'll be too busy oohing and aahing over all the cute little outfits and being amazed at the amount of stuff new parents need these days, even with a second child."

"True—and you'll be doing the same. Mark and Rebecca are bound to produce a grandchild before long."

"Hopefully before I need a walker."

"How does Samantha seem? I haven't been with her since we went food shopping. Holed up in her room except for work?"

"The opposite. Miss Congeniality! She loves her job. The 'crew' at Starbucks is 'fab' plus she's made a 'ton' of new friends. Apparently the corporate world was 'sterile' and now she's, and this is a direct quote, 'realizing what is really important in life.'"

"And that would be?" Faith was amused, but also knew how worried Pix was. This was so not Samantha, an overachiever from birth.

"Something along the lines of finding inner peace and happiness. I suppose I should be glad it's Starbucks and not a cult."

"You mean it's not?" Niki walked in at the tail end of the conversation. "I would have been here earlier, but I swear no matter what route I take it's being paved. Yet the number of potholes seems to stay the same."

"Just one of life's many mysteries, like disappearing socks in the dryer," Faith said as they all got to work.

Alexis had been Alexis Abbot for so long that "Alexis Reed" on the envelope was a slight shock. She could see the Santa Monica pier from the balcony where she was sitting, going through the mail that had accumulated while she was shooting a commercial in

Vancouver. It seemed like every offer the last couple of years, whether TV or film, involved trekking there. She ought to apply for Canadian citizenship.

The view was soothing, as always. She'd grown up by the ocean, okay, the Jersey shore, but still beautiful. She was forever grateful that when she'd started making real money out here all those years ago she'd had the sense to buy this place.

Careful of her newly manicured nails, she reached for the letter opener on a small table next to the chaise, careful also not to knock over her Pellegrino.

She read the invitation and enclosures. Rodeo Drive would take care of wardrobe, and as for the body beneath, she'd little need to polish what had already stood the test of time with a little help from skilled professionals and a whole lot of hard work on her part. The first thing she'd done after purchasing the house was install a home gym. She was sure that cow Eve would be on the guest list, and although she hadn't seen her in person for twenty years, Alexis had kept track of the aging actor's career. A career that had robbed her of her big chance, thanks to Max Dane. Revenge was a dish best served cold, she reminded herself, and Massachusetts in winter would be frigid.

She reached for her cell and tapped in a number.

The Friday five o'clock shower was already in full swing when Amelia's sister-in-law, Jennifer, clinked her wineglass with a knife blade to get everyone's attention. "Weekends are so busy, I mean I live in my car, driving to soccer in the fall and now hockey, gymnastics, plus all the errands I never finish. Anyway, everybody has had or been to so many baby showers, I thought I'd give Amelia a 'baby sprinkle' for baby boy or girl number two!"

"Thank you so much! I love you, Jen," Amelia said, wiping away a tear. "I'm at the weepy stage, guys."

Jennifer gave her a hug, and Samantha, standing on her friend's other side, passed her a tissue.

"So," Jen continued, "I thought what we—and Amelia—needed was a party! I do have some games . . ." She paused while the expected groans came from all sides of the room. ". . . but they aren't stupid. Have Faith catering has lots of yummy stuff to eat, so you don't have to cook dinner, and I've created a special girl or boy cocktail for Amelia—a Cosmo with a dash of blue curaçao. Plus there's plenty of wine. Sorry, none for you." She gave Amelia another hug. "Now, before I forget, ladies, there are envelopes already stamped on the table. Address one to yourself and save Amelia the work. You know how good she is about thank-yous. And there are slips of paper for you to write your guesses for birth date and weight! Winner gets a gift card to Starbucks, which an anonymous donor has generously given us!"

Faith could hear everything from the kitchen. Jennifer was in her starter house, she speculated. A small cape that would serve until her two kids were older and her husband was further up the ladder at the financial planning service where he worked, and where, Faith heard from Pix, who was seated with the rest of the guests, the couple had met. Faith took a tray of warm hors d'oeuvres out to pass. A cheese platter and a smaller crudité assortment were on the dining table. After many years of experience with the veggies, Faith had learned people liked to treat themselves on occasions like this, and she would end up taking the healthy stuff back to work virtually untouched. She had added artichoke hearts and tiny baby beets (appropriate) to the ubiquitous peppers, carrots, and broccoli florets. She'd also provided two dipping sauces—blue cheese and Asian ginger. The changes were attracting more interest.

The women were having a good time, she noted as she moved around the room offering small Cuban sandwiches, smoked salmon blini, stuffed mushrooms, and mini quiches. She was surprised to see a look of apprehension on Pix's face, so different from the laughter in the rest of the room. Samantha was talking to someone Faith didn't recognize. She seemed older than the other guests, but maybe it was because of her perfect makeup, hair that appeared streaked by the sun, and a cut so artfully casual both screamed a pricey Newbury Street salon. She was wearing a black pencil skirt that showed great legs. An ivory sweater was just this side of too tight and paired with very high heels. Faith could only assume she must be going out afterward, not home to tiny hands that would leave marks on the sweater. Faith had only just started wearing ivory or white again herself.

"Faith, this is Denise Walker. Denise, Faith Fairchild of Have Faith in Your Kitchen. Denise and I were at Aleford High together," Samantha said.

"Oh, Faith, I know who you are. Such divine food. I was just showing Samantha my ring. Why, here's a thought. I'll talk to Mummy about doing a tasting with you. The wedding isn't until Labor Day. Oh, such a joke here at the shower! Labor Day!"

Just as Denise knew her, Faith knew Denise. Everyone, male or female, has had a high school nemesis, and Denise was Samantha's. She'd been the leader of a pack of girls who slyly and not so slyly attacked others—the followers out of fear they might become targets, too. Studious Samantha who had been a late bloomer had been one of Denise's favorite victims. No matter how often Faith and Pix told Samantha to ignore the girl, that she was jealous and so forth, Samantha had been hurt each and every time.

Faith wondered whether there might be some Ex-Lax in Jen's medicine cabinet that she could slip into a stuffed mushroom to give Denise an uncomfortable hour or two later. But no, she was a professional, and tampering with her food was a mortal sin. Heaven or hell? No problem there.

"I would be happy to talk to your mother, although unfortunately we are booked solid for Labor Day weekend and those before and after. It's a popular time for weddings."

"Oh, we've had a caterer for ages. I just thought we might get a better deal from you, seeing as you're local." Translation: small town, Faith thought. She'd heard it before.

Pix stood up. "Well, congratulations, Denise. I'm sure your parents are very happy. Why don't I fill another tray, Faith, while you pass the rest of these? Everything is delicious."

Samantha jumped up, too. "I'll help."

The years since high school had done nothing to change Denise.

"I hear your boyfriend dumped you," she said loudly to Samantha. "What was his name? Something like a farmer? Caleb, right? You'd better get going or you could end up on the shelf." She laughed heartily, expecting the room, which had gone quiet, to join in.

"I'm pretty proud to be on that shelf, Denise," a pretty young woman with a chin-length bob said. "A lot of us here are. I mean why grab the first one to actually go down on one knee? Better to wait for the real thing."

Now the room did erupt in giggles.

"Denise's older brother is Jen's husband's boss," Amelia whispered to Faith. "I didn't want her here, but I thought she'd behave. Nobody believes anything she says anyway."

"Prezzies now, cupcakes later," Jen announced, and the party was back on track.

After a while, when it became apparent that no one was making an attempt to talk to her, Denise teetered out. Faith saw and smiled at Samantha, who was helping to organize the gifts. She raised a hand and indicated "score one for you" with her finger. Sam grinned back.

Maybe the road to happiness *was* paved with lattes and Frappuccino.

The shower or "sprinkle" had been a great success. Pix was helping Faith pack up.

"It *was* fun looking at all those weensy clothes," Faith said. "Can't imagine Ben and Amy were ever that small. I know I have pictures, but I also seem to have amnesia."

"I pretty much had amnesia for the whole first year after each of mine," Pix said. "It's a wonder poor Dan got any notice at all when he came along. I do remember being in the same sweatshirt and sweatpants for several years, however."

Amelia's mother, Susan, came in. "Thank you, Faith. Everything was delicious and looked so lovely! I'm afraid Amelia's father will be getting soup and a sandwich or takeout on his way home from work tonight—I've eaten so much!"

"Takeout. What a great idea. Sam can swing by Country Pizza and get himself a grinder," Pix said. "Neither Samantha nor I will need dinner." She looked pleased at the idea of not having to cook.

"I saw Ursula at Symphony," Susan said. "She is amazing. I hope I am as spry at her age—and as beautiful."

Pix smiled. "I know. She runs rings around me most of the time."

"Certainly having a beau must help," Susan said over her shoulder as she left, adding "and such a handsome one, too. A lovely couple."

Pix was standing much as Lot's wife may have.

"Beau?" she said, her voice barely audible. "Mother has a beau?"

She tore the letter open after seeing the name on the front: "Bella Martelli." It didn't take long to read the invitation or look over the rest of what was inside. Taking a pen from her purse, she made a dark check next to "Will Attend," pressing so hard there was an indentation on the back. Placing it in the stamped envelope—so thoughtful!—she licked it closed, went out, and was about to drop it into the first mailbox she saw.

And then changed her mind, stuffing the RSVP into her pocket.

But, oh yes, she was attending.

CHAPTER 5

"Did you know about this?" Pix asked as she and Faith got into the van.

Faith was rarely at a loss for words, but at the moment the only response that sprang to mind was "Um." Her thoughts tumbled about. Pix and Ursula had gone shopping for what was a very different wardrobe for the older woman. Hadn't Austin Stebbins come up? And why had Amelia's mother described him as a "beau"? Had she spotted the two holding hands during intermission at Symphony, a public display of affection in the august hall tantamount for a New Englander like Ursula Lyman Rowe to canoodling in the orchestra pit? And what *should* Faith have told Pix after she'd met Austin? She hadn't known exactly what to say and so had said nothing. But she should have mentioned something. A good friend would have figured out a tactful way to share what now seemed a time bomb.

"Um. Yes, but I don't exactly know what 'this' is? Ursula introduced Austin Stebbins to me as an old acquaintance who had recently moved back to the area. Seems like a nice person and obviously has good taste in food. He took her to lunch at L'Espalier," Faith said awkwardly.

"L'Espalier! That expensive place in Back Bay?"

"Um, yes."

Pix snapped her seat belt shut with a loud click. "First Samantha, now Mother. I don't think I can handle any more surprises, although as a mother of three, one would think I should be used to them." She pressed her lips together and then opened them again. "She told me she had a friend staying with her for a while. Of course I thought it was a female friend. Did you know this, too? That he was staying with her?"

Faith let go of the "ums." Time to woman up. "Yes, but I don't think it's anything to worry about. I understood that it was for a short time while he's looking for an apartment or condo in town. Ursula thought it didn't make sense for him to waste his money on the hotel when she had extra room." Ursula was the embodiment of Yankee thrift, ironing wrapping paper and saving string—even pieces too short. "He wants her advice, since he has been living in California for many years and doesn't know Boston anymore."

"And why haven't I heard his name?" Pix fumed. "Mother has never mentioned an 'Austin Stebbins' to my certain knowledge, and over the years I've repeatedly heard the names of all the people she went to school with, met anywhere in fact, even every pet she's had."

Faith took it as the rhetorical question it was. She knew that not being kept in the loop was behind Pix's tirade. And yes, it was another surprise so close to Samantha's news. When her friend calmed down, she'd see it was a good thing. Arm candy, pleasant male companionship for Ursula—Austin was definitely good-looking, a very well-preserved older man. Once Pix met him, she'd be happy for her mother. And the sooner the better.

Before they'd left Jennifer's house, Faith had assembled a new platter from the crudité and cheese leftovers and put the hors d'oeuvres in the boxes she'd brought ready for the hostess to slip in the fridge or freezer. They'd packed up the unopened bottles of wine—no charge for them—and left a surprisingly small container of the Blue Cosmo mix. The ladies had taken to the creation enthusiastically. There were also a few of Niki's cupcakes left, but Jen insisted Faith take them. "Please, my kids don't need more sugar. They bounce off the walls as it is, and I won't be able to keep away from them either. Ellery is three and I still have my baby fat. And my husband is on the no-carb protein diet."

Thinking now of the box in the rear, Faith said casually, "How about we drop the cupcakes off at your mother's? We drive right by the house."

"But it's after seven. Much too late."

"I'm sure she'll still be up," Faith said, although Ursula would have had supper long since and could well be brushing her teeth, getting ready for a long winter's nap. The combination of January dark and early-to-bed habit might not have been broken by her houseguest's presence.

"Best to call," Pix said, and Faith noted a hint of anticipation in her tone of voice. She got out her phone. "Hello, Mother. It's Pix. Faith and I are on our way back from Amelia's shower." There was a pause. "It was lovely and yes, Samantha was there, but she had to go straight to Boston for her shift. We're near the house and have some treats to drop off if it's not too late." Another pause. "Okay, we'll see you soon."

Ursula, as was her custom, opened the door before they had crossed the wide porch. "Such a nice surprise. Come in. Pix, you haven't met Austin Stebbins, who is staying with me until he decides where he wants to settle now that he's back in the Boston area."

She motioned them into the living room. Every time Faith entered the space, she was reminded how much she loved it. On this cold January night, it radiated comfort from the jewel tones of the Oriental carpet that covered almost the entire floor to the heavy gold and Prussian blue damask drapes, which picked up the colors of the comfortable wing chairs and Federal-style couch. A mahogany gateleg table stood against the wall beneath a bull's-eye mirror. Ursula, or someone else, had placed a large blue and white export china vase filled with dried yarrow and other flowers on the table. The mirror reflected the yellow blossoms, surrounded by flames from the fireplace, on the far wall.

Austin stood up, came over to Pix, extended his hand, and said, "I've heard so much about you, Pix, and it's past time we met. It was a pleasure to see your daughter when she came by here the other day, but I've been especially looking forward to meeting you." He smiled as they shook hands and continued to smile as he turned toward Faith. "Lovely to see you again. I hope the call from your husband that interrupted us last time wasn't anything major."

Ben's Mandy Meltdown. Nothing major. More like catastrophic. "Oh no. Everything is fine," Faith said.

"Good," Ursula broke in. "Now sit by the fire Austin made. I'm hopeless at this sort of thing. You'll have some sherry? Or brandy? I seem to have acquired a very fine bottle of Remy Martin as a gift." She was wearing another blue dress—cowl necked—and Faith thought she detected traces of makeup.

Pix shot Faith a look. Ursula had an ancient merit badge for fire making and could get a roaring blaze going with a few twigs and a piece of flint. And the brandy was Ursula's favorite; there was always a bottle tucked away for what she termed "a tipple."

Faith said, "I'd better be getting back" at the same time as Pix answered, "Love some brandy."

"Which is it?" Ursula asked, looking amused.

Pix sat on the couch, leaned back, and folded her arms across her chest. "Brandy. Faith, you said Amy's at a sleepover and you left supper for Ben and Tom. Sam is picking some up for himself, so we have all the time in the world."

"I'll put the cupcakes—you'll love the orange mocha, Ursula—in the fridge, and I can get the drinks," Faith said. She'd noted that Ursula and Austin both had snifters.

The Rowes' home had been built when thick plaster walls and

heavy wooden doors were the norm, so she couldn't hear the conversation from the kitchen. Quickly she put the cupcakes away, poured herself a glass of water, and grabbed the brandy, which was on the counter, and another snifter. In a matter of moments, she was back in the living room.

Pix had settled farther back against the cushioned couch and had the kind of determined look on her face that Faith knew spelled trouble. She hoped that Mrs. Miller wouldn't embark on some version of twenty questions. Not that Pix would be rude, but if ever inquiring minds wanted to know, this was one of those times.

She'd hoped in vain. Pix got right to it. "I'm curious. How are you acquainted with my mother, Mr. Stebbins? I don't believe I have ever heard her mention you," Pix asked, taking a generous swallow of brandy from the snifter Faith had handed her.

Oh dear, Faith thought. Her friend's question was phrased not just in a rude way, but a belligerently rude way. As if her mother had met the man, wearing a Brooks navy blue blazer, seated calmly by the fire, in a Kasbah drug den.

Austin had been holding his snifter in both hands, warming the brandy. He carefully put it down on a coaster on the table by the side of the chair. Ursula was giving her daughter the look that in childhood would have meant sitting on the stairs for a while.

"Please, call me 'Austin.' I think you probably haven't heard my name, because your mother and I knew each other a very long time ago. When I called recently it was nice to discover she remembered me." He gave Ursula a fond look, which was returned. "I'm afraid that when you get to be my age, the numbers of friends from one's youth are sadly few."

Pix looked chagrined, but another gulp of alcohol spurred her on. "Then you grew up here in Aleford? You knew my father as well?"

This was treading on shaky ground. Faith was familiar with the story of Ursula's childhood and the tragedy that had led to the way she met Pix's father, Arnold Rowe, but Pix seemed to be forgetting it—accidentally or on purpose. Arnold had *not* grown up in Aleford.

Austin shook his head. "I knew your mother and her family when we all lived in Boston on Beacon Hill. I was at Browne and Nichols when Ursula was at Winsor. My older brother, who has since passed away, was at Harvard with Ursula's."

Faith looked over at both women expecting to see—what? Faces stiffen, tears threaten? Theodore Lyman had died while still a student under heartbreaking circumstances.

Pix's face had, in fact, stiffened. She looked apprehensive. Ursula's on the other hand was almost radiant. "It has meant so much to me to talk with someone who remembers Theo, even a little bit. We were much younger than our brothers."

"I lost touch with the whole Lyman family when they moved out here to Aleford," Austin said to Pix. "I didn't even know where they were, just that they moved suddenly. My late sister had gone to Winsor as well, and the old girls' network makes the FBI look shabby. I had tried to no avail to find B and N friends when I planned to return here, then wondered whether any of my Winsor pals were still, well, alive. When I called the alumnae office, they were obliging, once I mentioned my sister's name and looked up my list of names. Ursula's was on the top and we've been corresponding until I came east a few weeks ago."

Pix's snifter was empty, and although her tone had relaxed somewhat, she was back to question time. "What was your line of work in California, Mr., um, Austin? And why Boston? Surely not for the climate."

He laughed. It was a pleasant one. Not too hearty and not a giggle. "I was a property developer, but it's a young person's game these days. Too much risk. And as for coming east, I've wanted to for some time, but my late wife was from California, and indeed the weather was a deterrent for her."

Ursula had had enough of her daughter's unsubtle interroga-

tion. "I'm feeling a bit tired. Austin and I went to Symphony today. I'll say 'good night' to you both and have an early night."

Faith leaped up, chiding herself for not realizing it really had
gotten late. Past eight thirty. Pix did the same, although not with
the same alacrity. "Shall I pick you up tomorrow for the garden
club meeting?" she said. Ursula and Pix were faithful members of
Aleford's Evergreens.

Giving her daughter a quick kiss on the cheek, Ursula said, "I
think not, dear. I may have other plans, and if I change my mind,
Austin can drop me off. But you go. I want to hear all about what
that dear man from the Arnold Arboretum has to say about winter
kill on lilacs."

Back in the van, Faith turned the key and headed for the parsonage and the Millers' house. "Feel better now? He's so pleasant
and wonderful for your mother to have someone with whom she
can talk about the past."

Getting no response, she glanced over, and then patted her
friend's hand.

Pix burst into tears.

Faith pulled the van into the driveway and stopped at the garage.
There was nothing that needed to go to the catering kitchen
tonight. Niki was baking cheesecakes in the morning and would
drive her back later after Faith had washed the plates, glassware,
and platters. The shower had been finger food, so almost no
cutlery.

Faith's plan, upon arriving home, had been to compose an
e-mail to Max Dane setting up a time to meet, ostensibly to finalize the menus that she'd sent. She wanted to pry some more information about his guests from him as they talked about what said
guests would be served. But right now she needed to make Pix—
who kept saying, "I'm fine, I'm fine" as she wept—something to
eat and a nice cup of peppermint tea, Pix's remedy for ills of body

and soul. Faith couldn't stand the stuff herself, but it seemed to work wonders for Pix. Years ago Faith had started to dry her own, and now she kept a tin stocked in the pantry.

The kitchen was empty, and seeing a light under the door of Tom's study, she surmised he was working on his sermon. She hadn't seen any lights on upstairs when she got out of the van, which meant Ben was off with friends.

One hour, three cups of tea, and a toasted cheese sandwich later, Pix was ready to go home. She'd been silly, she confessed. It had been a shock. Yes, Ursula had been widowed for many years, but Pix had never thought of her mother as someone who might want for, or need, male companionship. Faith hastily assured her that Austin Stebbins was no doubt simply an old friend Ursula was helping out, not a replacement for Arnold Rowe, truly the love of Ursula's life. By the time Pix left, both women were laughing about the notion—"I could be the flower girl," Pix had said, "and the Evergreens can be attendants."

Faith closed the door, cleaned up, and went to see if Tom wanted anything. He was slumped over his desk, snoring softly. Assuming all he desired was sleep in his own bed, she shook him awake and they made their way upstairs, leaving the hall and out-door lights on for Ben.

The next morning, Faith got up early to take the van back to the catering kitchen. She'd have coffee with Niki and tell her about the shower and maybe about the Ursula/Austin impact on Pix.

Ben had left the lights on, but she didn't want to wake him up to nag at him. It could wait. He'd done it before and he'd do it again. Same with her nagging.

Niki was in a rush. She'd left little Sofia with her mother, since her husband was out of town and her mother was going to Foxwoods with the women's group from her church. "And, no, I don't know how they square the whole gambling thing with the guy above, although the priest organizes the trips, so he may have some sort of special pull."

Faith poured herself a large mug of coffee and, as Niki worked, filled her in on yesterday's events.

"Ursula is still a beautiful woman and the notion that people her age are not interested in nookie—save for my parents, do not want to go there—is more than out-of-date. Wasn't there something about a town in Italy where they're all living to be a hundred because they have sex and eat a lot of rosemary?"

Faith laughed. "I read about that, too. Apparently it's some kind of highly potent variety of the herb, and you're right. Men and women are never too old for a little roll in the hay."

"Listen to us with our euphemisms!" Niki laughed. "I'm sure Sofia will think her parents are as ancient as dinosaurs by the time she hits her teens and starts scoping out ice floes for us—if global warming has left any."

"Whenever Tom gives me a hug or kiss in front of the kids they look shocked. That we should be well past such shenanigans. How's that for a euphemism."

"Good one, but my favorite is 'Slap and Tickle,' not that I've ever actually gotten to that page in the Kama Sutra!"

Faith almost snorted coffee through her nose. "Enough! I have to compose myself and write a serious e-mail to Max Dane about the final menus."

"As I recall from reading British country house novels, there was a lot of this sort of thing on those weekends. You'll need to keep an eye out to make sure the names on the guest room doors don't get switched around."

"I don't remember nameplates for cards on them, but you're right. It does all suggest the Edwardians, especially the king himself, creeping under covers."

Faith sent the e-mail, briefly asking to meet, and Niki dropped her off at the parsonage.

Tom was in the kitchen. "I was just about to call you. Amy needed to be picked up, and my car wouldn't start. One of the other parents dropped her off—she's upstairs—but I have to go out to Emerson Hospital to make a call. Give me your keys." He looked out the window. "Did you leave it on the street?" He seemed puzzled.

"It's in the garage. I didn't use it yesterday. And here are the keys." Faith dug them out of her bag.

"No, it isn't. Only my car is. Didn't you take the van this morning?"

Faith nodded. "I parked it here last night in the driveway. Niki just dropped me off. But, Tom, who would steal my car? Don't they go in for snazzier models?" Faith's Subaru was five years old and had seen a few brushes with the Canadian hemlocks.

Amy came running into the room. "Ben's bed hasn't been slept in!"

The Fairchilds looked at one another. Car gone, untouched bed. Ben was missing.

Faith grabbed her phone from her bag and called Ben. It went straight to voice mail. She closed her eyes and tried for a deep cleansing breath, that and being good at corpse pose, the two things she'd taken away from a brief foray into yoga. She opened her eyes. It hadn't worked. Her heart was still pounding.

Tom was on his own phone: "Hi. It's Tom. Is Josh around? I wanted to run an idea by him."

Josh was Ben's best friend and also the current First Parish youth group leader. How could her husband sound so calm? Faith wondered. More on-the-job practice?

There was a pause while whichever parent had answered was speaking. "Great," Tom said. "What an opportunity. Tell him to give me a call when he gets back. No rush. Yes, I will. Bye, Elaine." He put the phone in his pocket. "Elaine says hello and

Josh is in New York City with his uncle who scored tickets for *Hamilton* from a client."

For a millisecond Faith was jealous. Then all her fear, and an undercurrent of anger, rushed back.

Amy was sitting at the kitchen table nimbly texting away on her phone. She looked up at her parents. "Ben drove to Bates to see Mandy. He just woke up. And he says he left a note on his bed. He's going to get something to eat now."

She should have thought of texting, Faith chided herself as she headed for the door, now very angry. It was the best way to get in touch with both her children for reasons she did not understand. What was so terrible about actually answering the phone and speaking?

All three Fairchilds ran upstairs. Ben had indeed left a note on his bed. Written on a sheet of white computer paper and folded flat against his white pillowcase. The intent was obvious.

"I'm sorry!" Amy said. "I didn't notice it. I should have, though, because he folded down his spread and he never does that."

Faith picked it up, skimmed it—it wasn't exactly a novel—and read it aloud.

"'I'm really sorry I took the car without asking. I had to talk to Mandy in person. Love, Ben. P.S. Sorry about the car.'" She looked at Tom. From the expression on his face, he was as close to the boiling point as she was, now that they knew Ben was fine. Ben was a good driver and they let him use one of their cars when it wasn't needed. Many of his friends had their own cars, and Ben hadn't pushed for one. Faith suspected he'd been driving for longer than he'd had a license, up on the back roads of the island with his friends there. He'd never taken the car without permission before, though, and Bates was a good two and a half hours away. He must have left when he came home from school and he probably had stayed up late or all night talking if he'd just gotten up. But what to do? Drive there and drag him home?

Amy was looking at her parents, her hands on her hips. "Look, he had to do this. I think he may have finally been able to see Mandy's Facebook page when he was over helping Samantha install some stuff on her laptop. I'm pretty sure Mandy didn't unfriend her. Maybe he saw that Mandy didn't have a new boyfriend or something else. Anyway if I was his mom and dad I'd leave him alone and then ground him for about twenty years when he comes back."

When had her daughter morphed into a combination of Ann Landers and Dr. Joyce Brothers?

Tom started laughing. "Honey, maybe you should be taking over for Mom and me. Sounds okay to me. Faith?"

"I agree—to it all. Possibly the *Aleford Journal* should start a 'Dear Amy F.' column."

Amy shrugged and gave her parents a tolerant look, at which point Faith's cell rang. She looked at who was calling. "It's Mandy," she said as she accepted the call.

"Put it on speaker," Tom said. Faith did.

"Hi, Mrs. Fairchild. It's Mandy. I just wanted to apologize. Ben should have asked for permission to come up, but it's really my fault. I should have waited to tell him what I had to say face-to-face. It wasn't fair after all we've been through together and how much your whole family has done for me."

"Well. He has been pretty upset," Faith said in one of her more major understatements, "so I'm glad you've had a chance to talk together now."

"I'm not with anybody else, but I've been feeling kind of penned in. It's taking every bit of my concentration to stay on top of the coursework here and I just don't want any other complications." The girl sounded a bit choked up.

"That's completely normal and I'm sure Ben understands now." Faith saw the look on Amy's face that mirrored her own thought. Ben would never understand.

"Anyway, we're going to get something to eat and he'd like to stay until tomorrow morning, if that's all right. The Franco

Center here is having a French film festival tonight and we both want to go."

After an exchange with a French family last year, Ben had decided that he would continue with French in college. He'd gotten Mandy to take it, too.

"Why don't I speak to Ben?" Faith said.

He came on the line almost immediately. "Hi, Mom. Look, I'm sorry . . ."

"We can talk about it when you get home. Enjoy your time and drive safely. We'll expect you sometime in the early afternoon. Oh, and sweetheart, you're grounded for roughly the next twenty years."

She heard a gulp and then a somewhat feeble good-bye.

Faith hung up and Amy brought them back to earth: "I'm pretty late, I was supposed to be at Cindy's a half hour ago. We're going to the mall and then maybe the movies. Her mom is driving."

"Okay, enough drama for now," Tom said. "Maybe I can work some of it into my sermon. What have we learned here?"

"That I will not be happy if you don't drive me right now?" Amy said.

"Sounds about right," Faith replied. The curtain was down on this production, but it was only a matter of time until the next. That reminded her of Max Dane and the Rowan House weekend rapidly looming. She needed to check to see if he'd replied to her e-mail and get out there.

What to do, what to do? Samantha Miller wondered. She'd finished her shift and was taking the MBTA to Porter Square, where she could get the commuter rail to Aleford. As if she didn't have enough on her mind. She wished she wasn't so sure about what she saw. Wished there was the shadow of a doubt, but there wasn't.

The doors closed and the car crossed the river, soon plunging underground. She was in one of the older trains—she'd heard some dated back to 1965, and this was definitely an ancient one. Shuddering and squealing along the tracks, it came to sudden halts in the dark—no explanation from the conductor. Then with a mighty grinding sound started up again. Maybe she should get a job with the transit authority. Do something good for Boston.

What she had just seen at Starbucks had sent her straight back to that horrendous day two weeks ago. The time seemed both longer and shorter. But she was feeling the same sort of disbelief that had started at work with the call from HR to come to its office. "Cost-cutting measures. Others as well. Not just you. Fine work." The words had merged into a kind of Tower of Babel with no single distinct phrase. She was accompanied to her small office, took only the BEST SISTER EVAH mug Dan had given her one long-ago Christmas and a photo from last summer of the whole family on the porch of The Pines in Sanpere. Then there was the endless wait while IT wiped her laptop, leaving only her personal e-mails.

Somehow she'd made it back to Brooklyn, thinking only of Caleb. Seeing him, feeling his arms around her, comforting her as he had done in the past when life was overwhelming. There were other jobs, she told herself. HR had been reassuring, and while she dismissed the platitude, maybe it was true. She got off the subway and decided to get Caleb a chai almond milk latte from their favorite coffee shop, one for herself, too, and some scones. Comfort food.

Stepping into the fragrant warmth, she looked around the coffee shop. Caleb was there with his assistant, Julie. His "indispensable right-hand gal," as he put it. *Hand* now being the operative word. He was holding hers across the small table, and from the way they were looking at each other, Samantha knew he wasn't congratulating her on a job well done. She also knew that all the recent late nights and weekends meant something vastly different from what she had thought.

Hands across the table today, too. And the smell of coffee. That had been what caused the flashback.

Back two weeks ago, she'd walked over to their table, startling them, said only, "Good-bye, Caleb. It's been—something," adding as she left, "I'll figure out a way to get the things from the apartment I'm not taking now." His "Wait, this isn't . . ." and the pain and embarrassment fighting for room on his face had stopped her for a moment, but only a moment. Julie had interrupted coolly—"I'll do it. Send your things. Aleford, right?" She'd managed to make the one-word town sound like an imprecation. And she had a smug look on her face, assuming Samantha would head for home. The way a little girl would. The fact that it was exactly what Samantha had intended made it more horrible.

The T car was stopping at Central Square. Samantha didn't think it was her imagination that the people who got off looked relieved to have made it without any further delays.

In the midst of her thoughts she'd vaguely noticed a guy who looked about her age staring at her from across the aisle since she'd got on at Charles Street. Samantha was attractive—tall like both parents and with her mother's thick brown hair.

This guy was smiling at her. He wasn't bad-looking. Maybe his face was a little thin, but his hair was a glossy black cap like some kind of bird feathers. A raven? It reminded her of her young cousin Dana's. There was something kid-like about the guy, too, and suddenly imagining him younger made her jump up and sit down in the empty seat next to him.

"I know you! Zach, right? The friend of the Fairchilds? The computer genius?"

"Zach Cummings, and I don't know about 'genius,' but the computer part is true. I was beginning to worry you might think I was some kind of perv staring at you. We haven't seen each other since their holiday party two years ago, but I recognized you right away. And your grandmother filled me in on what you were up to when I went out to help her with her iMac a few weeks ago. Home for a visit? She said you were in New York."

Samantha tossed her hair back in slight annoyance. No secrets in her family—at least when it came to her. "I moved back here recently for good. Let's just say the company wasn't a good fit."

"And the engagement? He's moved here, too? Congratulations by the way."

"Caleb and I were never engaged." Samantha felt her face flush. "Turned out that wasn't a good fit either. It's, well, complicated. Oh, here's my stop!" The subway was lurching into the Porter Square station.

"Mine too. Do you have time for a cup of coffee? Porter Square Books has a great café."

There was really no rush to get home, Samantha reflected. She could easily take a later train and be back early enough to make dinner, the job she'd taken on. "Sure," she said.

As they walked across the large parking lot she was aware that their strides matched, and soon she became aware of their reflections in the store windows, too. They made a nice couple. Not that she was in the market. She didn't want to have anything to do with men for a very long time. If ever. But she recalled Faith talking about Zach's IT skills—a wizard she'd said. Who was it who said there was no such thing as coincidences?

He held the door open and they walked into the café. The fragrance of brewing coffee was no longer producing a bad memory but was energizing—a caffeine contact high. And Samantha had always loved the bookstore, with tantalizing volumes piled on tables and filling the shelves. All a person needed right there.

At the counter she ordered a latte—good for a comparison—and Zach asked for a large flat white. "My treat," Samantha said. "And how about a chocolate croissant or something else?"

"I'm good, but you go ahead. And thank you. I'll accept if you agree it will be my turn next time."

When Zach smiled, his whole face joined in. Even his eyes. "Sounds like a plan," she said.

Monday morning Faith had no trouble locating the button on the gryphon's eye that activated the intercom. Pressing it firmly, she heard Ian's voice with the same instructions. Perhaps it was recorded.

Ben had arrived back from Maine around two o'clock yesterday, penitent but looking happier than she had seen him in weeks. His "I don't want to talk about it" was uttered with much less anger—almost a pleasantry. Tom was back at the hospital, keeping a last watch with a parishioner's family. Faith merely said, "Fine. No one's asking. Now, go to your room and do the homework you didn't do this weekend." At the kitchen door she called him back. "Take a snack. I made a sandwich for you. It's in the fridge." His "Thanks, Mom" sounded particularly heartfelt—or he could just have been starving as usual.

Apologizing for the short notice, last week friends of the Millers and Fairchilds had called to offer their condo near the Loon Mountain ski resort in New Hampshire to the two families for next weekend. It was happily accepted and the details worked out. Faith would be at Rowan House, but the others were all free. Tom was even taking an unaccustomed Sunday off. The assistant minister would preach. Faith skied but was just as happy to read by the fire in the lodge. Yesterday Tom and she had talked about leaving Ben, an avid boarder, home. Samantha would be next door. But it seemed too mean. Besides, he was grounded otherwise for the foreseeable future.

No sunshine today. A cold gray day much more typical of the time of year. The grasses in the fields looked sere and when the house came into view it reminded her more of a dark mansion from a Gothic novel than the Richardson architectural masterpiece that had shone so spectacularly in the morning light on her last visit. There were no cars in the drive. She parked, walked up the stone stairs and across the veranda. She was about to ring the bell when the door opened.

"Good morning, Mrs. Fairchild, please come in. I'm afraid Mr. Dane has been delayed, but perhaps we could use the time to completely finalize the menus and go over a few other details?"

Ian had phrased the request as a question, but it wasn't. Faith realized that whatever she was to Max Dane, she was the help to Ian Morrison. She followed him to the kitchen, wondering whether his polite tone would always have this edge. But Faith had been Morrison's choice for a caterer. Maybe he was regretting it?

He offered tea, but she declined. It didn't feel like a particularly cozy occasion. He sat on one of the stools at the kitchen island and indicated a stool across from him for her, opening a large notebook in front of him. He leafed through printouts of her e-mail suggestions and set them to one side. The page he was on seemed to be a list—good, she was a list maker herself—and she took her iPad from her purse to take notes.

"We like all your suggestions. Max wants to talk about the birthday banquet, so we'll wait on that. Your idea of a buffet for Friday will work well."

Ian had e-mailed that all the invited guests had accepted but offered no further information about them.

"I'd assumed that arrival times might differ," Faith said, "so a buffet where we could keep the food warm seemed the best choice. They are arriving at different times, yes? Or possibly some might be coming out here together, especially those coming from New York?" Ian had mentioned on the phone when she'd asked about Friday night that a car service would be picking everyone up at Logan. All would be traveling by air.

"Each guest will arrive here separately. Max most particularly wanted them to greet each other for the first time in front of him. He also wants the drinks and meal served in the summer parlor.

There's a small butler's pantry there, as you may recall, and I will set up several tables."

Faith nodded. She planned to be as close as possible to Dane's side, watching each guest's entry herself. Ian would be answering the door. Besides the convenience of keeping food hot, she'd selected a buffet for this very purpose. It meant she could stand behind the table under her cloak of invisibility.

She picked up the Friday night thread again. "I thought we could wait for the *Heaven or Hell*–themed food until the banquet and go with one of the menus I sent, or selections from them. Since it's New England, clam chowder as one of the soups with wild mushroom bisque for the other." The men had said they weren't catering to food preferences or allergies, but Faith planned to have plenty of alternatives for any possible vegetarians, vegans as well. The mushroom bisque was one of her favorites—not too much cream overwhelming the earthy mushroom flavor.

She began going down the rest of the list. "People always like the Dijon mustard–encrusted baby lamb chops."

"Max wants the poached salmon."

Okay . . . "Great. How about both of those as entrées and one of the pastas I suggested as a third?"

"A tortellini. Easier to eat than linguine or fettuccine. We don't want the guests messing up their clothes." He grinned. Faith had never seen Ian smile so broadly. Maybe he was getting excited. Maybe this would turn out simply to be a fun birthday weekend with fine food, drink, and good cheer. And maybe Tinkerbell was real.

"Any of the sides will work with these choices," Ian said. "The roasted vegetables—oh, and Max likes creamed spinach. And no leafy salads. Iceberg wedges with bacon and blue cheese."

Faith got it. "Steak house menu food. Should I do steak fries or oven-baked potato wedges?"

"Oven-baked wedges will be fine." Ian wrote something in his notebook.

"I thought we'd offer an assortment of desserts, fruit as well," Faith said. "There is a small fridge right? I'll do some individual mousses—chocolate, lemon, and other flavors. You're taking care of the alcoholic beverages, but I'll bring soft drinks, flavored and unflavored sparkling water, plus the breakfast juices. And a variety of coffee and teas."

Ian gave her a somewhat sardonic look. "This crowd will be hitting the hard stuff, but yes, bring them."

"I think that's it for Friday night. No hors d'oeuvres, although I could put some out on the buffet."

"Didn't we tell you?" Ian looked surprised and perhaps disappointed. "I am sure it was mentioned last time you were here. Max wants an ample raw bar, mounds of caviar, foie gras, and the embellishments for each set out on top of the casket."

"Of course." Faith *had* remembered but hadn't thought they were serious. But they had been—deadly serious. She didn't want to say this, however, and merely made a note and then looked back up at him.

"Max wants to talk about how to arrange the room, so once he's back you can have another look at the casket."

Can't wait, Faith thought and then pulled up her breakfast suggestions to fill the time. They all met with Ian's approval. She mentioned she'd have snacks available in the kitchen throughout the weekend. Someone in the hard-drinking crowd might want a cup of coffee or tea—and she'd better bring an analgesic and some Pepto-Bismol. Large sizes.

"I think we're all set," Faith said at last. "You are using your own florist, and the linens, china, and cutlery you showed me should be more than enough for all the meals. And lovely."

Ian cocked his head. "I hear Max's car. Just one more thing and we'll go meet him in the foyer."

He got up and Faith did the same, following him to a rustic-looking hutch at the far end of the room. It looked as if it would have been at home in a Yorkshire farmhouse but still went well with the modern kitchen. The shelves were filled with toby jugs of all sizes, many of them political figures and literary ones. Faith spotted both Churchill and Dickens. Ian must want to show her some kind of serving dish from the cabinet below, she thought. Instead he opened one of the top drawers.

"I want this on your person the whole time you are here."

It was a gun.

CHAPTER 6

"The Sig Sauer P two-three-eight is perfect for concealed carry. Lightweight—only a little over fifteen ounces. And the recoil is mild. Here." Ian took the gun from the drawer and held it out to her. "About an inch wide. Good for small hands. A woman's gun."

Faith's recoil wasn't mild. She took several steps back.

"Not this woman. Forget about it being completely illegal for me to carry a weapon for which I don't have a license. Let's talk about what you think may be happening this weekend that would require it."

Suddenly she was siding with Tom, Niki, and a whole lot of others if they knew—that this qualified as a must-miss job. "I am being hired to determine who might be a threat to Mr. Dane—and cook—but am definitely not on board with the possibility of putting myself or the others in lethal danger. A bodyguard-type scenario that you seem to envision in which I carry a gun—incidentally I have never fired one and intend to keep it that way—is completely off the table."

Ian sighed. "I thought you might feel this way." He was holding what looked like a revolver in his hand, with what could only be described as affection. "Max doesn't know about this. I was simply thinking you might want a little insurance. Like having a spare tire in the trunk. You are not a target—and no one else on the guest list is, either. There is no danger whatsoever. Whoever sent the casket is after Max and Max alone."

The spare tire was ludicrous, and Faith was about to expand on just *how* absurd it was when Max Dane walked into the kitchen. "I thought we were meeting in the foyer. Something wrong? You both look a little down in the mouth. No Beluga available?"

Faith had to admire how fast Ian slipped the gun away and shut the drawer. "Sorry," he said. "We got to chatting about your collection of toby jugs. Faith was particularly admiring the Red Queen and other *Alice in Wonderland* ones."

"Well, she can't have them. Now I imagine you've finalized the menus, so why don't Mrs. Fairchild and I talk over the rest of the weekend? I won't be needing you for the moment, Ian."

"Yes, master," he said with a click of the heels. The two men laughed. It was obviously a well-worn routine. He appeared to have been working at Rowan House for a while—the way Max had described Ian's quarters suggested as much—but what was Ian's background? The theater? Some other performing arts? A stint on *Upstairs, Downstairs*? He had all the right moves. His name hadn't been in the *Heaven or Hell Playbill*. She'd ask Max at some point.

"I'll be back in an hour or so. Do you need anything?" Ian asked.

"Nope. Now let's get going, Mrs. Fairchild. Friday is fast approaching," Max said.

Don't I know it, Faith thought. And, should I or shouldn't I?

It was almost as if Max Dane knew of her misgivings. He led her into the beautiful library where they had met the first time, and once they were seated, he immediately began to talk about his possibly having overreacted to the bizarre gift.

"When one has the kind of theatrical background I have, one tends to see all life as a stage, a play in production. Maybe

I was impulsively leaping to the conclusion that a coffin at center stage meant a murderer in the wings, but I did—and Ian thought so, too."

"I've read the bios of your guests in the *Playbill* and done Internet searches, but it would be helpful if you could provide more input. Why invite these ten, or eleven, counting Jack Gold? Plenty of other people were involved in the musical. I know you think I am some kind of latter-day Miss Marple, but even she had village gossip to help her out."

He smiled. "I thought—and still think—it is better for you to meet and observe the guests without preconceived suspicions, especially mine. I can assure you each has very strong, and maybe even good, reasons to dislike me. Even to want me dead. I'm afraid I'm not a very nice person, Mrs. Fairchild."

Exactly what Chat had said, Faith thought. She hadn't mentioned her connection to Charity Sibley's PR firm and didn't intend to, since Chat had mentioned Dane's ill feelings toward her. But her insatiable curiosity kicked in. She wanted to see the weekend through, and Dane's explanation was enough to reassure her after Ian's dramatic moment with the gun. An impresario like Max Dane would have had an over-the-top reaction. There would surely be some awkward moments, but everyone, including Max, would be in one piece by the end of the party on Sunday. She pulled out her iPad and went to the guest list.

"You listed James Nelson as 'original director.' Why that designation?"

"I had to step in myself. It was a mistake to hire him in the first place. He'd never directed a major show, never directed a musical." He paused a moment in thought. "There are basically three kinds of directors. A maestro, who keeps a finger on the entire pulse of the production, then what I call the 'daddy' director, who sees the cast as family, and finally the mediator, who is big on collaboration, asking for and offering input on every detail. You've heard enough about me to guess which category I fall into.

James fell into both the second and third categories. A nurturer. Big on consensus. Like the Quakers. He may even have been one. Anyway, it was obvious very soon that we were in trouble and rather than work with me, he quit. Well, maybe I encouraged it. Oh, and why did I hire him in the beginning? The show was different from any other I'd ever done, and he was different from any director I'd worked with. You know the basic plot right?"

Faith shook her head, not wanting to mention the synopsis Chat had given her. She also wanted to hear Dane's version.

He proceeded to tell her about the wager between God and Lucifer. "We were a little sketchy when it came to the prize, leaving it at bragging rights, fodder to win the faithful or enticement to the opposite. There were some pretty good production numbers. Tony Ames was a helluva choreographer—pardon the allusion. Especially the opening and the finale. And that was a great song. Betty and Phil made a few pennies from it. Anyway, the show focused on a small group of people from above and below. One of the angels had been a good girl all her life, gave up college, career, marriage, to take care of a sick parent, and just after she's set free, like the day after the funeral, she's hit by a car. The driver was drunk. He gets out and she dies in his arms."

"And that was Eve Anderson's role?"

"Yes. Looking back she may have been a little long in the tooth for it, but she was the money—along with Baker and Sinclair."

"The money?" Faith asked.

"The carrot for the backers. I couldn't expect investors to cough up even for one of my shows with total unknowns. So Eve Anderson got the lead and I had a team with a string of hit songs. Back in the day George Abbot could get backers with two bottles of booze and potato chips in a tiny apartment living room, but that changed, especially since the 'widows law'—you have to have all your financing in place before you sew a single costume, build a set, etcetera. A safeguard against cheating little old ladies."

"Not like in *The Producers*."

"Sadly, not. I want a drink. You?"

"I'm okay, thanks."

He walked over to the largest of the built-in bookcases and touched the spine of an impressive leather-covered volume. A door swung open, revealing a well-appointed bar. Faith was impressed. The books had certainly looked real. Thinking of the pistol in the kitchen drawer, she wondered what else might be hidden away at Rowan House.

Max poured himself a generous tumbler of scotch—Laphroaig, she noticed, Tom's expensive favorite and doled out in much smaller amounts on special, or stressful, occasions. Max shut the cabinet and returned to his chair.

"Long story short. It was boy meets girl, boy instantly falls in love—but not the best circumstances. He was the drunk driver, kills himself in remorse, and goes to hell. And then the girl is chosen to descend. As part of the bet. Aurora—that's the young cutie whose life he cut short—comes upon him in her wanderings. She's frightened, as well she might be. Great special effects and lots of deadly sinners. Harvey—always thought we should have changed the name, but too late now, audiences back then associated it with a giant rabbit—recognizes her right away and offers his protection. Travis Trent, who had just started to be a name, played him. Eve's and his voices were well matched, but there wasn't a lot of chemistry. I figured it would build. That happens. Anyway, Aurora is grateful and of course falls madly in love with him, too. And he's been in love with her since he held her dying in his arms. Bunch of subplots with the other characters and a good, pretty raunchy song by Naomi Stein. She's gone to one or the other herself now. Great character actor—started in Yiddish theater. She played an eighty-something who had never had any fun in life and is having the time of it now in Hades. Some more stuff and at last comes the choice for the two lovers. Will Aurora go back or will she stay?"

"Certainly an unusual plot. But who would choose eternal damnation even for love?"

He gave a broad grin. "Me for one. Not necessarily for love, but I'm with those who think if it exists, heaven would be pretty boring, not that I'll have a chance to find out. Anyway, I picked up Adrian St. John's script and pretty much all the others for the same reason I hired James Nelson. I wanted new, out-of-the-box stuff. Even Naomi hadn't been in anything for years. And I got it," he added ruefully. "So out of the box that the guys packing them were the only ones with jobs in a few weeks."

"What happened to everyone once the show closed? It closed pretty soon, right?"

"It should have the next day after we'd seen the reviews. 'The Dane Touch Goes to Hell' and so forth. Reviews sell tickets no matter how good the production and actors. But technically we limped along for a couple more weeks. As for what happened to everyone, I haven't been in touch. So far as I know Adrian never wrote another word. Went back to England. May be raising sheep in Yorkshire."

"Wasn't it a London address?"

"Yeah, but you know what I meant. Now James Nelson really could be raising sheep on some island in Maine. He was always kind of a nature boy. Walking ad for L.L.Bean. I have no idea what either of them have been doing all these years."

Reflecting that James could actually be raising sheep—a small herd or more likely goats—on Haute Mers, Faith said, "But they stopped doing what had been a career?" She was looking for grudges. "And others as well?"

"Dammit, Faith—keep forgetting you're married to a sky pilot, so forgive my language in advance for the whole weekend—I didn't force them to upend what they were doing. I didn't destroy their careers. Most of them didn't really have any to start with, and if James or Adrian had any real passion for the stage they never would have left."

"But you had it—and you left, too."

"I retired! Completely different situation."

"Any others who left the theater?"

"In a manner of speaking they all did except for Travis briefly, Jack Gold—and he never worked on a big show again—Tony Ames, too. Some have gone on to success in related work. Eve a few movies, TV. Alexis was the youngest and she got snapped up for a sitcom gig, made a lot of money. Changed her name to 'Abbot,' which may have helped break the jinx."

"The jinx?"

Max waved his hand. "Forget I said that. We have more important things to think about now. I want to do a walk-through for Friday night in the summer parlor." He freshened his drink—the glass was almost empty—and said, "Coming?"

Faith had seen the invitation Dane sent out and she had the feeling she was being cast—a "walk-through"!—but she fully intended to come to the party as herself.

Samantha had called Zach on Sunday after she got home. Somehow what had started as a brief call asking him if he would like to meet up for coffee again soon turned into a long one as they discussed everything from favorite films to whether alien life existed—on Mars or elsewhere. Samantha found herself comfortably chatting as if she and Zach were old friends while she stirred the bacon butternut squash risotto, tonight's dinner. She was recalling more about the events that led to Zach's meeting Faith when he was in high school and the way she had helped him out— more like saved his bacon. And then he had done her a similar turn some years later.

"How about we continue this over hamburgers at Christopher's— it's near the Porter T stop?" Zach suggested. "I like them even better than Bartley's."

"Wow, that's blasphemy around my house. My parents even celebrate their wedding anniversary there!" The venerable and

legendary Harvard Square burger place had been the Millers'—
and thousands of other couples'—first date.

"You seem up to a challenge. Are we on?"

They agreed to meet for lunch the next day, before Samantha was due for a long shift. Zach seemed to have very flexible
hours and when she commented on it he said he didn't have to be
physically present in the office much. "Which is a pain, because it
means I'm always working, or thinking I should be anyway."

There was no way it was a date, Samantha told herself as she
added hot broth to the rice mixture after she hung up. She needed
his help. But still, it didn't hurt that he was smart, good-looking,
and as far as she could tell, not involved with anyone.

"You look happy, honey," Sam Miller said, coming into the
kitchen. "And if what you're making is as good as it smells, I'm
happy, too. Easy to please. That's what they say about me."

"I think that's a song lyric," Samantha said as her father kissed
the top of her head. "And you seem pretty happy, too."

"Ah, that's because there's a Planning Board meeting tomorrow night. The developer is presenting his preliminary requests.
He doesn't know we have a secret weapon."

"Weapon, what weapon? What's going on?" Pix came into
the room. Samantha noticed the slightly guilty look on her mother's face and suspected she'd been upstairs measuring Danny's bedroom for a sewing room for herself. She'd said she wanted a place
where she could quilt and not have to put everything back in
boxes and into a closet each time. What her mom hadn't said, but
Samantha knew, was it also meant her brother wouldn't be able to
move back easily.

"Come to the Planning Board meeting and all will be clear,"
Sam said.

"That sounds like a miracle. In any case, Faith and I will be
there." She gave her husband a hug. "Open a bottle of wine. We
can drink to making improbables probable."

"You two," Samantha said as she watched her father dance her mother around the room in an impromptu tango. She turned back to the stove. She didn't want either parent to see the tears springing to her eyes. Caleb used to do things like this. Grab her and spin her around singing cheesy love songs until they would collapse in a heap on the couch, then collapse into another kind of dance. Damn him.

The fact that it was gray outside, the bare trees ungainly sharp spokes, made the casket in the summer parlor look almost appropriate. Max turned on the ceiling lights, which did not bring a warm glow to the room but rather bathed everything in white light, creating shadows in the corners.

"I'm thinking more welcoming light?" Faith suggested. "Use different bulbs and place a few table lamps around?"

"Each to his own. I like this effect, but you're right. Doesn't have a party feel to it."

"I think we can count on the coffin to dampen any party feel," Faith said dryly.

"Oh, but you will have transformed it with linens and all that sumptuous food. My hope is that only the person who sent it will react visibly at first."

"That would make my sleuthing job easy," Faith said, doubting anyone clever enough to arrange such a difficult delivery would be stupid enough to react to seeing it in situ. "I'll try to transform it, but you are planning to let everyone know what it is?"

"Of course. Otherwise, what's the point of the whole weekend?"

Maybe it was the scotch, or maybe Dane was getting excited about his birthday, but he was definitely in a good mood.

"Now let's talk about seating. Three round tables for six will be more than enough. The tablecloths are in the butler's pantry. Big enough tables so people can change seats—a moveable feast—

and also keep a distance from each other, as the need may arise with this troupe. Votive candles—tapers are too perilous—and more of them scattered in other parts of the room, but not too Transylvanian."

They were sitting on a curved window seat at the opposite end of the room from the fireplace. "And a fire in the fireplace or not?" Faith asked. The casket was well away from it, and the andirons had been moved out onto the floor.

"Not, I think. The andirons are serving another use in any case. I don't have another set this large, and since this is to be a one-time event, I don't want to purchase others. I want prime rib for my birthday dinner. What else have you planned?"

"It's been fun tracking down celestial and not-so-celestial dishes in keeping with *Heaven or Hell*," she said. "Instead of mashed or baked potatoes with the beef, how about *Himmel und Erde*— 'heaven' represented by apples and 'earth,' below ground, by potatoes. I've been testing several versions and I think you'll like it."

"Go for it, but better keep a bowl of good old garlic mashed for me in case I don't."

"The first dish I thought of was some kind of pasta Fra Diavolo—with lobster, of course, as befits the elegant occasion. It's so rich, though, I'd suggest it as a primo piatto, and sticking with the theme, use capelli d'angelo—angel hair pasta—instead of linguine."

"I'm loving this. What else?"

"Well, your birthday cake is obvious: devil's food, angel food, or both."

"Definitely both, and make the devil's food as decadent as possible. Also think of something to go with the angel food so it's not so namby-pamby."

Not the words Faith would use for her rich version, but she knew what he meant. "I could make a whipped frosting in soft peaks like clouds and sprinkle some edible confetti—Funfetti rainbow sprinkles have made a big comeback."

They discussed a few other side dishes—no salad, "rabbit food," and Max also nixed an antipasto course served at the table.

"We'll gather on the second-floor landing by the fireplace I showed you the first time—it's plenty big enough. You and Ian can pass hors d'oeuvres. I'll be pouring the champagne. By the way, only Ian and I will be opening the wine and other liquor bottles, although guests can pour their own—and they will—once we've opened them."

This was a little too 007 for her taste, but Faith didn't say anything. Should she be keeping her eyes out for a hypodermic plunged into a cork?

"Oh, and you," Max added. "Should the need arise, feel free to play sommelier."

"I sent a list to Ian that you may not have seen yet of things we'll serve during the birthday aperitif: several versions of Deviled Eggs, cheeses like smoked gouda, puff pastry deviled ham squares, smoked nuts, and two kinds of Devils on Horseback— bacon around an oyster and bacon around a cheese-stuffed date. They'll get the idea."

"Better make plenty. Some of this crew make locusts look like picky eaters. I'm impressed, Faith, you've done a splendid job. I've never heard of those horseback things. Who dreamed them up? You?"

She shook her head. "Nobody knows for sure. There are many explanations, some pretty outlandish, such as the Normans using rashers of bacon as armor—sounds more like Monty Python—but the dish either originated in Britain or was popularized by it after the French made a trip across the channel."

He laughed. "There's a Steinway baby grand in the foyer that I'm sure will see some use over the weekend. Maybe I'll print up the words to Eric Idle's 'Always Look on the Bright Side of Life.' Do you know it? From their *Life of Brian* film."

Faith did know it. The song was terrific, but as it was sung by a chorus of men about to die, perhaps another choice. "Happy Birthday," for example.

"I know you plan to serve champagne before the banquet, but I also came across a cocktail called Fallen Angel that was invented at the Savoy Hotel bar in London at some point during the thirties. It's gin with lime juice, a dash of bitters, and a larger dash of white crème de menthe. Offer it as an alternative or along with?" (See recipe, page 233.)

"Definitely along with. And is one a fallen angel before or after imbibing?"

"I think that's one of those chicken-or-the-egg questions. It should make for some witty speculation." In her mind Faith had dressed the guests in period costume, as if gathered at the Savoy bar next to Marlene Dietrich, Noël Coward, and Bogie.

"Ian will whip them up. He had a stint as a bartender at the Savoy when he was resting."

Faith knew this was the term actors employed when unemployed, but she hadn't known Ian was one. She wondered again how he had come to be in Max's employ.

"Ian was on the stage in Britain?"

"Kind of. He was a dresser—the guy who makes sure you're wearing the right clothes for a scene and that those clothes are in perfect shape. He'd been the dresser for an older actor friend of mine for many years. I was in London while Rowan House was being renovated and I mentioned to my friend that I was in the market for a kind of butler/housekeeper type. I didn't want a woman. They talk too much." Max appeared lost in thought for a moment. "Nice chap—and talented. Died while I was there. I'd met Ian once or twice, had even asked him if he knew someone who might want the job. Saw him at the funeral and well . . ."

Biting her tongue at the obvious gender slur, Faith said, "That was how Ian came here?"

"He wasn't sure he'd like the States—not a fan of Yanks—so

we settled on a six-month trial, and he's been here ever since. He'd never been to Manhattan and that was what convinced him, plus the salary and perks like first-class tickets home—he's going off Sunday when the bash is all over. He gets a yen for real fish and chips. Apparently the ones here are 'rubbish.' Despite his manner, Ian has some plebian tastes. Likes his pint, too."

The conversation seemed to be trailing off. Max was staring out the window. Faith thought about saying it was time for her to go, but she didn't want to interrupt whatever train of thought was going on inside his head. Bang—she was startled when he kicked the wooden window seat with his heel.

"My grandmother used to lock me in here to punish me. One of the first things I did when I moved in was have the lock removed. Why they needed a lock in the first place is a good question—the silver was kept in the safe in the pantry. But I suppose it was for decorative effect. The mortise was engraved with lion's heads."

"How awful! You must have been terrified." Faith pictured a Max Dane small enough to fit in the seat, confined in the dark. Whatever the length of time, even a few minutes, would have seemed like ages. It was child abuse.

"I was, but what became more terrifying was what would lead up to my incarceration. I could never figure out how to avoid putting the particular foot wrong that would send me here or up to my room. When I was old enough to realize that any trace of Brooklyn—that's where I grew up, I think I told you—in accent or behavior would result in instant punishment I would avoid even the merest hint of the borough. The other things were unpredictable. Playing with the chauffer's son, making a pet of a field mouse—that didn't last long. The housekeeper followed her nose and found it. Literally cut off its head with a carving knife. And one memorable time I'd hoped to please her by bringing a bouquet of flowers I'd picked in the garden. How was I to know it was look, don't touch?"

"But why were you here alone? Weren't your parents here, too?"

Dane got up and walked over to a beautifully carved Morris-type panel next to a window, pressed on it, and took out another bottle of his scotch. There were hidden liquor cabinets in every room, it seemed, and Faith was realizing why. He returned and sat down, giving her what she believed was an apologetic smile. "Shouldn't be drinking alone. Ian will be annoyed. Sure you won't join me?"

Faith shook her head, hoping he would keep talking. He did.

"I was here because my grandparents, particularly Grand-mamma, believed in doing the proper thing, which meant having her grandson for a week sometime during the year. I never knew when the ax would fall. What season. Summer was best, but often it was the dead of winter. My parents weren't with me because my father, Henry Dane, was dead and my mother, Helen, wouldn't darken the door."

Faith settled back. Here was what Ursula had alluded to in describing her friend Helen. That there had been some sort of problem. And now she was looking at it, or its result.

Max took a small sip of his drink, seemed to relish the taste, and continued, "My mother grew up here. As a wedding present to her parents, her grandparents had turned the place over to them. It had just been completed. The Frosts didn't suffer from the Crash as so many others, even in their rarefied layer, did. My grandfather believed in real estate, not stocks. He was very good at wringing every rent penny from his tenants, high and low, in Boston. My mother was the younger of two. Her brother died pretty young but managed to form a desirable marriage with a Lowell before he went off to the equivalent of the Somerset Club in the sky."

Faith knew the Somerset Club in Boston, though she had never been inside the massive stone mansion at 42 Beacon Street that suggested a fortress more than the convivial social club, founded in 1851 or even earlier according to some accounts. Asking about membership was a guarantee of exclusion. It was the snootiest and perhaps the wealthiest of Boston's formerly all-male social clubs. The story most often told about the Somerset was an accurate one: when a fire broke out in the 1940s, the firemen were made to use the servants' entrance.

"The precious Frost name continued, and still does, but that branch did not have the business acumen shall we say of *moi*? I was able to purchase Rowan House—it had, of course, been 'Frostcliffe'—and then move in roughly twenty years ago when my uncle's widow died. It gave and gives me enormous delight to think of my grandparents, and other relatives, spinning rapidly in the family plot at Mount Auburn Cemetery."

He started to stand up, but Faith wasn't about to let him leave without the whole story. "It must have pleased your mother to have her childhood home back?"

"She died when I was in my early thirties and no, it wouldn't have pleased her. She hated the place growing up and the feeling intensified as an adult. You see, she had been kept locked up in the equivalent of this window seat. Only allowed to associate with the right kind of people."

Faith thought of Ursula. The right pedigree, although the family was not wealthy after the move to Aleford. "I have an older friend who was in school with your mother in Aleford. Before you got in touch with me, I had never heard of Havencrest and I asked her about it. She came here occasionally and remembered one of your mother's birthday parties. A sixteenth, I think she said."

His face softened. "After all this is all over I'd like to meet your friend. I don't know many people who recall my mother, and I adored her. And she me, despite the fact that I wasn't a good little boy, particularly after a trip here. I suppose I was doing what I wanted to do on those visits. I'd pick fights with other boys, get in trouble at school."

"But she kept sending you."

"I never told her what it was like—the tiny room in the attic, the food—I ate in the kitchen, and if the housekeeper wasn't around, other servants would slip me some of the good things to eat. Otherwise it was plain soup and yesterday's bread. I came to understand as an adult that she sent me so I would know what you give up for love. The importance of it."

"Sounds like the theme of *Heaven or Hell.*"

Max's eyes narrowed. "I suppose you're right. I've never thought of that." The look quickly vanished. "Anyway, my mother wanted to go to college, but that wasn't going to happen. She did convince her parents to let her go to a kind of finishing school on Beacon Street near the Public Garden that later became a junior college. She loved it and if mater and pater had known that the girls were allowed to stroll in the park without chaperones—although they had to be in twos or more—they would have had her out of there in a heartbeat. Dad was living with relatives in the North End—the fact that he was 'Eyetalian' made things all the worse when it came out. He had shortened 'Danetelli' to 'Dane' when he was still a teenager. He came to Boston from Brooklyn to learn watch repair at the North Bennet Street School, a block away from where he was living. My mother said he figured it was a good trade. That no matter how poor people were they would need to have a watch. He'd laugh today to see that kids only use their phones. Dad wasn't about to stay in just one part of Boston. In his free time he wandered all over the city. On one of those afternoons—cue lights—fate stepped in and he met the beautiful Helen Frost. One of her school friends was happy to act as beard, and it wasn't long before Helen and Henry . . ."

"H and H—heaven and hell," Faith murmured.

Max grimaced, and said, ". . . were madly in love. Helen knew her parents would never approve, but she gave it a try and brought Henry out here. The butler admitted them, assuming Henry, who was quite the looker—although a carrottop like me—was one of the Frosts' kind. He wasn't and after what I can only imagine was a rip-roaring scene, Helen left the house with him that very day. She never returned. They got married and at first lived in the North End. Helen worked in a bakery and I was born more than a year later. She sent her parents a note. There was no reply. Remember, they still had her older brother and his family. Mother wrote again to tell them where she was living when they moved to Brooklyn and again when Dad died. Still no replies until after her brother died—she hadn't even known of his death. They asked her to come for a week, bringing me. She had to work, and I'm pretty sure wouldn't have come anyway, but she took the train up with me, handed me over to the chauffer who met the train at South Station, took it back, and did the whole thing over again until I was old enough to go on my own. How I loved those return trips! It was like being let out of jail."

Faith couldn't help herself; she reached for his hand and gave it a squeeze.

"Then Charles Frost—Ian mentioned he had a small part, a walk-on—is a relative?"

Ian entered, looked pointedly at the empty glass in Max's hand, but before he could say anything, Max answered Faith's question.

"Yeah—and the only one left."

Faith drove home, her thoughts somber. It seemed to her that the person with the greatest need for revenge was Max himself. By buying the Havencrest property he had struck a blow on behalf of his parents, especially his mother, and for the child he had been. But wasn't there something deeply twisted about returning to a place of such misery? The return coincided with his one large career failure—punishing himself?

Heaven or Hell wasn't just the title of the musical; it was Dane's whole life.

She'd been able to get a fuller picture of some of the guests, but there were notable exceptions. Bella Martelli, the costume designer, for instance. She was listed as living in Brooklyn and "Martelli" was an Italian last name. Had she and Max known each other there or only through the show? She'd try to track down more information about Bella online. There weren't going to be any more tête-à-têtes with Max. Early Friday morning she'd be out at Rowan House setting the stage. Wherein to catch the conscience of . . . ?

When Samantha emerged from the Porter Square station, Zach was waiting by the tall wind-driven revolving sculpture. She had always thought the bright red flat metal pieces looked like hearts, and in today's breeze they were spinning rapidly. It may have been the long climb up the subway stairs, but her heart was beating a little faster, too. On the train, she'd realized how much she was looking forward to the lunch. In New York, she'd had an active social life, mostly with friends she and Caleb had made in their Park Slope neighborhood, but she had also had regular girls' night outs with Wellesley and Wharton friends. She liked her coworkers at Starbucks, but everyone was on different schedules, and talk of meeting up never went far. Aside from asking Zach for his help, she was eager to have some of her kind of grown-up conversation. And from their increasingly frequent and increasingly longer phone calls plus texts, Zach filled the bill. They agreed on everything, from politics to food. Well, she was being put to the hamburger test, so that might change.

It seemed natural to give him a quick hug and slip her arm through his as she greeted him, "Oh, the pressure! Bartley's versus Christopher's! I may have to order something other than a hamburger."

"No cheating. You'll have a hamburger. Fair and square. You have to tell the truth."

"I always tell the truth," Samantha said.

They were waiting for the light to change so they could cross

Mass. Ave. Zach looked at her with a slightly serious expression. "You know, I think you probably do."

The walk sign blinked and Samantha started across, pulling him along. "A good thing, I hope. Now lead me to this mecca of ground beef. Am I allowed cheese, condiments?"

"What do you have on your burger at Bartley's?"

"I'm pretty hard-core—medium rare leaning to rare, a dollop of catsup and always cheese. American cheese. The orange kind."

"Okay, so you need to order exactly the same."

"And fries. I always have fries. Sweet potato."

"Hmmm. I don't recall fries entering the competition, but heck, let's go for it."

When they entered the restaurant it smelled so good Samantha realized she was starving. She hadn't taken time for breakfast. There was a table available and Zach got right to it, telling the server their burger choices, or "burgah" on Christopher's menu, which put Samantha off a bit. But hey, when in Boston . . .

Zach wanted grilled onions on his—"I always do"—and ordered a basket of sweet potato fries, warning Samantha they were the waffle chip kind. "And two waters please. Plain tap, no lemon." Once the server had headed off, he explained, "No other flavors intruding on the palate. And no fries until you've had two bites of your burger."

"Yes, Dad," Samantha said. "And may I stay up until nine tonight? There's a *Gilmore Girls* marathon."

"Definitely not. Now were it something like *The IT Crowd* I might consider it."

"I love that show! My brother Dan, who may be even more nerdy than you, introduced me to it. 'Have you tried turning it on and off?' Sorry for my terrible British accent."

"A good try—and hey, who are you calling a nerd?" Zach laughed.

The food arrived quickly. "Shut your eyes tight," Zach instructed. "The food's here. I considered bringing a bandanna of some sort to use as a blindfold, but it might give people, including you, the wrong idea. We eat first with our eyes, and I didn't want you to be swayed one way or the other by the plate's appearance."

Obediently, Samantha closed her eyes. She heard a slight clunk as the dish was set on the table. She was about to feel for the burger with both hands when she felt Zach's fingers guiding her. She'd noticed his long slender fingers, nails cut short for keyboarding, when they'd had coffee together. No tattoos on the knuckles. Nothing like that of any sort that she could see. Caleb had several studs in one ear and Samantha had always thought it was cool—artsy without going overboard. Now she thought it was slightly clichéd. Or something that he should have grown out of, like the taste for wine coolers and Slim Jims.

Zach was still holding her hands in his, raising the burger, which smelled heavenly, closer and closer to her waiting lips. She felt the bun brush them, opened her mouth wide, took a good-size bite, and chewed. "Oh my God, Zach, I can't believe how good this is! It's sinfully delicious."

She started to open her eyes. "Keep your eyes closed," he said. His hands were still holding hers, his fingers clasping them harder. "Take one more bite, then open. You need to be sure."

She took another, and it was even better than the first. She opened her eyes wide. "I'm sure," she said.

He dropped his hands and picked up his own burger. "You should try it with grilled onions sometime."

They talked food some more, arguing about where to get the best dim sum in Chinatown. Zach was a regular at Hei La Moon—they brought him specials from off the menu. He was convinced it was because they thought he was part Asian because of his hair.

The sweet potato fries were a draw. "Think we have to try Bartley's," Samantha suggested. She looked at her watch, a present from the Fairchilds when she had graduated from Wellesley. It had the school's seal and motto, *"Non Ministrari sed Ministrare"*—"Not to be ministered unto, but to minister." She had to minister to a horde of thirsty Starbuckians all too soon and she hadn't come close to asking Zach for his help.

"You know you said you thought I was an honest person?" she said.

"Yeah—now don't tell me that you're really spying for my competition or something else heinous."

She laughed. She seemed to laugh a lot with Zach. "No, but besides wanting to do the taste test, I did have another reason for lunch today."

He leaned back and braced his hands on the table. "Let me have it."

"Nothing horrendous. I just wondered if I gave you someone's name, you could find out more than I've been able to simply by Googling him. All I know is he recently moved here from California."

"You have come to the right man. But I must warn you: I'm a White Hat. No funny business that could land me in federal prison."

Zach took out his phone. "What's the name—and are you sure it's real? Can still track him down, but it's harder. Approximately how old is he? And do you mind telling me why you want to find out about this guy?"

She took a deep breath. "His name is Austin Stebbins and he's in his eighties. Was in real estate, I think, but probably long retired. Widowed. Grew up here, a Beacon Hill Brahmin. He knew my grandmother when they were both young and that's the name she said when she introduced him, so not an alias. She's why I want to know more about him. They are spending a lot of time together. He's staying with her right now at the house while he looks for his own place. And she's bought all sorts of new clothes, different from her usual." Samantha flushed. She was about to tell him more, but he leaned in, his face close to hers.

"Okaaay. Let me get this straight. You want me to investigate your grandmother?"

CHAPTER 7

The Planning Board meeting had been moved to the largest room in Town Hall. It seemed all of Aleford had turned out once the agenda topic was announced. "Strip Mall," although not mentioned as such in the wording of the topic, was not merely a red flag, but also a call to battle—reminiscent of the one heeded by Aleford's feisty 1775 forefathers and mothers.

Faith and Pix took seats at the back, Faith because she always sat in the back row at these things in case she wanted to discreetly slip out; Pix because she liked to see who was in attendance and constantly turning her head from the front upon each arrival was a bit rude, plus it caused a crick in her neck.

"Do you think Millicent has been camped out here since this afternoon? She's grabbed a prime front-row spot," Faith said.

"Definitely," Pix answered. "And it's no secret which side she's on."

Millicent Revere McKinley—"Miss," not "Ms."—was an authenticated descendent of the famous silversmith and clarion. Her small white clapboard house was positioned nicely to afford her a clear view down Main Street and across the hallowed Green unchanged from that famous day and year. She was the custodian

of all things Aleford, as well as a long list of things she considered
her moral obligation to protect: manners, language usage, proper
dress. She was not opposed to progress, she once told Faith, just
change.

When the board entered, Faith was disappointed to see that
the new town counsel was not among them. She knew everyone
taking a seat—the only comfortable ones in the room—behind the
long table. An AV kid from the high school was taping the meeting for the local access cable channel, perhaps the most watched
one in town. Nobody wanted to miss, say, a vote on signage—no
sandwich boards on town property or others hanging over the
sidewalk. Tree removal petitions brought before the board gar-
nered higher ratings than the Oscars.

Pix nudged her friend and nodded toward the door. "I believe
that's Ms. Sommersby," she whispered.

Blake Sommersby, slender and tall, was indeed stunning. She
was wearing the requisite navy attorney suit, but hers suggested
designer, not Brooks, and her matching heels were Cole Haan.
Faith had the same in black. Not over-the-top as Manolos would
have been, but not generic. Under her jacket Ms. Sommersby wore
a white silk blouse with a soft, not overly deep cowl. Her only
jewelry were pearl studs and a watch that even from far away Faith
spotted as a Cartier Tank. Understated and classy. The overall effect was surprisingly sexy. Like the old movies where Miss So-
and-So removes her glasses, unbuttons her jacket, shakes her hair
out, and Cary Grant falls in love, or lust. Blake Sommersby's hair
was rich auburn and grazed her chin in a blunt cut. Faith had always wanted red hair, particularly auburn, ever since reading *Anne
of Green Gables*. It wasn't too late, but even if Tom didn't notice—a
distinct possibility—Amy would point it out.

The developer arrived next, and this was a surprise. In her head,
Faith had pictured a caricature: a short, slightly sweaty, paunchy
middle-aged man with a bad comb-over and several wardrobe
mistakes. Beady, shifty eyes and thin lips, too. Instead, this man

looked to be in his early to midthirties and easily Blake's counterpart in appearance, save for the watch, which was a Breitling. He was tall as well and accompanied by two men, virtually clones. One got busy setting up a laptop for the presentation. Faith had the sense there would be no mishaps with focus and file finding as regularly happened at Town Meeting when Alefordians tried to go high tech.

There was a palpable air of both anticipation and dread in the packed room. Everyone wanted to get the matter settled, but not if it meant what many were calling "the thin edge of a wedge," development that would alter the town's basic character. Condos might be next! Streets without the town's treasured potholes to discourage traffic!

Marian Cho, Planning Board chair, was welcoming everyone. She introduced the board members and then said, "I am especially pleased to welcome our new town counsel, Ms. Blake Sommersby." The lawyer flashed a warm smile around the room. Faith decided to hate her, but only because she appeared so perfect. No other reason.

"We have only one issue before the board tonight," Marian said, "and I want to emphasize that this is just the beginning of the process. No votes will be taken. Bradley Peters of the Peters Development Group will present his proposal. The board will then direct questions and comments to Mr. Peters and his associates. Following that, we have scheduled forty-five minutes for questions and comments from the floor directed either to the board or Mr. Peters."

Pix yawned. "It's going to be a long night."

"You said it," Faith said, feeling her eyelids already getting heavy. And the room was warm, which made it worse. But she couldn't leave. She had to see how this first foray went. Bradley and Blake. What was with these last names as firsts?

The two suits stood up with Bradley as he positioned himself where he could address both the board and the audience. The equivalent of the AV kid stationed himself at the laptop pointed toward the screen, and the third sat next to him, an iPad in hand. All three men exuded confidence and competence. Bradley's presentation was clear, starting with several slides depicting the plans and a rendering of the finished building. Red brick with faux columns on either side of the entrance doors and topped by a white cornice along the flat roof, it suggested a cross between a bank and a 1940s elementary school. "As you can see, it will fit in with Aleford's traditional architectural style well," Peters said.

At that point, a loud "Ha!" from the front row echoed throughout the room "Miss McKinley, there will be time for comments later," Marian Cho said sternly.

"I'm just sayin'," Millicent retorted. Since Benjamin Fairchild had instructed her on the use of the Internet for genealogical research at the library, Millicent had acquired her own computer. Her recent vocabulary—and diction—indicated she was surfing more than Ancestry.com on the Web.

Peters went through additional architectural site-specific drawings, spoke of the contribution the building would make to the town with its combination of business and affordable housing rentals. "Affordable housing" caused several on the board to visibly perk up. Always a problem in Aleford. Faith watched as those board members glanced at Millicent—no question about her expression—and returned to their blank-canvas faces immediately. The same thing happened when Bradley Peters mentioned the increase the new businesses and apartments would produce for Aleford's tax rolls, since the prior occupant had been a nonprofit.

Faith was having an extremely difficult time staying awake. When she'd returned from Rowan House—was that just today?— she'd retrieved Tom and the kids' skiwear from the attic and packed it in large duffels. Besides the prep work and baking for Rowan House, she had to make up some casseroles, soups, and other food for her family to take for their weekend. Pix tapped her arm and Faith's head snapped up. The board was addressing a series of questions to the developer, the boilerplate ones Faith had expected about parking, maximum occupancy, and safety codes. Then Ms. Sommersby firmly took over; firing a series of queries relating to state ordinances with so many House Bill numbers that Faith's head was soon reeling. From the looks on the developers' faces, theirs were, too. Clearly they had not expected this kind of expertise in what they surely thought was a backwater. Blake barely let them get a word in edgewise. Faith decided not to hate her after all. The woman was a force of nature.

Finally it was time for questions from the floor. Much to Faith's surprise, Millicent was mum. Peters had shown photos of other sites he'd developed, and now Patsy Avery, the Fairchilds' dear friend, read a list of Peters projects Bradley had not included in his presentation, most of them in Dorchester and Roxbury, citing the fact that the renters he'd turned out of the buildings he'd razed with the promise of affordable, better dwellings were unable to come close to meeting the increased prices once the new dwellings were completed. "What exactly is your idea of affordable?" Patsy asked. "We need to hear some numbers and percentages. How many of the units will meet the State's definition?" Patsy and her husband, Will, were both lawyers; her law firm was known for civil rights cases, while his specialized in family law. Both were active in the Youth Advocacy Foundation.

Peters smiled at Patsy. "Great question. We will be detailing this in our final proposal, but I can promise you our commitment to the community in this regard is genuine. I believe at the moment Aleford just makes the percentage required by the Commonwealth. We intend to increase that considerably." He was a cool one, Faith reflected.

Before Patsy could come back with a follow-up, Randall Foster, the town gadfly, who proudly admitted to being ninety, jumped up and as usual went off topic, grumbling about the police department's newest patrol car—"Why are our tax dollars being used for such a fancy vehicle?" Marian patiently reminded him that Town Meeting had voted on the model and make, also applauding that it was a hybrid. "Do you have a question or comment on the matter before us? The proposed demolition and change of use to what is known as the Grayson House?"

"Grayson House! Nobody can take that down! My grandfather designed it and lived there, too. Plus the First Parish burial ground and a Native American one are in the side yard. When I was a boy we used to dig up all kinds of things. I remember Ralph Lee, some of you remember Ralph and his birdcalls, well, he once found a bone. May have been a deer. Didn't have this DNA stuff back then. Bits of pottery, too. Young man"—he shook his finger at Bradley—"you need to back off."

Marian decided to adjourn after that.

"That was fun," Pix said. "Think Tom and Sam will be pleased. Peters should back off. Randall was perfect as usual."

Faith shook her head. "They're just getting started, and now they pretty much know our objections, so can come back with modifications. He'll bring in experts to refute the burial ground claim and remember, the heirs want to sell to him. Grayson House is an albatross for them and he's offering a way out."

"I'm afraid you're right," Pix said, "but I'm still betting on Ms. Sommersby. I have the car and Sam has that 'Let's get out of here look.' Talk to you tomorrow."

Faith and Tom had come separately. She told him she was leaving and he said he'd be home soon. On the way out she stopped at the restroom. Before the recent Town Hall renovation, it had been in the basement at the end of a musty corridor lined with teetering piles of boxes of what Faith assumed were town records but that looked more like hand-me-downs from the Collyer brothers. The facility itself dated from the early days of plumbing and it was a brave and/or desperate soul who used it. Now the new restroom was on the main floor, handicapped accessible with environmentally up-to-date fixtures. Faith made a point of stopping in when she was in the building as a reassurance that Aleford *could* move with the times.

Outside in the parking lot the environmentally friendly lights made the dark periphery look even darker. Take one step away and you'd effectively be lost. There were only three cars left, Tom's not among them, and Faith was about to head for hers when she noticed a couple standing close to one another. She stepped back into the shadow cast by the building and stood still. As she watched, one of the figures leaned in still closer, suggesting even further intimacy. Despite the dark, Faith had no trouble recognizing them.

Bradley Peters and Blake Sommersby.

Working at Starbucks had proved to be exactly the kind of job Samantha wanted for now—and maybe always. The pay wasn't anywhere near what she had been making, but she'd managed over the years to put away a hefty chunk working for her—financial advising had been part of her job, after all.

Starbucks had excellent benefits and she was a devout coffee drinker. She didn't even mind when her father told her she smelled like a freshly ground bean after a long day. No worries about wardrobe—was loving the green apron look. Better still were her incredibly friendly, noncompetitive coworkers. One of them, a veteran of several years, had explained that Starbucks' workplace ambiance all depended on the manager, and they had a jewel of one in Ken. Organized, affable, and supportive. Under him, the store was kept happily humming—Samantha found the only stress involved was keeping up with the morning and noon rush. And the customers were pleasant, too. Her coworkers told tales of demanding ones—"This isn't the hot grande sugar-free triple shot caramel chai soy latte with a quarter inch of foam I ordered and waited forever for!" (All of forty-seven seconds; the barista had kept track)—but so far Samantha was happy to comply with the most complicated and weirdest requests. She enjoyed getting to know the regulars and what they ordered, teasing the cashier who came on his midmorning break from Deluca's market next door when he occasionally went rogue and ordered a venti macchiato instead of grande.

She liked that her mind was free to wander as she prepared the drinks, kept the cases stocked, and helped clean up. Ken was a stickler for no spills on the counter where they kept the sugars and containers of milk. At the moment her thoughts were wandering back to Christopher's and what had followed Zach's accusation, or what had felt like one.

"Not investigate Granny! Investigate Stebbins!"

Zach had called for the check, which Samantha had insisted they split. She'd dug out some cash and said, "I know it sounds like I'm poking my nose into her personal life. But I have a reason. I wish I didn't have to get to work, I need more time to tell you why I'm not feeling comfortable about his friendship or whatever it is with my grandmother."

"Easy fix. I'll ride with you. I have to go to Kendall Square anyway."

They'd retraced their steps across Mass. Ave. and waited for the next train. The car had been almost empty and they took seats away from the few people on it. Not that what she was going to tell Zach was so hush-hush, but Samantha hated hearing other people's conversations in public, especially the noisy cell phone ones—the "Like it was like really awesome" type.

"Okay, spill." Zach had sat so close to her she'd become momentarily distracted by trying to figure out what shampoo he used. Definitely not AXE. Something subtle. Could it be Johnson's No More Tears?

She took a deep breath. "I think he may be some kind of Lothario."

Zach had burst out laughing. "I have never heard anyone say that word aloud. 'Lothario' or maybe you mean 'gigolo'?"

"It's not funny," Samantha said, although it kind of was. She had meant "gigolo." "I was at work, fortunately you can't really see me behind the machines, and Stebbins walked in with a woman. About my grandmother's age, maybe a little younger. Attractive, but I think she's had work."

"Meow," Zach said.

"No, this is to give you an idea of what to think about when you dig stuff up. She looked like money. Her clothes, purse, jewelry. Overdressed for Starbucks, but it seemed they had just nipped in for hot chocolate. He had the peppermint. Neither had a pastry. So maybe they were off to dinner later and didn't want to spoil their appetites." She caught herself rambling and stopped.

"When was this?" Zach said.

"Saturday afternoon. I didn't think anything much about it. He grew up on Beacon Hill. She was probably a childhood friend, like Granny. I even thought about going over to say hi, but then he reached across the table and took her hand. I could see both their faces, and they weren't 'how great I bumped into an old acquaintance.' They were flirting! She finished her cocoa and put her other hand on top of his. And *then,* she made a kind of blowing a kiss with her mouth. A young couple at the table next to them were smiling, like 'get a room'!"

Zach had frowned. "You don't think your grandmother might know about this other woman? That Austin has a friend he's serious about?"

"I wish. No. Granny hasn't gone nuts, but she's dressing up for him, wearing makeup! And they've been going out to fancy restaurants—his choices—plus someone saw them at Symphony and referred to him as 'Ursula's beau' to my mom, which did not go over well, especially because she hadn't known about him or that he was staying with Granny. He says it's while he finds a place in town of his own, but I bet he has no plans to move out until he has another well-feathered nest."

The train had pulled into the Kendall/MIT station and Zach stood up to leave.

"It does sound as if he's using your grandmother as a place to live while double-timing her with the woman you saw. I'll start seeing what I can find out about him right away. It could all be very innocent . . ." But his face belied his words.

The next memory made her face redden, and not from the steam from the latte she was preparing.

He'd leaned over and given her a kiss on the cheek that ended up close to her mouth before slipping out the door onto the platform. She was pretty sure he had winked at her as the train left.

Years ago Niki had given Faith a bumper sticker to put up in the catering kitchen: DATES IN THE MIRROR ARE CLOSER THAN THEY APPEAR. It had never seemed more true than today, Faith thought. She'd awoken at dawn, wired to the point where she thought she might as well leave breakfast for everyone and go in to work. She'd told a sleepy Tom who muttered, "You're crazy," before drifting off again.

Things were well under control for the weekend. She'd ordered all the meat from Savenor's Market. Jack Savenor had been Julia Child's friend and butcher. His son, Ron, was continuing the family tradition of excellence. Out at Rowan House Ian would take delivery on Thursday. Savenor's was also supplying some of the cheeses and charcuterie. Her other suppliers would deliver to the kitchen, and she'd bring everything out Friday morning. Niki was baking two devil's food cakes, one with a traditional dark chocolate frosting and the other with something she'd found online and thought appropriate—angel frosting, fluffy white marshmallow. Faith would make the Angel Food Cake on Saturday. She'd also had a middle-of-the-night idea to make a few dozen mini cupcakes—red velvet, mocha, vanilla bean, and gold cake—frosted with tiny fondant halo and pitchfork decorations. Max Dane wanted an over-the-top weekend, and that was what he was going to get.

Besides the weekend, Have Faith had one small private dinner party Wednesday that the hostess wanted to serve herself. They were to drop off the meal with instructions on preparation, which mostly involved heating it up. Faith received this request often, and she was always curious to know whether the host or hostess in question smiled and nodded when complimented on the food or came clean.

Niki arrived at nine and they got to work. Adrenaline was a useful commodity, Faith thought around eleven, when she still felt full of energy despite her short night. She'd have to get more sleep before Friday, though. She had the feeling she wouldn't be sleeping much out at Rowan House.

She'd been compulsively checking the weather since early last week. No blizzards, or any snow at all, in the forecast. It was going to be cold, but that wouldn't be a problem. This didn't sound like a crowd that would be up for wintry walks around the grounds. She was pretty sure that whatever their locales, their walks were ones that took them past or to shops and restaurants—maybe a museum and of course a theater.

At noon the phone rang and Niki picked it up. Faith intended to keep the work landline with its answering machine for a long time to come. She'd probably have to get a business cell eventually, but for now she was able to keep hers personal, calling into the machine to check messages.

"Just a moment, please." Niki covered the mouthpiece and said softly, "The Brit from Rowan House."

"Hello," Faith said, taking the phone from her.

There was a pause while she listened. "Thank you for letting me know so I'll be able to set the tables correctly."

Another pause. "I think Mr. Dane—and you—will be pleased. See you Friday."

A last pause, then, "Good-bye."

Niki hadn't moved. "For a moment I thought they were canceling. Your face looked so serious."

"No, and if they do, we still get paid. He was calling to say that there would be only nine guests, not ten."

"Well, there will certainly be enough food!"

Faith smiled, but it was only on the outside. Inside she was trembling. Bella Martelli, the costume designer, wasn't going to be able to make it because Bella Martelli was dead.

Wasn't a "good death" an oxymoron? In any case there had been nothing remotely good about it. For months they'd waged a battle to stay ahead of the excruciating pain, a battle more often lost than won. Watching the beloved face of the woman who had given up everything for her became harder and harder to bear as each day went by. "You can go. I'll be fine. You know that," she had implored her—wishing the end would come and provide blessed relief, even though she knew she would always want one more chance to look into those eyes, still so beautiful. Liquid brown flecked with gold, clear until the final moment when at last there was no breath, no pulse, and the lids closed forever.

She wanted to die herself, but first she had something to do, somewhere to go. She made the arrangements, was the sole mourner, and went back to the tiny apartment they'd shared to pack a bag. She hadn't shed a tear. They had dried up long ago, forming a hard shell that felt like a second skin. Armor. It was her constant companion.

Samantha hadn't expected Zach to come up with information on Stebbins immediately and she didn't want to be a nudge, but when she dropped in to see her grandmother late Tuesday afternoon and the man came downstairs into the living room to whisk Ursula away for a special event at the Boston Museum of Fine Arts, it was all Samantha could do to keep her fingers from texting Zach "Help!" Granny had looked beautiful. Another new dress—a deep burgundy satin shirtwaist that showed off the tiny waist she'd never lost. And she'd had her hair done. Nothing outrageous, just a trim, but the change was still obvious. Ursula's short, shiny white curls were more platinum than anything else, and she could easily have passed for a very well-preserved Jean Harlow.

"I'm so sorry we don't have time for a real visit, but always lovely to see you," Ursula apologized.

Seeing that Stebbins already had his topcoat on, Samantha quickly said, "I'll be back soon. And I'll call first."

Ursula looked bemused. "No need, sweetheart. Just drop by whenever you have some free time." They were getting in Stebbins's car as Samantha pulled away.

Nobody was home when she got there. She'd expected her father to be at work but had no idea where her mother was. Given that Pix's fingers were in not just town pies, but pretty much all of MetroWest's, Samantha wasn't surprised. She didn't intend to say anything about Ursula to her mother, but she wished Zach would get in touch so she could vent to him. Austin was too charming. If he broke her grandmother's heart she'd kill him. It would be justifiable homicide.

Faith had given her a recipe for what she called Pantry Soup, which involved sautéing onions, garlic, and any other veggies kicking around before adding chicken broth, canned chickpeas, rosemary, a can of diced tomatoes, and slices of chicken sausage. Samantha had learned to keep packages of the sausages in the freezer in all different flavors. She defrosted Italian ones in the microwave and added them to the mixture she had on simmer. Before she served it she'd bring the soup to a boil and add a cup of ditalini pasta. Maybe she could train as some sort of chef. She was enjoying the part of her job that involved interacting with people and food, even though it was mostly coffee. Something to bring up with Faith.

Dinner just about done, she poured herself a glass of the box wine her parents kept in the fridge and sat down to look at the paper. A print version still arrived in the Millers' driveway before six every morning. Samantha smiled to herself and said aloud, "How quaint," thinking also of the stack of road maps in both cars' glove compartments, which her mother insisted were more reliable than "that lady" on the GPS.

Her phone rang. Seeing Zach's name, she answered immediately.

"Sorry it's taken me so long, but the project at the Kendall Square firm is eating up all my time."

"It's fine, "Samantha fibbed. "No rush."

"If you say so." She knew he didn't believe her.

"Okay, so I am a little anxious."

"A little? I won't keep you in suspense. Austin Stebbins is a retired property developer who has lived most of his adult life in various parts of California. He was born and grew up in Boston, attended Harvard University and the Harvard Business School. I have more details—final club at Harvard was Porcellian and so forth, but for now that's not important. His wife passed away a year ago and from the obit's suggestion that memorial tributes go to the American Heart Association, it's safe to assume she died of some sort of heart failure. No kids. No relatives mentioned at all."

"How about money?"

"Judging from the news articles I turned up he was successful. Lots of business-type awards and still the owner on record of a number of office buildings in and around Orange County."

"What else? Anything?" Samantha was beginning to feel extremely disappointed. "Arrest records? DUIs? Income tax evasion?"

"Sorry, honey, he's clean. But I've only scratched the surface here. Sit tight. We may be able to uncover something juicy like bigamy."

"Hmmm. This reminds me of a newspaper article I read a couple of years ago. A guy had two families living several states apart. He traveled a lot for his job so he could pull it off. He was so meticulous he had one set of keys, the locks the same at both houses, and even two duplicate wardrobes exactly the same so his wives wouldn't ask where a new tie had come from or a new sweater. Maybe Austin was doing that?"

"For the last twenty years he's been living at the same address with a Mrs. Olivia Stebbins and he wasn't a traveling salesman. He had an office in Montclair, California, before retiring and others before that."

"Well, something about him just doesn't seem right. He's too nice, for one thing."

"And that would be bad because . . . ?"

"You know what I mean. False nice, not nice nice."

"I think this merits further discussion. Why don't you text me times you're free and we'll repeat the burger challenge at Bartley's, adding the fries?"

"I'd like that." A lot, Samantha said to herself. "And there are other worlds to conquer. Like the best Pho."

"What's that?" Zach said, clearly to someone else. "Sorry, Samantha, but I've gotta run. Text me when you know your schedule."

He hung up before Samantha could thank him. She took a sip of wine. The sun was setting and the low winter horizon was ablaze with streaks of deep purple and fuchsia. Her soup was filling the house with a tantalizing aroma. I'm happy, she thought, very happy.

Samantha recognized the fur coat before completely registering the face above it and the man following close behind. You didn't see that many full-length dark mink coats in Boston, especially during the day. She darted over to her boss, who was taking bags of beans from a cupboard beneath the counter. "Ken, sorry, I know it's not time for my break, but I need to make a quick call. It's very important."

"Sure, Samantha, no problem. I can cover."

"You're the best!" Samantha said and ran into the back, taking her phone from her locker. Please, please, please pick up, she said to herself after hitting Zach's number. She'd put it on her favorites list for convenience. At least that's what she told herself.

Luckily he did. "Hi, what's up?"

"I'm at work. Stebbins just came in with the same woman as before. They're in line to order and it's a long one. Is there any way you could get here and follow them when they leave? I know it's a lot to ask, but we may be able to find out where she lives and then her name." Samantha was breathless.

"No worries. Always fancied myself a sleuth. Fortunately I'm at Kendall, so it won't take long to get to you. I'm leaving now. And stay cool, okay?"

"I have a break in half an hour, so I'll check my phone. And then I'm off after another hour. Go!"

"I'm gone."

Samantha went back, thanked her manager profusely, and was relieved to see that the couple had only just reached the front of the line. She heard them order cocoa again. This time Austin went for the Chile Mocha. Maybe he thought he was in for a hot time soon, Samantha thought bitterly. His lady friend stuck with the traditional, no whipped cream.

Soon the two were seated at one of the tables near the big window looking out over the Common. It seemed Samantha had just hung up with Zach when she saw him strolling by. It was a short ride on the T from Kendall to Charles and he must have sprinted down the street. He came in, ordered a cascara latte, and she leaned over when she handed it to him, whispering, "By the window." He nodded and tapped the side of his nose with his finger. Samantha could tell he was getting a kick out of this.

After more holding hands and kissy faces on her part, the couple left. Once the door closed after them, she went to clear their table—so inconsiderate to leave the cups—and was relieved to see Zach trailing behind them as they crossed the intersection toward Robert McCloskey's *Make Way for Ducklings* bronzes in the Public Garden.

No swan boats. No reason to linger this time of year. They must be headed for the Back Bay. Samantha went back to cope with the line, which had suddenly gotten long again. When it was time for her break, she checked her phone. Zach had sent a text: "Slow walkers. Went past the Taj and down Newbury Street. Have been in Burberry's for a while now. Am across the street in the Garden. Getting chilly."

She called him right away. "I'm so sorry. Why don't you go into the store to keep warm and pretend to be a customer?"

"Really? Sam, I'm not exactly dressed like their target clientele."

"Oh, that's silly. You could be a famous rock star who goes for the slightly scruffy look."

"Who are you calling 'scruffy'! I didn't have time to shave this morning. But no, I'm not chancing it. It's the shoes. You can always tell by shoes, and mine say New Balance outlet store all over. Oh, hallelujah! They're leaving. Austin is carrying a rather large store bag. Wish I had her coat, even for a few minutes."

"Which way are they turning?"

"Down Newbury away from me. I'm off. The game's afoot!"

Reluctantly she put her phone back in her bag. The rest of her shift was a madhouse and so busy she almost didn't think about what was going on outside, except to note worriedly that it was getting darker and colder, judging from the way people were clutching their coats and scarves.

At last her shift was over. Shrugging her parka on, Samantha hit Zach's number. "Where are you now?" she said before he said anything. "Are you freezing?"

"Yes, and I'm headed back toward you. They're waiting for the walk light just opposite. Are you free now?"

"I'll stand just outside. I have a hat and I'll pull my hood up so they won't recognize me."

She spotted all three immediately. When Zach saw her he made a beeline, quickly crossing the street and calling, "Hi, darling! Sorry I'm late." He gave her a bear hug when he reached her and whispered, "Thought I would divert any possible suspicion. And, darling, you wouldn't happen to have an extra hat or gloves on you by chance?"

Hugging him back, she said, "Take this one. I'll tie the hood tight. Oh, they're turning up Mount Vernon Street! Hurry!"

"Believe me, there is no need. They do not sprint."

"Where have they been all this time?"

"Serious shopping. Armani and Chanel. I crouched in the vestibule of that church across the street. Made a new friend. He wanted to share what was in his brown bag, but I needed a clear head. Gave him a fiver when I left. Oh thank God, they've stopped and she's got her purse open."

The couple stood on the brick sidewalk in front of a town house, then started up the front stairs. "She's got keys out!" Samantha said. "Let's wait a little longer and see how long he stays," she added after the door closed behind them. "I wish you could have seen who paid for the purchases. Stebbins was loaded down with shopping bags."

"Did you know that the original *Thomas Crown Affair,* the real one with Steve McQueen and Faye Dunaway, was filmed in that big house up the street?"

"You mean the Harrison Gray Otis House designed by Bullfinch? The chess scene? Yes, in fact, I did."

Zach grinned. "You don't happen to play do you? I'm getting a very sexy image here or maybe I'm hallucinating."

Samantha ignored the remark. "The lights went on in what must be the front living room. These town houses had double parlors. Darn it! She has those half shutters, so we can't see in. Go over and make sure there aren't any names next to what looks like an intercom. I doubt the house has been carved into apartments."

Zach sighed audibly. "And then can we go to some sort of interior space, preferably one serving alcohol?"

"Yes! Go quickly!"

"You can be a tad bossy, you know," he said over his shoulder as he crossed the cobbled street.

Samantha started walking slowly down the hill toward Charles Street and he soon caught up with her. "Single-family dwelling. Quintessential Beacon Hill Federal by the look of it. Have the house number, nothing so crass as a nameplate. I can look the name up in a reverse directory as soon as we go someplace warm. The closer the better. Like Toscano. I'm thinking osso buco. Not too early to eat, is it?"

"Not too early at all," Samantha said, tucking her arm through his. To warm him up a bit. That was all. It was her fault he was freezing. It was the least a girl could do.

It was a crisp, very cold morning, and once again Faith had been awake for hours. When the alarm went off she made sure the kids were up and went down to make brioche French toast for her family, which they devoured happily, chattering away about Loon Mountain's black diamond trails. Ben was particularly happy because Dan Miller was joining his parents. As she watched them she felt a pang. She'd been away from them longer in the past, but today she had the feeling they were all embarking on a much lengthier journey.

The ski resort was not close. She wished this wasn't the weekend that would put them hours away from home. She would have preferred imagining them all safe and sound in their wee little beds while, much closer, she dealt with—what exactly?

"Mom, we're going to miss the bus," Ben complained as she gave him an extra tight hug.

"She's just nervous," Amy said. "Don't worry, we'll all come back in one piece."

Faith hadn't really been thinking of the dangers posed by the slopes. "Don't forget to wear your helmets," she shouted after them.

The bus door was open and Faith could hear hoots of laughter from inside. Moms!

Tom was laughing, too, and his tight hug was welcome. "We're not going to Siberia. They have stores. Restaurants, even. And we're not leaving until after school, so you have plenty of time to call me and tell me what not to forget."

"I know. Besides, Pix will be with you." Nothing bad would happen. No broken legs, hungry kids. Pix would be in charge. Oh, and Sam too. And of course Tom.

The landline rang. It was Pix. "I know you're crazy busy and about to head over to Rowan House, but I wanted to say have a ball and take notes, photos if you can sneak them. Can't wait to hear all about it and I know you're going to get rave reviews!"

Suddenly Faith felt better than she had for days. The news that Bella Martelli had died had been unsettling. She had no idea how old Bella had been. There was no publicity photo in the *Playbill* next to her name. She'd checked obituaries in New York and then nationwide to be sure and hadn't come up with one, but local papers or even big city ones often didn't link up to Google. There was no reason to think the death was anything but natural. Hearing Pix's excitement was contagious. She knew Dane had hired Winston's, Boston's premier florist, to decorate the house, and she was now itching to get out there.

"And," Pix continued, "I know you're making Tom check his list twice or more, but don't worry about a thing. The condo is fully equipped, very comfy, and near everything."

"It sounds ideal and my gang can't wait to hit the slopes. Thank you for this."

"See you Sunday night!"

Faith hung up and said good-bye once again to her husband as he took off for his day as a chaplain at the local VA hospital. He assured her he would be checking texts even when his phone was on silent.

She would be leaving her car at the catering kitchen and taking the van. It was surprising how much space the food for the weekend took up. She had decided that well appointed as Rowan House's kitchen was, she wanted some of her own batterie de cuisine. Her small suitcase was ready—she'd be wearing her chef's clothes for the most part but had packed slacks and turtleneck sweaters as well as nightwear. Dane's house was large, but it had been toasty warm both times she'd been there. Ian had mentioned that they had a substantial generator, so even if by some chance there were a power failure, everything would still work.

Before leaving the house, she looked around one last time, sure she had forgotten something. But just as her family wasn't going to Siberia, neither was she. If need be, she could always run home or to the catering kitchen.

Outside her breath hung suspended in a cloud. She half expected it to form icicles. It took a while for the car to warm up. When she pulled into the small parking lot, she was surprised to see another car. Niki was home today, and in any case, she had a Mommy SUV, not a cute bright red Mini Cooper. Faith's surprise increased when she saw Blake Sommersby get out, looking even taller in contrast to the car, or maybe it was her high-heeled boots.

Faith got out as well and walked over to the woman. Before she could say anything, Blake did.

"Mrs. Fairchild, we need to talk."

CHAPTER 8

Could the timing have been any worse? Faith said to herself as she walked across the icy parking lot covered with sand. No salt or commercial products for Aleford.

"This really isn't a good time," she said as she got closer. "I'm due at a job. Why don't we pick a day next week? My schedule is pretty open."

Blake shook her head. "I have to go out of town and I'll be gone a week, maybe more. And this shouldn't wait. Could we go inside? I'll be as quick as I can."

While Faith was a little annoyed at being overruled, she was also very, very curious. She flashed on the image of the two figures in the shadows Monday night. Was Blake going to confess to a mad passionate affair with the developer and give Faith a letter of resignation for the board? No, she'd give that to Marian Cho. But whatever it was it had to have something to do with the proposed scheme. Faith couldn't think of anything else Blake and she might have in common save taste in clothes—and Tom, of course. The two had been seated next to each other Monday night, and even from the back Faith could see they were scribbling notes to each other. Next thing he'd be carrying her books home from school.

Yesterday she had loaded everything into the van but perishables and the baked goods—they would possibly have frozen. She didn't have all that much left to do. She'd planned to have a cup of coffee while she worked and leave. "Come in then, but I have to be out of here soon, so I'll be packing things while you tell me whatever is so important it can't wait a week or so. I'm going to make some coffee. Would you like a cup?" Offering coffee to Blake might encourage her to stay longer. But Faith wanted one.

Blake followed Faith into the kitchen. "Thank you, no. If you have some herbal tea that would be great. Mint?" She sat down at the counter, making herself at home. Ms. Sommersby didn't seem like the mint tea type, but Faith had it and soon put a steaming mug down in front of her unwanted guest.

"Okay, here it is," Blake said. "I want your help, but I don't want anyone to know what we've talked about."

"Since I don't know what we've talked about that shouldn't be a problem."

Blake smiled. "I know you're in a rush. I'm sorry. I'll get to it."

And I'll stop acting bitchy, Faith decided, sitting down with her coffee.

"This whole strip mall thing could drag out for years," Blake said. "It won't cost the town anything, but Peters is going to have to pay his lawyers. Even now I have enough to tie up their plans."

"And this isn't a good thing, because . . . ?"

"I obviously haven't lived here long, but the Averys are long-time friends of mine. It's why I chose to move to Aleford. I have a pretty good idea of what makes the town tick. Dragging this out means endless wrangling, meetings, and ultimately divisions among the town's population. Quite a few people want to see the Grayson property put money in the coffers, and Bradley Peters's plan makes sense to them."

She was right. Faith thought back to some of the school and other proposals that had acrimoniously split the town, even households. "So how are you going to get Peters to back out? The threat of a lengthy process would probably be viewed as just that by him—a threat, possibly not a viable one."

Was Blake proposing that Faith somehow catch the lawyer and the developer in a compromising position? Had she been setting it up last night, starting to come on to him? The camera on Faith's iPhone was pretty good. But Blake would be relieved of her position, so to speak, not Peters. She added, "I still don't get it."

"Sorry," Blake said. "I haven't been clear. My mind is a bit preoccupied these days. As soon as I saw Grayson House, which included touring the inside, I thought that it would make a great assisted living facility if modernized. Aleford has an aging population that wants to stay in town, not go to one of the nearby facilities. But I want Peters to think of it himself. He'd have to partner with a health care facility, but half or more of the residences could be apartments—some affordable, some high end. The place is in bad shape, but I've gone over the building inspection the heirs had done to put it on the market, and most of the work would be cosmetic plus expansion. There's enough room to add another story on the wings next to the main building where there's already an elevator. It would need updating, but the space is there."

"It's a wonderful solution," Faith said, "but I don't see how it's going to happen."

"That's why I need your help. I can't mention it to Peters, conflict of interest big-time. But a board member could. As in 'have you considered this way out?' Say over lunch?"

"And I happen to be married to one."

Blake beamed. "I knew you'd get it. Again, I have to emphasize I can't intervene. As counsel I'm there to listen, advise, but not propose, especially in such a major way. A board member can arrange a casual meeting to go over the presentation. I checked— there's nothing that prohibits it. However, Tom needs to come up with this idea himself. I thought of Sam Miller, but he'd immediately think I had a hand in it all."

"Whereas my husband wouldn't. Being as he is great at one-on-ones with God, but often a bit naive with interactions down here on earth," Faith said. Ms. Sommersby had certainly figured her husband out quickly. Must be from picking jurors.

"Exactly! He's such a good man and I know you can talk to him about the idea in such a way that he will believe it was his own—or the man upstairs."

Faith had to laugh. "Why do you think I would be able to do this?"

"Patsy Avery has told me a great deal about you, particularly when all that business at Mansfield Academy was going on."

The mention reminded Faith of Zach Cummings and his IT skills. "At Monday night's meeting, Patsy had a list of dubious projects Bradley Peters was involved with. Couldn't we dig up some more online and go that route?"

"I thought of that, too, and I've already done that. Bradley never broke any laws. Again, it would drag things out even longer. No, this is the best solution for the town. A win–win. The facility is needed and the strip mall is not." She drained her mug and stood up. Mission accomplished. "Now, I need to let you go."

Much as Faith wanted to say "Not so fast, lawyer lady," she found herself agreeing. "I admit it would be good for the town."

Blake stood up and buttoned her coat. A nice shearling. Looked like Searle, Faith thought. She had opted for her Michelin Man one this weekend.

"All right. I'll talk to Tom. Not manipulate him. We don't do that"—well, maybe sometimes she did, but she wasn't about to share this with the woman she still had doubts about. She kept thinking of the scene Monday night. What if Blake and Bradley were partners of some sort, business or otherwise? Could this new scheme be the one the developer, and Ms. Sommersby, wanted all along? Dangling the prospect of the mall so the real one could go through easily?

Faith opened the door for Blake and said good-bye but didn't wait to see her jazzy little car zip off before shutting it. She had a weekend to cater—and a possible murderer to uncover.

The gates swung open after Ian's instructions, which Faith was now sure was a recording. She pulled the van around the back of the house. Ian came out to help her unload.

"Best pull your vehicle into the garage when we finish. You won't be using it until Sunday, but I'll give you a remote just in case you do have to run out for something."

He was eyeing the mound of things in the van and Faith had to say, "Thank you, but I can't imagine needing anything." He smiled. This was good. They were bonding, Faith thought.

"Remember that besides the refrigerator here, there are small ones in the butler's pantry and the service area off the summer parlor plus another full-size in the basement. Max doesn't care for defrosted foods, so there is no large chest freezer anywhere. You'll have to take any leftover food away and deal with it as you wish."

"I hope there won't be too much," she said, but the amount of supplies as they emptied the van, added to what was already spread out in the kitchen, suggested otherwise.

"Now I have a few last-minute errands to run, including picking up Max's birthday present. An antiques dealer in Lexington has found an Alfred Hitchcock toby jug in mint condition finally. Max has been trying to locate one for a long time. I also need to fetch a few things for my vacation. Did Max tell you I was leaving for a well-earned reward on Sunday once the party's over?"

Faith had forgotten, but she nodded. She was struck by the obvious pleasure Ian was taking in the gift. She sensed that over the years employer and employee had become the closest of friends, each other's sole company, and confidant? Ian was zipping up a Canada Goose parka. Even a simple one could run close to a thousand dollars. Max seemed to be paying his friend, albeit employee, a very decent salary.

"It shouldn't take long. I'm assuming you'll want to put every-thing away yourself where you'll have it to hand."

The subtext was: not my job. Faith got it and said, "Yes, ex-actly. Thank you." Or not.

He left and she got to work as fast as possible. He'd be gone at least an hour. Max Dane slept until noon or even later. For now she was virtually alone. As soon as she finished, she wanted to look at the whole house. All the guest rooms, everything. She needed to have the lay of the land fixed firmly in her mind.

She also wanted to make a quick call to Tom to check in and remind him that her cell wouldn't work here and he'd need to use the landline number. Ian had told her this the first time she'd been at the house but said that occasionally one could get a signal out-side on the hill behind the house. Faith had successfully tried it, but besides not being convenient, she'd discovered it was treacher-ously slippery. Tom wasn't picking up, but she left a message on *his* cell, knowing full well she'd told him all this several times before.

Afterward she went up the servants' back staircase to the third floor, envisioning a very young Max doing the same. Not be-ing permitted the main parts of the house, fetched down for his meals in the kitchen with the help. The kind ones slipping him some of the food his grandparents and whoever else was visiting were having in the dining room. The outdoors must have been a blessed release for him, although she was sure he had to keep out of sight from Grandmamma. It wasn't just Dickensian; it was un-imaginable cruelty.

Clearly the rooms on this side of the house were being used for storage. All save the one where Max had stayed as a child had an air of disuse—not musty, but still. The tiny room barely large enough for the bed did not. There was even a slight indentation on the bed itself that indicated someone had been sitting there. Did Max come here to remind himself of the past? To nourish a justi-fiable hatred? To think of his parents and what might have been?

The quiet here was so profound it was disconcerting. Not

a single squeaky board or rustle of any sort. When she had first moved to Aleford from Manhattan after her marriage, she had found it hard to get used to the lack of noise, or rather different noise—the bullfrogs and crickets changing with the seasons and constants, like the Fitchburg line train whistle. Cars passed by the front of the parsonage, but any after eight o'clock were an aberration.

She went down a floor. The florist had been hard at work. Each guestroom had a Winston's signature arrangement: tight, perfect blooms in simple crystal vases, some lined with glossy banana leaves. The colors of each room were echoed in those of the roses, orchids, parrot tulips, hydrangea, and more. Every door had been labeled with the occupant's name—more calligraphy that she suspected was Ian's handiwork. The cards were suspended on white ribbons attached to those very handy removable 3M hooks. Next to each bed was a carafe of water and a glass, a silver biscuit box, selection of books, and small flashlight. She opened one closet to find extra pillows, blankets, and a cashmere throw, padded and wooden hangers. A luggage rack. She assumed all would be the same. Each bathroom contained a spa tub and separate rain forest shower. A thick terry cloth robe with ROWAN HOUSE in gold script on the breast pocket hung on the back of the door. A basket mounded with high-end Molton Brown products—Ian again?—was placed on each double sink counter.

There was one other notable detail in each room. All had the *Heaven or Hell Playbill* carefully placed in the center of the bed. And the message was . . . ?

She took the small pad she had tucked in her apron pocket and made a quick sketch, indicating who was staying in each room before heading for the landing at the top of the grand staircase. Here Winston's had outdone themselves with the kind of arrangement she associated with the Metropolitan Museum of Art or the Boston MFA—a green bronzed urn with white cherry blossoms, the branches a backdrop for masses of white amaryllis and large white tulips edged with pale green. About to head down to the ground floor—she didn't dare cross over to Max's quarters—Faith took a second look at the arrangement and paused. She'd learned enough from Pix to recognize the small white flowers encircling the rim of the urn. Black hellebore—the color referred to the roots. Toxic and often the cause of accidental death when used as a purgative. She looked at the arrangement more closely. There were sprays of white foxglove with black flecks. Foxglove—digitalis—another toxin. As she took some shots with her phone, she wondered what instructions Rowan House had given the florist. Were all the arrangements not in the rooms going to be the same? Beautiful but deadly?

She moved through the downstairs rooms rapidly to check out the summer parlor and noted as she went that all the flowers continued the subtle theme.

Switching on the lights as she entered the room, she was glad to see they had taken her advice and amped up the wattage. It was cloudy out and the room looked warm and inviting. It would glow even more at night. Dozens of votives had been placed on the tables, which were covered with black damask cloths shot with silver threads.

The casket, no longer on the andirons, had been raised up to serving height and Faith went over to see what had been done. The same black cloth was covering the kind of support on wheels used to transport a casket into a service. The wheels were locked in place, but looking at it gave her a chill. She dropped the cloth. The casket had a runner of similar fabric just covering its surface. From a distance it looked like a sideboard, although the handles were noticeable from the front. They were brass and could be mistaken for drawer pulls.

In this room all the flowers were shades of red—roses, carnations, ilex, amaryllis, tulips. She went to look at the large silver vase in a niche next to the window seat. It was filled with the most perfect roses she had ever seen. Nothing else. She stepped back and was startled by a voice almost at her side.

"The variety is called Black Magic. We've been having fun with the flora and hope to with the fauna as well. What do you think?" Max Dane looked well rested, his rust-colored hair brushed back. The word that sprang to Faith's mind was *vulpine*—as if he were on a hunt. Which he was.

She wasn't sure what she thought about the decorations or Max Dane. Was he the victim—or the perpetrator? She let her breath out. She'd barely realized she was holding it. "I think . . . I think you've done an amazing job."

"I thought you would. Now let's have a party."

"Mom! First of all I'm not a twelve-year-old—or sixteen and going to give a wild party, not that I did," Samantha added hastily. "And second you're only going to Loon, not the Alps."

"I know, I know. Habit, I guess. Good-bye, darling. We'll see you Sunday night. Probably not late. I'm picking Dad up at work now and we're going early to get everything ready for Tom and the kids."

"You mean you are. Dad will hit the slopes the moment the car stops." Samantha gave her mother a hug and gently pushed her toward the door. Pix had been leaving for more than twenty minutes.

"Now why is that U-Haul pulling into our driveway?" Pix said. "They must have the wrong address."

Samantha went over to look out the window with her mother. "Oh shit," she said.

"Language," Pix said automatically. But when the person got closer, she added her own version. "Oh dear."

It was Caleb.

He came to the back door and knocked. Samantha looked at her mother. Pix said, "Answer it. I'll wait to leave if you want."

"I want," said Samantha grimly, opening the door just enough to speak to her ex. "What are you doing here, Caleb?"

"The couch was yours, also the coffee table, plus there were a lot of boxes once other stuff was packed. I thought I'd bring it up instead of hiring someone."

Samantha felt her mother poke her in the back. "Well, you'd better come in and then I'll unload it with you. I have to be at work soon." She bit her lip. She hadn't meant to tell him about her job. But he just nodded and didn't ask her where.

"Would you like something warm to drink?" Pix offered. "It must have been a long drive. Coffee? Or soup, and I can make you a sandwich?"

Samantha glared at her mother. "I doubt he'll have time," she said just as Caleb answered, "Soup and a sandwich would be nice. Thank you, Mrs. Miller."

Pix went into the pantry to check her stock of Campbell's and Caleb leaned close to Samantha. "I wanted to tell you how sorry I am. It was a big mistake. My mistake. I miss you and I want us to be together again."

Moving away from him and sitting at the kitchen table, Samantha said, "What happened? Did you get dumped, too?"

He sat down, and she could tell from his expression that she had guessed right. "We decided to take some time apart and I realized how much I missed you. We were together for so long, Samantha! You're my best friend besides being the woman I love."

Pix came out holding a can. "Cream of Mushroom okay? And a ham and cheese sandwich?"

"Sure. Thank you. I didn't want to take time to stop for lunch."

"Best friends don't do what you did to me," Samantha said. "And lovers don't cheat on each other."

"It was just Julie. Never anyone else. I don't know what I was thinking!"

Samantha saw her mother looking over her shoulder at them. Her mother had always liked Caleb. "Okay, great of you to bring everything. Maybe we can stay in touch. I'll think about it."

Caleb grabbed Samantha's hand. She pulled it away, looking

straight into his face. "Just tell me the truth. How long did it go on—when did it all start?"

"Not long. Just after I hired her." His face was the picture of relief.

Samantha leaped to her feet. "You hired her almost two years ago! You're telling me this has been going on since then?"

"It wasn't a thing the whole time," Caleb mumbled.

"'A thing'? Is that what it's called? Mom, turn the soup off. No soup for him!" She enjoyed using the Seinfeld expression. "Help me unload the truck so this rat can get out of here and my life as soon as possible!"

Unloading went swiftly; Caleb seemed as eager to leave as they were to get rid of him. As the truck backed out, Pix urged, "See if you can get the time off and come ski with us."

"I'm fine, Mom. Really. This was exactly what I needed." She decided to tell her mother exactly what had happened. "I saw them together near the apartment in a coffee shop—Caleb's and my favorite—the same day right after I got axed from my job. They were totally into each other. They probably, well, you know, 'hung out' in the apartment, too. All Caleb's workmates must have known. I felt like a fool. I don't now. Well, maybe a little. How could I not have known, when it was going on so long?"

Pix hugged her daughter. "I believe those very words have been said by many others."

"So suck it up, right?"

"Right."

The curtain was rising. Faith, in her chef's clothes, stood behind the sumptuous spread: the caviar, foie gras, cherrystones, and oysters requested. The aromas from the warm dishes were making her a bit hungry herself. Max had come to check it out and eaten one of the oven-baked potato wedges. He gave her a thumbs-up but declined a plate with the baby lamb chops, or salmon, creamed spinach, and other food. "I'll wait."

The plan was that Ian would greet each new arrival, escort him or her to the appointed guestroom, and then after they had freshened up, he'd walk them into the summer parlor. He and Max had some sort of small pager devices with which they were communicating.

She'd made a quick call earlier to check in with Tom, who had made good time and was already at the resort. They were all heading out for some night skiing. Faith was extremely happy to be where she was, especially after she'd put away the few things she'd brought. The housekeeper's suite was even more luxurious than she had recalled. If Mrs. Danvers had had such digs she might not have preyed on the second Mrs. de Winter.

Max was wearing a dark chestnut smoking jacket with an open-necked cream silk shirt, black trousers, and the kind of velvet slippers with gold embroidered crests favored by English aristocrats. He wasn't drinking. At least not yet. Faith wondered whether this was Ian's doing or Max's own inclination to stay sharp. He grinned at her after glancing at his pager. "The first doth approach," and went back to stand by the arch at the other end of the room.

"Max, darling! Happy birthday!" The woman Faith recognized as Eve Anderson made an entrance worthy of a full house, her smile sweeping across the parlor, her eyes taking in everything. She was wearing a white strapless tightly fitted gown, her pale blond hair—champagne blond, Faith recalled the shade was called—pulled back into a sleek chignon. Her makeup was flawless, and the only jewelry she wore were long dangling Elsa Peretti gold mesh earrings.

"You look as gorgeous as ever, Eve," Max said, kissing her cheek as she leaned in to deliver two air pecks. "You could pass for fifty any day."

"Naughty, naughty as ever, I am fifty as you well know, and

thirty is what I am passing for." She paused briefly and said, "Surely I am not the only guest." Her face looked jubilant, a cat with a full bowl of cream. If she thought she was the only guest, could that mean Eve had sent the casket? It would make her job easy—and as for being fifty, Faith knew the woman was over sixty, but she certainly was doing her best to keep the depredations of age at bay.

"There will be a few other familiar faces. Now have a drink and something to eat." Max gestured toward the end of the room. Eve teetered over to the buffet on her Louboutins, watched closely by her host and Faith herself. If Eve recognized the coffin as such, however, she gave no indication. Of course, she was an actor.

"Give me a vodka tonic. Better make it a double," she said. With Ian manning the front door, Faith was tending bar tonight. Dressed butler-like in a dark suit, he was ushering in two more arrivals.

"Maxie, Maxie, Maxie," the man said. "I ran into Betty in the airport and it seemed simpler to take one car." He put one arm around her and the other around his host. "Just like old times, eh? Happy birthday!"

If Max was annoyed that his plan to have each guest arrive alone was spoiled, he didn't show it. "Good to see you, Phil—and Betty. Don't tell me you two kids are back together."

Betty Sinclair shrugged off Phil's arm. "Not a chance. Now that I'm here I intend to come as I am at this shindig of yours and not be cast, just in case you were thinking of a role for me." Her voice was surprisingly deep for a woman, but not unpleasant. Very Bacall.

"Wouldn't dream of it. 'As you are' has always been fine with me." Faith noted the fondness in his tone, as Betty's had been despite the words. Had there been something between the two?

Max was gently pushing them in her direction. "Drink up, drink up! Nobody's driving—or performing—tonight."

"Oh, I think everyone's performing," Betty said, "but I am

thirsty, and that young woman looks like she knows how to make a Manhattan."

Faith did, of course, and the next arrival walked slowly into the room as she was straining the rye, sweet vermouth, and bitters into a cocktail glass.

Neither Philip Baker nor Betty Sinclair had seemed to note what the serving table was. Phil, who sported a deep tan as well as a potbelly, was going for the food. He was dressed casually—V-necked melon-colored sweater, tan pants, and loafers without socks. The look a much younger man would have pulled off better, or a much older one living in Miami. Faith knew he was in his midfifties. He had kept his hair, or had plugs. Betty was a few years older. She was wearing a designer—Carolina Herrera?—black cocktail suit and major gold jewelry. Faith remembered her address was the Upper East Side in New York, and the uniform proved it. She had kept her figure, and her hair, though streaked with gray, was cut short and chic. Neither was wearing a wedding band.

They had both greeted Eve Anderson without much enthusiasm, but when they turned to see who had arrived there was no mistaking the delight on their faces. He seemed to be of two minds about whether he wanted to enter, and Ian, behind him, was firmly keeping him on track.

"Adrian!" Betty called out. "I never dreamed you would be here. Oh, this is wonderful!" She moved swiftly back across the room, put her arms around him, and kissed him soundly on both cheeks. Phil followed, his hand out. "Ditto from me, chum. Heard you'd gone back across the pond, but, well—it's been too long."

Eve Anderson had come for a refill and Faith heard her mutter, "Not long enough."

She hadn't heard him speak, but Faith could tell Adrian St. John was British from his Savile Row suit with a Turnbull & Asser shirt peeking out to his bespoke James Taylor & Son brogues. He was a small, slight man. The overall effect was that of a between-the-wars-pen-and-ink drawing of a gentleman from *Punch*. She couldn't hear what the group was saying, but the subject was making them laugh, including Max. A real laugh. A kind of laugh she had never heard from him. She was tempted to eliminate these three because of it. There seemed to be genuine affection among them—and more to the point: for Max Dane.

Ian had been in and out, barely pausing between guests, but now he walked into the center of the room. "Please don't wait for the others but help yourselves to food and drink. If there is something you require that you don't see, speak to Mrs. Fairchild or myself."

"What have we here? Jeeves?" Phil quipped.

Max stopped laughing. "Ian's right. Chow down. It could be a while before everybody gets here."

But the next to come followed rapidly one upon one another. Alexis Reed, or Alexis Abbot, as she was now known, also sported a California tan, but Faith was sure it had been acquired with much SPF protection, or not by lying in the sun at all. Alexis's skin was flawless. All of her was. In Victorian times, she would have been known as a "pocket Venus." Perfectly proportioned. Only her eyes—soft gray pools with dark lashes—were oversize. Her brunette hair, artfully tangled, brushed her shoulders, which were bare above a turquoise strapless ballerina-skirted dress. Unlike the other women, she was wearing flats, satin with silver filigree buckles. Alexis was greeted much less effusively than Ian, even somewhat offhand. Faith remembered that she was the ingénue, much younger than the rest of the cast and crew at the time *Heaven or Hell* was produced. She had no history with them prior to it and definitely not afterward.

Alexis drifted toward the buffet and asked Faith for some tonic water, not too cold, with a twist of lime. She didn't notice the casket, or if she did, showed no indication. Faith was beginning to think having everyone file in one by one to note reactions was going to be a flop. Kind of like *Heaven or Hell*.

There was a pleasant buzz of conversation, although still no one was eating much, when Tony Ames, the choreographer, literally danced into the room. He swept Betty Sinclair up into his arms and waltzed her around a few steps. Next to Alexis, Tony was the youngest in the group and he looked it. He'd maintained his dancer's figure and he had a boyish face—a shorter version of Tommy Tune.

"Get some champagne, Tony—you too, Adrian. You both liked it in the old days," Max said. "It's a celebration."

"I know," Tony said, "and I intend to do just that."

Max had ordered Taittinger, among some others—"Perrier-Jouët, the ladies like the bottles"—and Faith poured two flutes, holding them out toward the men as they came toward her. She'd found a few mentions of Tony Ames among shows since *Heaven or Hell*, but Adrian St. John seemed to have returned to London and disappeared. Not a single writing credit of any sort.

Despite Max's urgings, no one was eating yet. The guests remained clustered around him. Curious to see who would walk into the room next.

It was more of a stagger than a walk. "Hi, cuz! Happy Birthday!" Faith hadn't seen a photo of Charles Frost, but he was the only relative, so the man who appeared to have slept in his clothes, or had a particularly rough flight, must be he. She immediately poured a tall glass of water to have at the ready.

"Chip, good to see you. Been a while," Max said. He did not appear upset at his relative's obvious inebriation.

"You think? Well, water under the bridge. Say, I know you!" He waggled a finger at Eve Anderson. "You were the lead, but there was a hot little number that should have had it. Tried to get off with her, but . . ."

Max took his cousin's arm and firmly walked him down to the buffet. "You must meet Mrs. Fairchild, Chip, who will be cooking all sorts of delicious things for us this weekend." He put the glass of water in Chip's hand and told Faith in a low voice, "Try to get some food in him. He's not that far gone and I don't want him any further."

Since Chip was eyeing the chops and other dishes with obvious relish, Faith had no trouble convincing him to take a loaded plate to the small table set nearest the buffet. She wanted to keep an eye on him lest he fall facedown in his soup.

Once he was settled she did a quick count: Eve Anderson, Phil Baker, Betty Sinclair, Alexis Reed, Adrian St. John, Tony Ames, and Chip—seven in all. Two to go: James Nelson and Travis Trent, the original director and the male lead. She didn't think it was her imagination, but people seemed to be getting edgy. Several drifted down to the buffet and filled plates, but no one seemed in a party mood except Max himself, who was looking like a benevolent uncle in a roomful of favorite nieces and nephews.

Travis Trent strode into the room well ahead of Ian, taking command of the boards. "The gang's all here I see!" Faith thought he might break into song. He looked quite natty in a three-piece suit with a deep maroon bow tie. Not a clip-on.

"Glad you could make it," Max said, shaking his hand. The others greeted him as well, although Faith noticed that Eve lacked any warmth whatsoever, as had been true for all the arrivals. Was she disappointed not to be the sole guest? She'd made several trips to the buffet, but not for food, and Faith was giving her a weaker drink with each request, all as rude a command as the first had been.

"Come on, everybody, this is a party! Mine! A little merriment, please. Who knows when James will show up, or if," Max said.

"James Nelson?" Betty Sinclair asked, adding, "I would like to see him. You should have let him continue as director, Max. He was doing a fine job."

"As my cousin here said, 'water under the bridge' or 'over the dam,' whatever. I did what I thought best, Betty dear."

"Yeah," Eve said. "Max was right. Jimmy was a disaster. And what do you know about it all, anyway, Betty?"

"More than you, sweetie," Betty almost purred. "Jim wanted Alexis to take your place. We all knew it."

"Now, now, claws in," Phil interrupted. "It's Max's birthday and time we really got this party started. Where's the piano?"

Would Max move the piano from the foyer in here? Faith wondered. It would certainly go far to help lift everyone's spirits. Phil seemed ready to assume the role of emcee. And then all eyes turned toward the entrance to the room. Preceding Ian by several steps was one of the handsomest men Faith had ever seen. Surely James Nelson, the last guest. She hadn't been able to find a photo of him, and this was a face, plus all the rest, you wouldn't forget.

"James!" Max called out gleefully. "You made it off that island!"

"Happy birthday, Max. What's with the coffin?" He pointed to it.

"You tell me."

So much for scrutiny, Faith thought. From the babble of talk that erupted, everyone had noticed the unique serving station and no one had wanted to be the person to point to the emperor's new clothes.

"I thought it was one of your little jokes," Travis said loudly. "Bad one, as usual."

"Well, it seemed to be part of the decor. Look at all the red and black," Alexis said, gracefully flicking the cloth at the table where she had been sitting most of the night.

Adrian began to recite—beautifully, Faith noted, as she recognized lines from Wordsworth's "Ode: Intimations of Immortality."

> "There was a time when meadow, grove, and stream,
> The earth, and every common sight,
> To me did seem

Appareled in celestial light,
The glory and the freshness of a dream.
It is not now as it hath been of yore;—
Turn wheresoe'er I may,
By night or day,
The things which I have seen I now can see no more."

"Very nice, Adrian, but even Max can't believe he is immortal," Betty said, her husky voice making the comment more of a joke than a slight.

"Right, as you usually are, but Adrian has come closer than you think," Max said abruptly. "Let's let the play unfold, and if you all put your thinking caps on, you'll figure it out before Sunday draws to a close and the curtain, as it were, comes down."

His words cast a pall over the room. Betty Sinclair stood up. "I don't like this," she said. "Phil, let's get out of here. Max, have your butler person call us a cab. If we can't get a plane out, we can take the train. You know I don't like games."

Max came over to her. "Please forgive my penchant for drama. I got carried away by Adrian's performance. You're here for a simple weekend of fun and relaxation to mark a milestone birthday. After midnight tonight I will officially be an old coot and allowed any eccentricities. Stay. It won't be the same without you. Or," he added hastily, "Phil."

Betty Sinclair had gone quite pale, Faith observed. "We can leave tomorrow if you still want to, babe," Phil said.

"Don't call me 'babe,'" she snapped. Some of the color was returning to her face. "All right. I'll decide tomorrow."

Max looked pleased. "Now, Travis had the right idea. It would be a bit difficult to move my piano in here. Let's all head to the foyer. You may have noted there is plenty of room there. We can roll up the rugs and dance. Ian, will you show everyone the way? I want to have a word with Mrs. Fairchild, who will transport all her delectable food. And drink, my pretties—drink up!"

Chip Frost was the first to follow Max's instructions and the others soon followed. An odd sort of Pied Piper, but Faith was quite sure what impelled them was a desire to leave this particular room. As she watched she wondered whether Betty's wish to leave now meant Faith could eliminate her. Max was still very much alive, and unless she stabbed him on her way out, she couldn't be the would-be killer. But, of course, she was staying . . . a bluff?

Max came over to her. "You may have noticed the casket is on wheels. I'll send Ian back for it and you can set up under the big window next to the front door."

"They haven't been eating much, but I'll replenish things and it will all look the way it did at the start of the party," Faith said.

Max nodded. "Good. How do you think it's going?"

"You mean, did I notice anyone specifically looking daggers at you, aside from everyone just now?"

"I like your sense of humor," Max said. "Yeah, I guess that's what I mean."

"Not at you, but a few at each other. I don't think Eve Anderson likes anyone here, for example."

"Easy one. Now I must attend to my guests. Keep up the good work."

Faith quickly reset the buffet, and by the time Ian returned it was ready to roll, literally. He'd brought a bar cart for the drinks.

"The food has been perfect. My compliments to the chef." Ian was in a jollier mood than Faith had ever previously noted. She hadn't poured a drink for Max all night. Had Ian been nipping at the scotch instead during his trips to and from the front door?

In the foyer, which was glowing like a stage set for a PBS drama—the golden oak paneling and the large floral arrangements illuminated—Phil Baker had indeed taken command and was tickling the ivories with classic show tunes. Tony Ames grabbed Betty Sinclair and the two started to dance expertly. Not to be outdone, Eve went over to James Nelson, but he shook his head and walked toward the buffet.

"Hi," he said. "What do you have for beers?"

"You might like a Peak IPA, the brewery is in Portland, Maine." Was this why Max or Ian had included it in the selection? "I also have pretty much everything from Heineken to Guinness, Budweiser, too."

"The Peak will be fine, thank you." He smiled and moved away toward the others.

The music definitely lightened the mood. People began to sing along and toes were tapping. As Phil ended a Cole Porter medley and was about to start something else, Travis sat down next to him. "Shove over and let a pro do this. I'm a lounge lizard now, you know. Don't mind singing for my supper tonight."

Faith heard Max say, "Trav, you don't have to. Sit back and enjoy."

Trent flashed a smile. "I want to, boss." As soon as he started playing the first notes, Faith recognized the famous song from the musical, as everyone else must. He began to sing the lyrics in a rich tenor that had not diminished with age. Alexis stood behind him and added her soprano. It was a magical moment that wasn't spoiled even when Eve pushed in, saying, "Hey, that's *our* song, Travis," and started to sing. She toned down her Ethel Merman range and complemented their performance. There wasn't another sound in the room until loud applause broke out after all the verses had been sung.

"Thank you," Betty called out. She had tears in her eyes. "It has always been my favorite."

Ian was whispering in Max's ear. They were close enough to Faith for her to hear him say, "There's a car at the gate."

"No one else is expected," Max said, "but we'd better see what's going on. Nothing on the camera?"

"Doesn't work well in the cold," Ian said.

"Do you want me to walk down the drive and see who it is?" Faith offered. Max was looking anxious. Some sort of delivery, she figured. One of the guests had sent something to arrive after he or she did? Flowers? A funeral wreath?

"No. Too cold, too dark, too far anyway. Let them in, Ian, and stay by the door."

Travis was playing other tunes from *Heaven or Hell* and the party had moved into high hilarity. Pairs were dancing and Faith noticed Adrian St. John singing along. What were they all thinking? And aside from Travis, who had made it clear what he had been doing, at least lately, what had they all been up to since the show closed? She knew about Eve, Alexis, and Tony in part; but she was sure each wasn't the whole story.

A loud banging noise put a sudden stop to the music. Rowan House's front door had a heavy brass lion's head knocker and someone was using it.

"Who else is coming?" Adrian asked.

"I guess we'll just have to see," Max answered, opening the door wide. A young woman dressed for the bitter temperature stepped in, pulled her wool hat off, shook out her long dark hair, and addressed him.

"Hello, Daddy."

CHAPTER 9

"Sorry, kiddo," Max said gently. "I'm not your father. You must be Angela. I heard about your mother. My condolences."

"But your name has been on the checks. I don't understand why . . ." The girl sounded bewildered and at a loss for words. "When Mom got worse, she gave me power of attorney. I *saw* your signature on the checks."

The room was quiet. Max glanced at his guests. Tony Ames broke the silence. "Well, guys and gals, I for one am for beddy bye." Travis Trent played a bar of "Goodnight, Ladies," and in what seemed like seconds the room had emptied, save for Max, Angela, Ian, and Faith.

Faith put it together right away. Angela was the late Bella Martelli's daughter and had received her mother, the show's costume designer's invitation, but for some reason decided to come unannounced. She believed Max was her father and wanted to confront him—reason enough.

Max rested his hand on the girl's arm, as if to keep her from taking off. "Ian," he said, "you've had a long day, so you should hit the hay, too." It wasn't a request. "Mrs. Fairchild, I'm sure Angela must be hungry. We'll be in the library." This *was* one.

Faith had hoped they would stay in the foyer. There was a large comfortable couch in front of the fire. That would have given her the opportunity to hear what they said as she finished cleaning up, but it was clear Max wanted privacy.

She addressed Angela, who was still wearing her coat and carrying a backpack. "Why don't I take your things? I'll make sure the guest room upstairs is ready and will put them there."

"Well . . ." Angela said.

"You're not going anywhere tonight," Max said. "Give Mrs. Fairchild your stuff and we can talk for as long or short as you want while you have something to eat."

"All right." She smiled. It lit up her whole face, a beautiful one. Beautiful, yes, but she did not resemble Max Dane. Not a redhead, and her face was more Mediterranean than New England. But then Dane's father had been Italian, like Angela's mother. Max had been quite definite though. He and Angela were *not* related.

Although Ian and Max had made a point of not catering to the guests' food preferences or allergies, Faith had decided to ignore it, mentioning ingredients to people at the buffet. She would do so now, too. So many young people were vegetarian or vegan. "Are there any foods you might have a problem with or just don't care for? We had a buffet dinner tonight, so there's quite a variety of dishes. I can make up a plate and warm some of the soup as well."

"I eat everything. Oh, except veal—no baby calves—or foie gras."

"That's fine, then," Max said. "Nix the foie gras, Faith, and give her some of the salmon and I'm sure she likes creamed spinach. Plenty of those potatoes, too. What do you want to drink?" Before she could answer for herself, he did. "She looks cold, Faith. Make both of us hot toddies, if you will."

Angela didn't say anything, so Faith assumed it was fine with her, but she'd offer some other choices when she brought the food. The girl might want hot cocoa, not hot whiskey.

First Faith took Angela's coat and surprisingly heavy backpack up to the room. Passing the other guest room doors, she didn't hear anything. The doors were thick, however. As she reached the end of the hall, one of them opened and Eve Anderson slipped out—her back to Faith—hurried down the hall past several rooms and entered another. Her own Faith remembered. She remembered who was in the one she'd left, too. Phil Baker.

Somehow Faith did not envision them having a pillow fight or exchanging midnight confidences. In fact, she'd noticed earlier that they had not interacted at all beyond a halfhearted initial greeting.

In the unused guest room, Faith was tempted to peek in the girl's pack but instead took a quick look around to make sure the bath was stocked with towels and sundries and that the closet had extra blankets and pillows. This would have been the room allotted to Angela's mother—or Jack Gold. There weren't any flowers, items like the carafe of water next to the bed or a stack of suggested reading. There also wasn't a copy of the musical's *Playbill* prominently displayed. Faith would bring the water and some flowers later.

From the weight of the backpack, Angela must be carrying her own books. And there was no need for the sad reminder the *Playbill* would be. How old was she? Faith wondered. The show closed twenty years ago. Angela looked about that age. She'd mentioned power of attorney. Didn't you have to be twenty-one for that?

However old she was, Angela had discovered that her mother was receiving checks signed by Max. If he wasn't her father and the checks weren't child support, what were they?

It didn't take long to assemble a tray with the food and drinks. Faith tapped on the library door, Max opened it and held it wide as Faith walked into the room. He didn't seem upset about anything—just the opposite—nor did Angela.

Under her coat, the young woman was wearing jeans and a deep turquoise wool pullover. Her earrings were oversize turquoise studs. A gold wedding band hung from a simple gold chain around her neck. She was clutching it like a talisman, dropping her hand when she saw Faith place the tray on a small table that Max had obviously just cleared. "Thank you so much. This looks delicious. I haven't had much to eat today."

If anything, Faith thought, and probably not much other days as well. Angela was model thin. Not a healthy look. Grief? Or was something else going on?

"Would you like anything else to drink besides the toddy?" Faith asked. Angela answered, "I'd love a Coke if you have one."

Max interjected, "There's some here in the bar, so we're all set. I'll leave the tray in the kitchen later."

Faith got the message, but said, "I'll be there for a while if you do need something."

He nodded and Angela thanked her again. She was already spooning up the chowder. A good sign.

Faith closed the door. They were resuming their conversation, but the only word she caught was "grandmother." Whose?

She headed to the foyer where there were still glasses, dishes, and other detritus to clear up. The first thing she noticed was that the casket cum serving table was gone. Ian? It wasn't in the kitchen or hallway she'd come from after leaving the library, and it certainly wasn't in that room. She walked back to the summer parlor, which was in darkness. When she turned on the lights she noted that the tables and chairs were all in place, but the casket was not. A quick search of the other rooms on the first floor didn't turn it up either. Having served its shock—and practical—value, had Max instructed Ian to roll it out of sight, placing it in the basement or one of the outside buildings?

Back in the kitchen she made herself a toddy too with plenty of lemon and honey but just a splash of rum. She needed to stay alert.

The house was quiet aside from the hum of the appliances, including the dishwasher with its last load. She sat down at the counter to wait, sipping her drink appreciatively. For a moment she allowed her thoughts to drift to her family, sound asleep she was sure after a night of skiing.

She got up and looked out the window. There was a light on in Ian's quarters. The yard was covered with a scant few inches of snow. Enough for a New England calendar look for the guests, but not too much to be a problem. She could tell it was very cold. The snow was a sheet of shining ice where the beam of light hit.

The dishwasher cycle ended and she unloaded it. She imagined the morning would mean a steady stream of breakfasters, none she suspected early risers. She'd be getting up well before the guests to bake the muffins and scones. Now, before she went to bed she crept quietly up the back stairs to the second floor and stood in the middle of the hallway. No more musical room switches so far as she could tell. It was as quiet as a tomb.

On a frigid night like this, Samantha thought she should either move closer to her job or apply at a Starbucks nearer to Aleford. The town did not have one—or a Dunkin' Donuts, no chain whatsoever except the Shop'n Save, which was one of three locations owned by a family, not a corporation. The lack of fast food and recognizable logos was a point of pride for the town, and once the Minuteman Café started serving exotic beverages like lattes to go, the few complaints about having to drive to Lexington or Waltham for such brews disappeared.

Despite the onset of the cold weather, Samantha was enjoying her commute—the feeling the distance gave her. Freedom to leave her comfy, albeit cloistered, nest and head out into the wider world. It was freezing tonight, though. She'd have to search through the Miller closets for warmer boots. It must be even worse up at Loon, but she knew both her parents would be warming up with night skiing. The condo was right by the slopes. Maybe she could get up there for a day or two. She certainly hadn't done much skiing when she lived in Brooklyn.

Was Zach a skier? She could ask him herself in a few minutes. Harvard Square was the next stop and they were meeting at Bartley's. Zach had texted earlier to see when she was free for the sweet potato fries challenge, suggesting a late dinner. Bartley's was open until nine. The official name was Mr. Bartley's Burger Cottage, but Samantha had never heard anyone use it. It was simply "Bartley's."

He was waiting just inside the door and came out to greet her. "I've been watching for you and I swear I saw a guy totally encased in ice. Man, it is ridiculously cold!"

It seemed only natural to give him a hug and once again Samantha wondered what shampoo he used. Good old-fashioned Ivory Soap?

The aromas inside the tiny restaurant were lovely, too. More than that—intoxicating. The burgers, of course, but also onions, peppers, and other grill items. She was starving within seconds. It was packed as usual. Zach spied a table by the back wall and they grabbed it.

"Too cold for frappes, want some coffee? Or working where you do are you off it? I have a friend who had a summer job at Baskin-Robbins and has never been able to eat ice cream since."

"No! Coffee is my life now and I love it even more than before. No sugar, and milk, not cream, please," she said.

A server arrived, and besides the coffees, they also ordered the same burgers and fries as they had at Christopher's. "I feel like a traitor," Samantha said. "I've always been a Bartley's fan. Maybe when I taste my burger tonight I'll realize I was wrong about which was better."

"Not a chance, but you can assuage your conscience by preferring the fries."

It was nice to be out but not on a date, Samantha thought. No jumping from the frying pan into the fire for her. How could she have been so wrong about Caleb? She was off men. Excluding

Zach. He was a guy, yes, but just a friend. Nothing complicated. She realized he was telling her something.

"Sorry, what did you say?"

He looked amused. "Where were you? From your face, it was a planet far, far away. Anyway, you don't need to tell me. I was filling you in on what I'd found out about Austin Stebbins's 'date.' I'll start over. Her name is Mary Cabot Pritchett and she's lived at the Mount Vernon Street address for seventy-nine years, which is also her age. It's safe to assume the house is a family one. Mrs. Cabot Pritchett is widowed, childless, and has no siblings— nor occupation. She's in a bunch of clubs—I have a list if you want to see them—and there's a summer address: Seal Cove on Mount Desert Island. The late Mr. Pritchett had been a partner in the law firm of Pritchett and Howell, founded in 1884."

"I'm impressed," Samantha said. "How about Stebbins. Anything more on him? Any dirt? A secret past?"

"Sorry, sweetheart, he seems to be exactly who he says he is. Boston bred, widower, California property developer with a more than adequate income. That doesn't mean he isn't a fortune hunter. Rich people always like to get richer. And the lady he's playing footsy, or handsy, with is definitely rich."

"But Granny isn't. She's not poor, but nothing like this Mary person. Why is he playing up to her?" Samantha said.

"Maybe the guy simply likes being with Ursula. I do." Seeing the disappointed look on her face, Zach added, "Don't worry. I'll keep digging. You could get lucky and he'll turn out to be an embezzler."

After this, the tone of their conversation shifted. They bantered back and forth, drank some more coffee, and when the food was in view, Zach insisted she shut her eyes again and fed her a fry.

I could get used to this kind of fun, Samantha thought as she concentrated on the sweet crisp morsel—and the feel of Zach's fingers when he fed her another "just to be sure."

Her eyes flew open. "Phew! They really are better."

"Well, that's good news. Now eat your burger, and if you don't have to be up early, we can go catch a movie in Davis Square."

"I'd love to," Samantha said. The burger—very close to perfection—and fries were soon gone. "Dessert later? After the movie? I'm pretty full now."

"Great," Zach said, motioning for the check. He was smiling. He really does have a nice smile, Samantha thought. And good taste in food. She realized she was smiling, too, and even the thought of stepping out into the cold to walk down Mass. Ave. to the T didn't wipe it from her face.

Samantha's phone rang as they were walking toward the movie theater. From the ringtone, she knew it was her mother and picked up. "Hi, Mom, having fun?"

"I've been checking the weather," Pix said, "and it's going down to the single digits in Aleford tonight. You need to crank up the heat and let the faucets drip."

"I haven't heard anything about the weather, but don't worry. I'll make sure the pipes don't freeze." The Millers' pipes had frozen during a very deep freeze years ago, and ever since Pix was religious about drips.

"Why don't you do it now while you're thinking about it?"

"I'm not home, but I will be in a few hours."

"It's kind of late, isn't it?" Pix said.

"Not that late, Mom." Samantha looked at Zach and rolled her eyes. Her mother wasn't usually this protective. Something about being in another state? She didn't say she was with Zach. Hadn't said anything about their growing friendship except for a comment that she'd seen him on the T that first time. She kind of wanted to keep him to herself, she realized.

"And I'll call Granny in the morning. I know the student is away this weekend. If she'd wanted someone with her tonight she would have called me or Dora."

"Is Mr. Stebbins still staying there?"

"I don't know. Look, do you want me to go by now? I can be there in about half an hour."

There was a longish pause. "I'm sure everything is fine and I'll call her in the morning as well. Maybe you can go by before work."

"I planned on it. Love you, Mom. Bye."

"Love you, too."

Samantha put her phone in her purse and said, "My mother tends to worry when she's not close at hand for her mother."

"Or you," Zach said and pulled her arm through his. "Who's Dora? I thought I knew everybody in Aleford."

"You'd know her if you needed TLC. Dora McNeill is the first call made for private duty nursing in Aleford. Anyway, she nursed my grandmother through pneumonia a while back and considers herself a kind of niece now—always on call for Granny."

"I like that. Aleford really is a special community."

"I suppose it is," Samantha said. For her it was simply home. "Now hurry up! I like to watch the previews."

"Me too. All those films I then don't have to go see."

"Exactly," she agreed, noticing again how well their strides matched as they set off for the theater.

It had been one of those uneasy-sleep nights. Faith kept waking up yet didn't hear any noises when she did. She'd turn the pillow—comfy down—to the cool side and slip back to sleep only to repeat the process in what seemed like a blink of the eye. At five thirty she gave in, took a shower, and prepared to greet the new day. Aside from the surprise guest, last night had gone smoothly. Max was still very much alive and there hadn't been any overt tension. A gathering of old chums, he'd said, and it had been just that. Fingers crossed it stayed the same until all the chums departed.

It was still dark out, but there was enough light for her to see the icicles hanging from the garage eaves and tree limbs bent brittle. Overnight the thin coating of ice had changed to Narnia under the White Witch. She hoped the sun would be strong enough to melt it all. And that the wind didn't pick up, sending branches crashing down on power lines. Power outages as a way of life were another thing she'd had to get used to in New England. But, she reminded herself, Rowan House did have an ample generator. She'd be able to cook and they'd all stay warm. Feeling better, she dressed and went into the kitchen to bake, but coffee first. Much coffee.

Adrian St. John was sitting at the counter drinking a cup of tea and reading what Faith could see was the London *Times* on an iPad.

"Good morning. Still on GMT. And do forgive my dishabille." He was wearing a dark maroon jacquard silk dressing gown, neatly tied with a tassel sash. An inch or so of navy silk pajamas peeked out below, brushing the tops of his matching velvet slippers. Nothing could have been less dishabille save top hat and tails.

"Good morning. Let me make you a pot of tea and proper breakfast," Faith said. "What would you like? Full English?"

He laughed. "No, I indulge only once a year or so in the artery clogger. Normally it's brown toast and a soft-boiled egg."

"I'm about to make some scones, so if you would like to wait for them with your egg, I could give you a nice fruit cup to start. And oatmeal. I've done Scottish oats overnight in the slow cooker." Faith found herself transformed into Mrs. Bridges, Mrs. Hudson, and definitely Mrs. Beeton simply by proximity to Adrian.

"Oatmeal and the fruit would be lovely and I'm sure if last night's repast was anything to go by the scone will be delicious."

Faith quickly got the food together, offering brown sugar as well as raisins for the porridge. It didn't take long to make real tea either. He'd taken a tea bag from the snacks and drinks she'd left out. That was all that was missing. Adrian was the only one who had been here—or wanted something from the tray. She'd asked

Ian to mention its availability throughout the weekend when he welcomed the guests.

While Adrian ate, Faith quickly put together two kinds of drop scones: lemon and mixed berry.

"Are you local or did Max hire a New York caterer?" Adrian asked.

"I'm local, but I started my business years ago in Manhattan where I grew up."

"It must have been quite a change to move here."

"An understatement," Faith said, "but I fell in love with a New Englander and he already had a job here." She decided not to be too specific, which always seemed to lead to clerical tangents. She wanted to seize this opportunity to chat Adrian up. Find out more about his fellow guests—and most especially him.

"I understand everyone here was involved with one of Max Dane's musicals."

"That's right." He eyed her speculatively. "His last as you may know. *Heaven or Hell.*"

"And you wrote the book. I mean the script."

"Yes. You seem quite up on the production."

Faith checked her scones. Nearly done. "I became interested when he asked me to cater the weekend. I've always been a fan of musicals and wish I could have seen it. An interesting dilemma."

"And not unique. People have to make choices like that more frequently than you might think. Not to burn in hellfire for eternity, but to give up what one finds comfortable for something less so when it's for love. Isn't that what you did?"

Somehow Adrian had turned the tables. He was now the interrogator. Faith thought back to her first months in Aleford and how much she longed for New York. She'd been quite horrible to Tom, complaining about not being able to get a proper haircut and missing what she then called the Three Bs—Balducci's, Barneys, and Bloomingdales, all nonexistent in the Boston area at the time.

"Well, it wasn't quite hell, but at times I suppose it was hell-ish," she admitted, putting a plate of scones with Irish butter and several kinds of jam in front of him. "What about you? After *Heaven or Hell*, what did you choose? A career as a writer or did you remain connected to the theater?"

"You know perfectly well that I didn't, dear lady. I'm sure you have looked all of us up on the Internet."

Faith knew she was blushing. "I was . . ."

"Interested," he finished for her. "I might as well tell you, since I plan to let the others know for purely self-centered reasons. Perhaps you have heard of Fiona Foster-Fordham?"

"Of course," she said. "She's one of my favorite writers and the BBC series based on her books has been fantastic."

"Well, I am Fiona. And it's been heaven, not hell at all."

Reading Fiona Foster-Fordham was a not-so-guilty pleasure along the lines of Sophie Kinsella and Helen Fielding. The books were marketed as such but emphasized the literary quality of the writing, and more than one critic had objected that the Booker Prize overlooked Ms. Foster-Fordham due to her commercial success.

Part of the marketing was also the mystique. Like the Italian writer Elena Ferrante, Fiona F-F as she was known, insisted on anonymity.

"Obviously I would not have been much of a success if I had written the books under my own name. The reverse of what Mary Anne Evans and Charlotte Brontë had to do." He reached for another scone. "These are the best I've ever had and I'm not going to think calories this weekend."

Faith was stunned by his revelation. "When do you plan to reveal your identity?" There was no question that Adrian topped the list this weekend in terms of success. Richer even than Max. How the writer must have been laughing up his sleeve last night!

"Tonight at dinner. After pudding, I think. After Max has

blown out his candles. Now I've told you the truth. Mrs. Fairchild, don't you think you should come clean with me? What are you actually doing here?"

"Good morning. Those look good. May I?" James Nelson glanced toward Faith as his hand hovered over the scones. Almost breathless with relief at being able to avoid Adrian's question, she said, "Please help yourself and tell me what you'd like for breakfast. The idea was to place things buffet style in the dining room, but I'm beginning to think I should take orders and then people may sit here or go there."

"Sitting here is fine by me. Gives me a chance to catch up with you, Adrian. What's on offer, Mrs. Fairchild? Breakfast is my favorite meal. I'm a morning person."

Faith had suspected as much. It was past dawn, but it was still very early. "First of all, coffee or tea? Then there's oatmeal, fruit, any kind of eggs—I could do an omelet and I have several kinds of quiche. French toast, waffles? The scones are warm and there are Morning Glory muffins in the oven now."

"Wow, I'm overwhelmed. I usually crack a few eggs and throw some bacon into a skillet. I'd love an omelet with whatever you want to put in. And coffee to start would be great."

The bacon meant he wasn't a vegetarian, so Faith decided to make a three-egg omelet with Niman Ranch ham, sharp cheddar, cherry tomatoes, mushrooms, and scallions.

"So, what have you been doing since last we met?" Adrian asked. "You left the show before I did and I haven't heard any show biz buzz about you, so I'm assuming you opted out of Broadway—or went for smaller productions."

"No, you got it right. *Heaven or Hell* was my first and last show. In a way, I'm glad it was hell, or I might have stumbled on for years more."

Adrian put his cup down. He was shaking his head. "You

were great. If you had stayed I know the show would have been a success—and you'd have gone on to more."

"But I didn't have that choice, did I? About staying, I mean. Max saw to that. I've had a lot of years to think about it all and I'm pretty sure he hired me with dumping me in mind. He needed a placeholder for a while. He was winding up another show, remember."

"Yes—and went on to another."

It was hard to pay attention to what she was doing while eavesdropping and Faith didn't want to burn James's omelet. She tried to recall what Aunt Chat had said about Max doing another show. A revival?

"Less said . . ." Faith caught Adrian nodding toward her and James Nelson's quizzical look back at him as she deftly slid his omelet onto a warm plate.

"Here's a basket of toast and croissants. Some muffins will be ready soon," she said. "What else can I get you?"

"Nothing. This is perfect. Thank you," James said.

The two then began to talk about travel. Apparently Nelson did leave the island in Maine on occasion. Soon they were deep into comparing trips they'd taken to what Adrian referred to as "Indochina" with trips made to South American spots. Faith knew Adrian could afford to go wherever he wanted in whatever style, but how did James? His address suggested a pared-back lifestyle and maybe that was how he traveled too. Bare bones.

Travis Trent and Betty Sinclair both came into the room. "I smell coffee. Black and a lot of it. I don't normally drink much—and seldom champagne," Travis said. "I'll be okay in a bit once my head clears. Say, this is some kitchen! The whole house is pretty unbelievable. Old Max always did well for himself." The sardonic note in his voice was unmistakable and Faith hurriedly put a large mug of coffee in front of him on the counter.

"Poor Trav," Betty said. "You never did have a good head for booze. And neither does Chip. I ran into him staggering around the hall. He wants water and, to quote, 'a truckload of Tylenol.'"

"I'll bring it up," Faith said, "but first what can I get you?"

"Two poached eggs, runny in the middle, whatever bacon you have, and I'll demolish some of these divine-looking baked goods the boys are eating, too."

Faith had Betty Sinclair pegged as a light or no breakfast eater and envied her metabolism. "Home fries with the eggs?"

"Of course! Now what's the plan for the day? It's like a skating rink outside, so unless it melts fast no rambles in the woods. Max never got up before noon and Phil is a lazy bastard, too. I imagine Eve and Alexis are not going to be up soon either—or they may be, but need time for their toilette. Especially Eve. There's four of us, so we could play bridge, or poker. You used to be quite good at both, Jimmy. I'm sure Mrs. Whatever here can scare up a deck of cards. We can catch up on the last twenty years. That should take us to lunch anyway." She delivered her suggestion as if reciting lines with special emphasis on certain phrases—"catch up on" for one.

"Fairchild," said James. "Her name is Mrs. Fairchild. Faith Fairchild to be exact."

"How sweet. Such an old-fashioned name. 'Faith' I mean."

Faith put Ms. Sinclair's food down on the counter in front of her, adding cutlery. "There's a room with a card table down the hall on the left, and Mr. Dane has left an assortment of games, magazines, and decks of cards as well as beverages there for your enjoyment." She felt a bit like a flight attendant and even more, a servant. Mrs. Whatever. Betty Sinclair knew Faith's name, Faith was sure. It was intended as a put-down.

Betty had omitted Tony Ames and Angela from her list. Tony and she had seemed close, but Betty might not be familiar with his morning routine. Although he could come soon in search of sustenance, Faith thought she'd check on Angela when she brought

Chip Frost the hangover cure she was assembling. She'd added a glass of a sports drink with plenty of crushed ice and some dry toast to his list and replaced the Tylenol with ibuprofen. Over the years one thing a caterer learned was how to help with a hangover's symptoms. Besides, Tylenol plus alcohol was an actual deadly combination causing liver damage—a fact few people knew. She wondered how bad Chip's was and whether she should look for some sort of bucket as well.

As she was leaving the kitchen, the back door opened and Ian entered. Faith had thought he'd be up earlier, although his apartment had a kitchen and he'd told her he'd get his own breakfasts over the weekend.

Rubbing his hands together, he unzipped his jacket. "Could be a nasty bit of weather moving in, but no snow. Just dropping temperatures. I called to have the drive treated and they said they'd be here soon. And I checked the generator. It's working fine, not that we'll necessarily lose power. Just a little taste of winter here for you Californians."

James Nelson stood up. "Mind if I have a look at your generator? I have some experience with them."

"Not at all. I'll show you where it is. You'll find it more than adequate—a monster. It's in one of the outbuildings past the garage."

Leaving Ian to see to the guests' needs, Faith went upstairs and knocked on Chip Frost's door.

"Come in," he groaned.

Apparently his idea of unpacking was to spread his garments over the floor and furniture. He was in bed and the drapes were drawn.

"How do you feel? I've brought what you asked for and some other remedies."

"You're an angel. Mrs. Fairchild, right? I feel like crap, but been there done that many times before and I'll be better in a few." He sounded better already.

"Do you want me to open the drapes?"

"Not yet." He was sitting up and regarding the bed tray. "I'll deal with this, then maybe you could come back in, say, an hour?"

Max had said no indulging any breakfast-in-bed requests, but Faith viewed this as more in the nature of first aid. "I'll check in an hour. Do you have what you need for now?"

"Yes, Mrs. Fairchild. Nice Mrs. Fairchild. Pretty Mrs. Fairchild. Too bad I'm so hungover. Besides making them, you're a tasty dish yourself."

"And a very happily married one," she said as she left.

There was no answer when she knocked on Angela's door, so she opened it a crack. The young woman might still be asleep or in the bathroom.

The room was filled with sunlight. The drapes were open. The covers on the bed had been pulled up neatly. There was no sign of Angela. She must have gone downstairs while Faith was in Chip's room.

Yet, entering the kitchen she didn't see her there either. "Has Miss Martelli come down for breakfast?" she asked Ian, the room's sole occupant.

"Not yet."

Not in her room, not here. Faith made a quick tour of the downstairs. Angela Martelli wasn't in any part of the house that Faith could see.

Where was she?

By one almost everyone had had some form of breakfast. Tony Ames had braved the ice and cold for an approximation of his morning run and then had had to "take a ninety-degree ninety-minute shower to thaw myself out." He ate at the counter, brightening at the mention of French toast, so Faith had done a stuffed version with strawberries. He'd cleaned his plate but refused seconds, saying, "You are a temptress, Mrs. Fairchild!" She told him where the four card players were, but he said that having a chance to spend time in the library Max had shown him was a rare treat and he'd be there. "He has a wonderful collection of books on the theater, as you might expect—history, memoirs. I may be there the rest of the weekend. Except for the birthday dinner bash."

This left Eve, Alexis, Phil Baker, Angela, and Max himself yet to make an appearance. Eve was the first. It appeared that Betty was correct about taking time to dress and apply maquillage. Eve looked stunning, especially if you didn't look too closely. No chicken neck. Faith was tempted to ask her secret hoping for a routine that didn't involve a scalpel.

She was casually dressed in black leggings, an orange chiffon shirt, draped low and cropped high, with a soft gold suede jacket, the sleeves pushed up to her elbows. Both wrists were adorned with what looked like multiple gold David Yurman bracelets. She was wearing opened-toed high-heeled cork sandals—a boon for Max's parquet floors and the carpets, Faith thought. She'd also pulled her long hair up into a topknot with a few tendrils artfully escaping. All she needed were Jackie O sunglasses.

"Am I the last?" she asked with a slight yawn. "Such a treat to sleep in. No early calls."

Faith was pretty sure it had been a long time since any studio had required Eve's presence, early or late, but she merely asked her what she would like to eat, listing the choices. Remembering how much the woman had drunk the night before, she added mineral water to coffee, tea, and juice.

"A little fruit. Mangoes if you have them. And toast. Wheat, no butter. Pomegranate juice and some Perrier. You can mix them together."

When Faith put it all in front of her with another plate of selected fruits she seemed disappointed. As if Faith had passed a test she was expected to fail. Before she could ask for anything more exotic, Alexis and Max entered the kitchen. Together. Very much together.

Alexis was wearing a short dress that could also have been nightwear and her hair was down again—and tousled. No makeup that Faith could detect and still the woman looked radiant. Max was dressed in his usual chinos, sweater, and open-necked shirt. He was grinning.

"I've just been giving Max his birthday present," Alexis announced. "And it was just what he wanted."

Eve made a noise that was somewhere between a choke and a scream, then left the room, overturning the stool she had been sitting on when the two had entered. No one went after her.

"Temper, temper," Alexis said.

"Hey, what's with Eve?" Phil Baker said. "She just about knocked me over. I asked her what the rush was and she told me to drop dead. Well, an equivalent that I wouldn't want to say in front of the ladies present. Anyway, I missed breakfast—great bed, Max. Slept like a baby. I looked in on the card players and Betty says they need sustenance. Can I get in on it? I'm going to take Adrian's place for a while."

"Of course," Faith said. He had a just-got-out-of-bed look, but it was very different from Alexis's—and Max's. Phil needed a shave and he hadn't combed his hair. "I can give you brunch or lunch."

"Betty says club sandwiches are the only thing to eat when you're playing bridge. Is that okay? And they're out of ice."

Betty Sinclair seemed to have appointed herself hostess for the weekend. Faith gave him a fresh bucket of ice and told him she'd bring in the food soon. First she needed to take care of Max and Alexis.

As suspected Ms. Reed, or Abbot, only wanted some fruit, yogurt, and green tea. Max said he'd grab a sandwich when Faith brought them to the others and left.

Faith's hopes of engaging Alexis in conversation were soon

disappointed. After a few nibbles of fruit and sips of tea, the actress left, too, saying something about a long soak in the tub.

Faith added a few Reubens to the platter of club sandwiches Betty had demanded. It was a somewhat childish gesture of rebellion but made her feel better. In addition to the platter she added bowls of coleslaw, potato salad, and other deli items with small plates and utensils. Ian came in as she was taking the first tray out and picked up another.

"This looks good. Max loves Reubens," he said. "I'm going to check the rooms to see if anyone needs more towels. I'll look in on poor cousin Charles, too. Max added him when, well, others weren't available. I'd never heard him mentioned before. Some sort of family falling-out I believe, but kin is kin I suppose," he said.

He sounded ironic, and maybe a little miffed. Chip might be family, but Ian seemed much closer. Faith put the thought from her mind, focusing instead on her disappointment at Ian's first words. She'd hoped to do the housekeeping herself and engage in some subtle sleuthing. "I'm quite free now, so I can do the rooms," she said.

"That's not necessary. I believe the kitchen is your domain." He softened his somewhat abrupt words with a compliment: "Everything is going splendidly. The food couldn't be better, and you are making everyone very happy. I know tonight's dinner will most certainly be the icing on the cake."

No mention of the reason for the birthday party and Faith didn't bring it up. She thanked him and started to get some of the preparations for dinner out of the way. She was whipping egg whites for Angel Food Cake when Angela came into the room.

"Hi, good morning, or I guess it's afternoon. I've been catching up on some reading for my courses. Max said I could use his office on the other side of the house. I didn't bring my laptop, so he's made one available. He has a Keurig there and I'm swimming in coffee. Could I make myself something to eat?"

"No," Faith said, "but I will, happily. That's what I'm here for this weekend. Breakfast or lunch? If you want to skip breakfast I could make a panini or another kind of sandwich, and there's split pea soup or more chowder."

"The chowder was great. I'll have that and a grilled cheese and tomato. I don't have very sophisticated tastes."

"You will." Faith laughed. "I'm sure as a student you exist on instant ramen and other microwavables."

After a moment, Faith added, "I was very sorry to hear about your mother. It's hard to lose a parent at any age, but especially difficult when you are so young. I know she did the costumes for *Heaven or Hell* and other shows. She must have been very talented."

"Thank you." She gave Faith a grateful look. "I still can't believe she's gone, even though she was sick for so long. And yes, she was a design genius."

"It must have been fun for you growing up. Lots of dress-up clothes from the productions."

"She never worked on another show after *Heaven or Hell*." Angela's voice was filled with acid—so strong a drop would have eaten away the thickest surface. "My mother sacrificed her career for me. Costume design wasn't steady enough, so she worked two jobs—tailoring for a small dry cleaning chain and doing alterations for a bridal shop near us."

Faith put the food in front of her. It was hard to know what to say. "I'm sorry."

"Me too. But it was what it was, although at the moment I'm not sure about even that anymore. What it was. I suppose you heard me—and Max's answer—when I came in last night?"

Faith nodded.

"Well, we had a nice chat in his library afterward. He's very kind and I learned that although he's no relation, he has been supporting us in part all these years plus paying my tuition at NYU. I'm a senior and have been commuting from our apartment."

She ate some of the sandwich.

"The problem now, Mrs. Fairchild, is I have absolutely no idea who I am."

CHAPTER 10

By now, Faith had been sure she would be able to point to the casket culprit. Or at least have a strong inkling about who sent it. Nothing. Not even a slight hunch.

With no immediate demands, she made herself a sandwich and sat looking out at the darkening sky. It was a good time to take stock and go over the guests. Funny to think that both Pix and Niki had been excited that she would be rubbing shoulders with stars, because aside from Alexis Abbot, none of the others had broad name recognition now. It was no longer a stellar group. Adrian alone was world renowned, but not under his given name. Would some have gone on to fame and fortune if *Heaven or Hell* hadn't been such a flop? A jinx?

And always, always the question of whom among them hated Max enough to both send the warning and carry out the implicit threat. She felt safe in eliminating Angela. Aside from the logistics of the casket delivery, and cost, the young woman believed Max was her father. She came to confront him, but patricide was a long way from "Hello, Daddy." So what about the others? "Grudges," Max had said, lethal ones.

Adrian may have had dreams of seeing his plays produced on

Broadway and in Covent Garden, but he also would not have achieved the heights he had if *H or H* had succeeded. In mystery novels, it was always the husband—or wife. Chat had said Max was much married. Was there an ex here out for revenge? Personal information about Max online was sparse. His Wikipedia entry was surprisingly brief, perhaps because the heyday of his career was before the online tool? No mention of spouses. Among this group, Alexis was too young and Betty was married to Phil at the time—an affair with each possible, but not a ring on the finger. What about Eve? Faith repeated the question to herself. *What about Eve?* She certainly seemed to have an agenda. If she wasn't married to Max once, Faith was convinced she wouldn't mind being Mrs. Dane now. Maybe not tucked away at Rowan House, but with the wherewithal to go someplace else.

James Nelson was a conundrum. What had he been doing all these years out of sight? He seemed tailor-made for a long-lasting animus. His career had definitely been cut short, and he blamed Max. So had Tony Ames's and Travis Trent's. Talented men, but stalled after *Heaven or Hell*. Faith knew that box office poison meant just that, and a colossal failure would keep an actor out of work for a long time, maybe always. Betty Sinclair and Phil Baker had been extremely successful before *H or H,* so the musical's closing so soon might not have mattered as much to them. Yet everyone wants to decide when to leave the party—not be thrust out. Which left cousin Chip. He'd been a walk-on in the show and was the same here—not on the original guest list. He would know Rowan House—or Frostcliffe in his parents' day— well. Therefore, he was the person most likely to know how to spirit the casket through the woods to the front of the house, and he did have a Boston, as well as a New York, address.

Both Jack Gold and Bella Martelli had been on the original list. Both dead. Maybe Faith shouldn't be so quick to eliminate Angela. Max must have thought Bella had a good reason to wish him dead. A reason she told her daughter? Up in Max's office studying, plotting?

Sleet began to rattle against the windows. Max had said cocktails at six, dinner at eight. Faith thought she'd better check on the card players. Ian had brought the dishes and empty platters into the kitchen almost an hour ago. Where was everyone now? And what were they all doing?

"Getting a bit nasty out," Max Dane said, entering the kitchen. "I'd like your help, Mrs. Fairchild. Not that you haven't been anything but helpful, but I wonder if you could go get Angela and pick out something for her to wear tonight? She'll feel out of place with everyone else in formal dress."

Faith was puzzled. She didn't have anything that Angela could wear, and while the notion of rifling through the other female guests' closets was an entertaining one, the owner would be bound to notice if Angela borrowed a frock.

Max saw her confusion and laughed. "Don't worry, I'm not asking you to grab some velvet drapes and do a Scarlett O'Hara. The Frosts were savers, and there's a big cedar closet at the end of the second floor, near my office where she's been studying. I should get rid of the stuff in it—clothes from who knows who across the generations. Well, I do know one, because she used to show it off. The white dress my grandmother was wearing in her portrait in the foyer. She would put it on and brag that she could still get into it."

"You've kept the portrait of her where you see it every day?" Faith blurted out. It struck her as masochistic in the extreme.

"First of all, it's a damn good—and valuable—painting. Although she was no looker, even at that age. Later it got worse. Mouth like sucking lemons. And next and last, I take pleasure in knowing how much she would hate my having it. But we're getting away from the topic here. Could you go get Angela and see if there's anything there she could wear for the party? There are even shoes."

It sounded like fun—and Faith had wanted an excuse to go to that part of the house. "Of course. And good thing about the drapes. I'm not handy with a needle."

"One more thing. I know I said Ian would do all the serving, but I've changed my mind. I want you in the dining room as much as possible. Leave only when you need to get more food and drinks. We're still having cocktails on the landing, and of course you'll be there passing things around. You notice I haven't asked whether your suspicions have fallen on anyone yet."

"They haven't," Faith admitted.

"They will after tonight," Max said and left.

"I wish my mom could have seen some of these. Look at the beading on this one." Angela was holding up a dress that a flapper must have worn. The closet was a treasure trove of fashion. The Frosts had indulged themselves with only the best. There was a Worth wedding gown and postwar Diors. Faith thought one of these, full-skirted after fabric wasn't rationed—the "New Look"—would be perfect on Angela. Knowing what the other women would most likely be wearing, Faith didn't want Angela to appear as if she was in a costume. Dior was timeless.

As soon as she'd seen the girl hunched over her laptop, Faith had crossed her off the list again. She'd looked young—and very vulnerable. Angela couldn't be a killer. But Faith would select a killer dress. A *My Fair Lady* Pygmalion urge was taking over, and she wanted Angela to outshine everyone else.

"How about this?" Angela asked, pulling out a long gown. "Should I try it on? It looks like it would fit."

The dress was a Dior, a pale pink satin sheath erupting just above the knee in a swirl of darker taffeta pleats—what was called a "mermaid gown" these days. When Angela put it on, Faith nodded in approval. Just as she was, in stocking feet, no makeup, Angela could have been on a catwalk.

"Look at these! Too much?" Angela had unearthed a glove box and was pulling on a pair of long white kid ones.

"Not at all, especially for the cocktail hour. And here's a stole to go with the dress, it's the same fabric as the ruffles," Faith said. "Let's see if we can find some shoes."

Reluctantly putting aside a pair of black suede Joan Crawford–type heels from the 1940s, Angela agreed to Faith's choice—simple white satin heels that may have been a bride's.

"I'll take everything and air them out," Faith said. "Why don't you get dressed in the housekeeper's suite? It's off the kitchen, and if you need help with anything, I'll be close by."

"Thanks. This is so not what I usually wear! What should I do with my hair? Up or down?"

"Hmmm," Faith said. Betty's hair was short, and the other two women would probably wear theirs up—the better to show off their tans and cleavage. "How about pulled back in a ponytail at the nape of your neck with a few strands loose around your face?"

"Good. I wouldn't want anything too fussy."

There was no need to select any jewelry. Angela was still wearing the wedding ring on a chain that Faith had noticed the night before—a piece she was sure the girl hadn't taken off since her mother's death and perhaps even before that. She was wearing simple gold hoop earrings now, and they would have to do.

"Having a good time, ladies? Everybody decent?" Max called out before he stepped into the room.

"Yes," Angela said. "The clothes are incredible. Thanks, Max."

He handed her a small box. "I thought you might like something sparkly. Don't want you upstaged."

Angela opened the box and took out a large diamond stud. Even in the room's somewhat dim light, the earring shone.

"These are fantastic, but I would be too nervous that I might lose them."

"They're for you, kid. I want you to have them. And you won't lose them." Max walked toward the door. "Now, I need to talk to Ian, then it will be time for me to get myself gussied up."

Angela put out her hand to stop him and kissed his cheek. "Thank you. Thank you for everything."

Faith shooed her off. "Take a long bath or shower. Whatever relaxes you. No more schoolwork tonight."

"Aye, aye, Mrs. Fairchild," Angela said, saluting. Faith gave her a quick hug. "Go on, now—and call me Faith, please."

She made sure everything was stowed in the cedar closet and went out into the hall. When she went to get Angela, Faith hadn't had a chance to get a good look at Max's office and she also wanted to see his bedroom. She was curious to find out if it was as beautifully decorated as the rest of the house.

The office occupied a room that stretched from the front of the house to the back. A large arched triptych window overlooked the meadows. The top panes were Tiffany stained glass. Elsewhere the room was adorned with what Faith had expected to see all over the house—framed posters of Max's hits, awards, photos with stars and other famous figures. She didn't linger. Max would be back soon to get dressed, so she walked rapidly down the hall, opening doors as she went—more closets and one small bath—until she found the bedroom.

It wasn't sumptuous, although it was large with a picture window overlooking the view from the front veranda outside the summer parlor. But the room was spartan. It looked more like a monk's cell than a Broadway luminary's. Or, Faith realized, like the room assigned to him as a boy. The bed, a simple double one, had been neatly made. There was a chest of drawers, an armchair by the window, several bookcases, and an uncarpeted floor with a small plain beige throw rug by the bed. This wouldn't have been

the setting for Alexis's birthday gift earlier. That must have oc-
curred in her room.

Faith couldn't risk exploring any longer. There must be a
dressing room, given the clothes she'd seen him wear, and a bath.
She didn't want to be caught prying.

Max Dane the ascetic. Was there no end to the roles this man
played?

Although it had been late when she got home—after the movie,
a drink at the Sligo Pub had seemed like a good idea—Samantha
was up early the next morning and called her grandmother.

"Hi, Granny, it's going to be another cold one and they're
talking about sleet and freezing rain moving in. I'm on a later shift
today and I thought I'd drive in, so I could come straight to you
and spend the night afterward." She hadn't had a sleepover at her
grandmother's in years. But if Austin Stebbins were still there, it
wouldn't be the kind of fun she had in mind. Popping some corn
and watching their favorite movies. With this in mind, she added,
"Um, do you still have company staying?"

"No," Ursula replied. "I'm on my own, and it would be delightful to have you."

Samantha didn't think it was her imagination. When her grandmother had said she was on her own, her voice seemed to catch.

Even though it would be well past Ursula's dinnertime, Samantha decided to make some stroganoff using chicken instead of
beef. It would do for Sunday dinner with noodles, and she'd bring
some of the butternut squash soup she had in the freezer in case
Ursula wanted more than popcorn late tonight. There was a loaf
of Faith's semolina bread, too. They could have toasted cheese.

Satisfied with her plans, she turned off all the dripping faucets
for now and went back to bed. She was tired and she'd been having such a nice dream . . .

When she got up the second time, she decided to add an apple crumb cobbler to her menu. Afterward, the house smelled scrumptious. As she was packing up, her phone rang. It was her manager, Ken.

"I don't know what it's doing out where you are, but it's sleeting here in sheets and all we have are the usual suspects. My nephew is with me helping and I'll put him up for the night." Ken lived on the Hill. "There's no need for anyone else to come in, especially from any distance."

Samantha knew what he meant by the usual suspects—and his tone was affectionate. They were the people who bought a tall regular most days and nursed it for hours to keep warm. Ken never turned them away.

"Thank you, Ken. My grandmother is on her own and I'd planned to go there after my shift, so I can head over now."

She finished packing the food and added a change of clothes plus one of her mother's flannel pj's. Ursula's house had a small generator, enough to keep food from spoiling and the furnace going if the power went out, but it was a big house, and its age made it impossible to fully insulate. Even without Nature's interference the rooms without fireplaces were chilly.

By the time she got to the car in the garage with her load, she was soaked, and she knew it would be worse parking in her grandmother's—Ursula no longer kept a car—and walking into the house. Somehow, the storm hadn't seemed bad from the inside. That was because it was a solid curtain of icy rain. The drive over was a slow one, and when she reached her destination, Samantha was glad she'd avoided getting hit by the numerous downed branches she saw.

"My dear child, you look like a drowned rat! Get yourself into a hot shower or tub right away," Ursula said, hugging her nevertheless. "I'll take the food—and you've done too much! There's a good fire in the living room. Come down when you're ready."

The appeal of the fire and the warmed-up stroganoff speeded Samantha along. She'd just pulled the pj's on when her phone rang. It was Zach. She'd decided it was sensible to give him his own ringtone: the theme from *The Thomas Crown Affair*, "The Windmills of Your Mind."

"I'm coming to get you and drive you home," Zach said when she picked up. "The weather is getting really bad. I'm sure your boss will let you leave early."

Samantha laughed. "He already did or rather, told me not to come in at all. But thank you. I'm at my grandmother's."

"Good. I'm going to head home now, but if you need anything, call?"

"I will. Love you."

The way she automatically said good-bye to her family slipped out and she was about to make a joke or something—say something!—when after a pause, Zach said, "You know, Samantha, I'm pretty sure I love you, too."

Samantha ran down the stairs, feeling a burst of energy. Her grandmother was building up the fire in the living room. She looked up and said, "That's better. You look very pink and rosy now."

"Would you like some of the stroganoff I made or some soup? Faith brought bread over the other day and I can do toasted cheese. And I have an apple cobbler."

"It all sounds very tempting. But let's just sit and relax a moment. Always lovely to be indoors on nights like this—not fit for man nor beast. You could get me a little of my brandy and some for yourself, or whatever else you see."

Samantha went to get the drinks. As she poured the brandy for Ursula and a glass of wine for herself, she wondered how to introduce the subject of Mr. Stebbins's departure. Or should she say nothing at all?

She brought Ursula her drink and said, "Well, this is fun. Like the old days when I would come for the whole weekend. Except when you had your brandy, I drank ginger ale with a maraschino cherry, not wine."

"I believe there is probably a jar of them somewhere still," Ursula said.

They sipped in companionable silence for a moment and then Samantha's curiosity could contain itself no longer. As casually as she could, she asked, "So, did Mr. Stebbins find an apartment on the Hill or somewhere else in town?"

Ursula put her drink down and looked at her granddaughter steadily. "Not an apartment exactly. I'll tell you what happened with Austin if you tell me what happened with Caleb and why you're back in Aleford."

Reflecting that her grandmother had always been a savvy horse trader, Samantha took a deep breath and told her the sorry tale, ending with Caleb's arrival at the house with the U-Haul and her mother's reaction.

"Oh, I wish I had been there, too," Ursula said, smiling broadly. "I would have taken a switch to him! But I'm sorry, Samantha. A broken heart is not a cause for levity."

"Is that what has happened to you?" Samantha said gently.

"Not broken, maybe nicked slightly. Let's move to the kitchen, heat up the soup and some of that bread—it will be fine just toasted by itself with butter—and I'll tell you all about it."

Ursula started talking even before Samantha ladled out the soup. "Austin didn't do anything terrible. In fact, I'm sure in his mind he was pursuing a sensible course of action."

"Why do I doubt I would agree?" Samantha said as she put all the food on the table. By tacit agreement Ursula and she sat on the side of the round table away from the windows and stormy scene outside.

"Because you're delightfully biased. This soup is delicious!"

"Okay, keep going. I know the soup's good, but what I don't know is what this Austin person did."

"I've heard that men who have been happily married are at quite

a loss when their spouse dies and waste little time looking for a replacement. Austin was lonely. He said so, and I believe him. He also
wanted to come back east, the place he always considered home.
Combining a return and a search for a bride made sense. Very ef-
ficient. I think you know he had been a successful businessman."

"Sounds pretty calculating to me."

Ursula shook her head. "No, it really wasn't. He knew where
he wanted to be and the kind of woman he wanted. The kind he
had grown up with. Someone like me—or Mary Cabot. She's
Pritchett now and widowed as am I."

It was all Samantha could do to keep from reacting, both to
the name and her grandmother's tone.

"Mary is a few years younger than I but was at Winsor, as was
Austin's sister. Austin got in touch with the school with a list of
names he remembered and hit upon someone sympathetic."

"Or not up on rules about giving out private information,"
Samantha said.

"I'm *glad* he found me, sweetheart. You have no idea. He knew
my late brother and all sorts of other people who have passed away.
It was a joy to bring them back."

"I'm losing you here, Granny. Happy or sad?"

"Oh, happy; but a bit embarrassed. Austin was shopping for a
wife. He and Mary are affianced now. He's living at his club until
the nuptials. I'm afraid my head was turned by the attention he
was paying me. When he told me he had proposed to Mary and
she had accepted I felt like a fool. You probably didn't notice, but
I actually bought some new clothes!"

"There's nothing wrong with updating a wardrobe every now
and then," Samantha said. Her grandmother looked skeptical. In
Maine she still wore outerwear that had been her mother's.

"I wouldn't have accepted his proposal and I'm sure he realized
that very quickly, which is why he must have continued on down
the list. But it was still a slightly unpleasant surprise to find I had
been displaced."

"Oh dear," Samantha said, moving over to hug her grand-mother close.

"It was nice to have some male companionship at Symphony, and the museums. And he does have extremely good taste when it comes to restaurants."

Samantha was trying to decide whether to believe her grandmother—that Austin moved on because he knew she was unattainable, or to believe he was after a higher priced model.

Granny read her mind, or rather her expression. "Mary is considerably more comfortable than I am." In New England parlance Samantha knew "comfortable" meant not ever having to watch your pennies. "But I am sure that is not why Austin is marrying her. He will now be living mere steps from his boyhood home. I've already given him my congratulations and said I will attend the wedding at the Boston Athenaeum. So that's it."

They cleaned up the kitchen and popped some corn. As Samantha turned out the light before they went back to the fire, she said, "Men!"

"Amen," Ursula replied.

As Faith walked up the stairs to the landing with a tray of Deviled Eggs, she thought back to the wording of Max's invitation: "Come as you are—or be cast." She felt as if she were walking onto a stage set. A Noël Coward drawing room comedy or Agatha Christie country house murder mystery. The men were all in formal wear of various vintages and the women in stunning gowns and jewels. Eve was in white again—her signature? This time the wow factor was revealed when she turned around and the demure high-necked Grecian drape dipped precipitously below her waist. Alexis was in black lace over silk that so closely matched her skin it appeared she was nude underneath. And Betty had abandoned what Faith was sure was her usual color choice—black—for a Fortuny-like pleated column of silver silk. But no one looked as exquisite as Angela, Faith was happy to note.

The lighting was kind to all. Firelight and subtle dimmed lights in the ceiling. The wainscoting glowed and the flickering flames picked out the colors of the Persian carpet. Max was glowing too, and Faith saw Ian give him a tumbler of what looked like scotch. It was the first drink Faith had noted all weekend. Most of the others were drinking champagne, which added to the elegance of the scene. A few had Fallen Angel cocktails. The conversation was muted, a pleasant hum.

The other hors d'oeuvres were on a table next to the bar cart Ian was using. The baked varieties that needed to stay hot were on warming platters. Faith passed the eggs and then went to make up a tray with all the selections. She slipped among the guests, the unobtrusive, invisible help, and as she did she pictured the various faces on cards—like a game of Clue. Tom's family, as well as the Millers, were board game aficionados and there were versions of Clue in all their homes. Ursula even had the British original Cluedo.

With the delivery of the casket, Max had been cast from the start as "Mr. Boddy," the victim, by one of the people in front of her. Who? Phil Baker had the look of Colonel Mustard and Adrian, Professor Plum. Eve could be Mrs. White, and Betty Mrs. Peacock, leaving Miss Scarlett for Alexis. The Reverend Green? James Nelson? Candlesticks were everywhere in the house. The other weapons: a rope, dagger, lead pipe, and wrench not so obvious. Nor was the revolver, which was still, she assumed, tucked in the kitchen drawer. She continued to shuffle the cards mentally. The guests, i.e. suspects, were in the hall now and would soon proceed to the dining room. All the other rooms in the game were present in the house, some with slightly altered names.

She was startled from her thoughts by the sound of someone tapping the side of a glass for attention. It was Max Dane. "I want to thank you for coming to help me start my next decade on what I hope will be a happier note than when we were last assembled."

"Hear, hear," Chip Frost said. He had an empty Fallen Angel glass in one hand, and from his flushed cheeks had fallen for a few others.

"Soon we will partake of what I am sure will be a heavenly and devilishly delicious dinner prepared by Mrs. Fairchild, during which I hope the conversation will be the same. I haven't had a chance to talk with some of you and want to know what everyone has been up to these last years. James, for example, we had a devil of a time locating you—and please everyone pardon the puns. After all, the musical is why we are here, isn't it? Adrian, you dropped off the radar as well."

James didn't respond, but Adrian said, "I was going to tell you at the end of the meal, but might as well now." He was the best-dressed man there—and not for the first time, Faith reflected on life's unfairness that made even the most homely of men look great in a tux. Tonight, Adrian, not bad-looking to start, was in white tie. He could have been about to present credentials at the Court of St. James.

"Do tell," Max said. "Ian, fill the man's glass up. Top up everyone's glass while you're at it."

As Ian poured drinks Faith passed the tray and then positioned herself by the Minton-tiled fireplace, where she could see all the guests.

Adrian had a pleasant speaking voice. "After *Heaven or Hell* closed, a friend offered me a cottage in Cornwall where I was to write my next dramatic opus. I did not merely experience writer's block, but the equivalent of writer's Stonehenge. I spent my days walking the countryside and my nights listening to storytellers in the local pub. They didn't think of themselves as storytellers, I'm sure, but that is what they were. The local woman who came in and did for me had been housekeeper to one of the 'gentry' and she had tales as well. Like Athena from the head of Zeus, an entire plot sprang up on one of my walks. I raced back and wrote a novel. A love story. Upon my return to London, my agent convinced me to adopt a nom de plume. For reasons of my own, I selected the name, Fiona Foster-Fordham."

Someone gasped and every face save Max's and Ian's registered extreme surprise—had they known? Faith wondered. Or simply stoic. Phil Baker said, "Jeezus, Adrian, you must be bringing it home in bushel baskets!"

Adrian took a sip of his drink. "Yes, I have had gratifying success."

Betty laughed. "But all you care about are your devoted readers, right?" Her sarcasm was more than tinged with envy.

"No, in fact, Betty, what I most care about is the money. I live in Eaton Square, have a manor house in the Cotswolds not unlike Morris's Kelmscott and a villa in the south of France—that a bit too predictable for those in my income bracket, but pleasant. England is so very rainy. Much like tonight." Clearly he was enjoying the put-down with its opulently detailed list.

Max put down his drink and started clapping. "Good on you, as you Brits say. I could always spot talent. Now anyone else have something to reveal or shall we go down to dinner?"

The room was quiet, and for a moment it seemed everyone was waiting for someone else to speak.

"I'm for hitting the old feedbag," Chip said, a bit too loudly. "No secret about what I've been doing, right, Max? A bit of this and that. Mostly that. It pretty much adds up to nothing. But I'm not complaining, cuz. Not complaining one little bit."

They'd arranged that Ian would see to cleaning up what was left on the landing while Faith plated the lobster Fra Diavolo pasta first course. On the way to the kitchen, she took one last look at the dining room to be sure everything was still perfect. Max wanted the Black Magic roses from the summer parlor moved to the sideboard here and placed in front of the large gilt-framed mirror that hung on the wall behind it. In addition to the roses, the mirror also reflected the table. The florist had created a low centerpiece with a number of small orchids. No fragrance and easy to see across. Max had told Faith to select whatever setting she wanted and she'd picked a Spode cobalt and gold-rimmed service with Tiffany gold vermeil Audubon flatware. Judging from some of the furniture and many of the paintings, she was certain he had purchased the contents of Frostcliffe as well as the house itself. The china and cutlery both appeared vintage. He'd approved of her choices and said he would do the seating placement himself. Ian had lettered place cards and Faith had found sterling holders, each a different bird that she was sure must have been selected to go with the Tiffany pattern.

Max was at the head of the table, and he'd put Angela on his right, Betty on his left. Phil was next to Angela, then Alexis, James, and Chip. On the other side Tony was next to Betty, then Eve, Travis and Adrian. Max had not picked a hostess—or host—to sit opposite him.

Besides the roses, Faith had placed the desserts on the sideboard: the two devil's food cakes, Angel Food Cake, and the *Heaven or Hell* mini cupcakes. There was a mixed berry coulis for the Angel Food Cake and a fruit epergne waiting in the refrigerator. She'd taken the four elaborate Victorian candelabras that had been on the long table and moved them to the sideboard as well, the tall tapers waiting to be lit. Max had said he wasn't sure he wanted them illuminated. Too over-the-top, or fear of fire? She would light the votives, which were etched with a delicate lace pattern and placed in abundance on the white damask tablecloth. There needed to be some candlelight as the chandelier, per Max and Ian's instruction, was dimmed. Coffee and after-dinner drinks would be served back in the foyer by the piano with plates of *friandises*—sweetmeats—and chocolates.

She heard the guests making their way down the hall and

darted into the kitchen to serve the pasta. Outside she could see the storm was getting worse. The lights had flickered a few times on the landing. She'd reached Tom earlier and he told her Pix had been worried about Ursula, but Samantha was going to be with her. No mention of Ursula's recent lodger, Faith noted. Had Austin Stebbins finally moved? The storm was to the south of Loon, Tom told her, and the skiing was incredible. He'd asked how things were going, and she'd answered all was well and that the house had some sort of behemoth generator, so they would be fine. "See you tomorrow night," he'd said cheerfully and in haste. She knew the slopes were beckoning.

Ian walked in with a full tray, which he set on the counter nearest one of the dishwashers. "You can deal with these later. We need to get the food out. I'll start pouring wine. You've filled the water glasses?"

Tempted as she was to say "Yes, master," Faith just nodded. "I can start bringing these in now while you open the wine."

Ian got busy with a corkscrew and also popped more champagne. Nothing had been placed out opened, the foil covering the corks intact. She left him to it and went across to the dining room with the loaded tray, which she set out in the hall on the stand she'd set up for service.

She'd saved the claw meat for a devilish-looking touch on top of each serving. Ian had lettered small menus for each place, so the guests would know what they were eating. If anyone had a problem with lobster, he or she didn't say, and everyone started to eat immediately, save Alexis. Even Eve was digging in—food to soak up the alcohol? She had been drinking almost as much as Chip Frost. Faith watched James take a bite and then look over to where she was standing by the door in a corner. "These have to have come from Maine, Penobscot Bay. Best in the world." They had, but Faith kept mum. She wanted to blend into the woodwork.

While Ian cleared the first course, Faith slipped out to plate the next. She disliked those fussy food towers so difficult to eat and an indication that the chef was more interested in presentation than the food's taste, but she did pipe rosettes of the *Himmel und Erde* potato dish and arranged green beans in neat strips. The prime rib was cooked medium rare as Max requested and smelled so good Faith was tempted to cut off a piece and pop it into her mouth. Later.

When she returned to the dining room, the first thing she noticed was that Max had another full tumbler of what she was sure was his favorite scotch with very little ice. Also evident was that the air of joviality, so apparent on the landing, had now become somewhat strained. Max picked up on it as well.

"How about a bit more birthday spirit? Some of you look as if it's a wake, not a party. Speaking of which, we haven't toasted absent friends." He stood up, raised his glass, and put his other hand on Angela's shoulder. "To those not with us tonight, especially Bella Martelli. She was one of my oldest friends, besides a colleague in the theater world. To Bella."

The guests repeated the toast and Angela said, "Thank you. I've been thinking of her all night. And we should also remember Jack Gold. I always called him Uncle Jack. He made me an amazing dollhouse and kept adding furniture for years. After my mother was too sick to leave the apartment, he'd come with fun presents, and he always cheered her up."

Max nodded. "A good guy and very talented. Tragic what happened. To Jack."

Again the toast was repeated and a few of the guests started to eat, but the tension in the air was more marked than before. It might have been because the lights flickered, but Faith thought not.

Tony Ames, who had been keeping a low profile all weekend so far as Faith could tell, broke the ice. With a sledgehammer. "You wanted to know what we'd all been doing for the last twenty years, Max. Well, we've heard from Adrian and we know about Alexis, although the role she played in the sitcom may not have been her career goal. Your cousin has survived in some manner outside the theater. As for most of the rest of us, we couldn't put *Heaven or Hell* on our résumés. It would have been the kiss of death. Even so, word got around. Travis is singing in a piano bar, Jack never got meaningful jobs again, and depression literally took his life. Phil is writing jingles, Eve doing ads for God knows what, Betty probably resting on her laurels, and as for me I get a gig now and then for some musical theater in the burbs and teach Boomers how to swing dance in adult ed. So, let's have it Max. Why did you really pull the plug? On the musical and on us?"

There was dead silence, and when it was apparent that Max wasn't going to answer, James Nelson spoke. "Yes, I went off the grid. All I had ever wanted to do was direct, and, Max, you made me feel completely worthless. I hit bottom and then a friend helped me crawl my way back. Much like the friend who loaned Adrian a cottage in Cornwall, this friend gave me his cabin on an island in Maine to use for as long as I wanted, eventually leaving it to me. In between, I went back to school. Back to my second love after the theater, now my first. The natural world. Since I finished my degree work, I've been involved in expeditions all over the planet, charting the flights of birds and mating habits of turtles. But Tony's question stayed with me as well. The reviews weren't that horrible. Tepid. And there were a lot of easy fixes. You knew that when we were out of town in Boston. It was as if you wanted a deliberate failure. One straight out of *The Producers,* only you didn't get a hit by accident."

No one was eating now, all eyes were on Max. His head was bowed. When he raised it, Faith was stunned to see the anguish on his face.

"You have a right to hate me and I know one of you does to the utmost extent."

No one said a word. Max drained his glass and Ian took it from him. Max waved him away.

"I needed a placeholder."

"For your revival that moved in right afterward," James said bitterly. "I've been digging, Max, and it's what I came up with. Only it wasn't quite the success you thought it would be. Revivals are funny that way. Even yours. So you took your money and ran here."

"Pretty much," Max admitted. His voice was steady. "The revival was in production. You all knew that, right? Or maybe not. I should have found places for you in it, but there weren't any that fit. The show before *Heaven or Hell* had had a three-year run and let's say it was part ego—there had been a Max Dane show on Broadway since Noah—and part business. I didn't want to invest much. You all came cheap. No, that doesn't sound right. I'm sorry."

He reached out his hand and Ian put another drink in it.

"Is this why you invited us here?" Betty asked. "To relieve you of your guilt? Let you die after a full confession?"

"No," Max said. "That's not why, and only one person here knows that. Unless this is a remake of *Murder on the Orient Express*."

Chip stood up, swaying slightly. "Got to see a man about a horse. Be right back." He left the room. Faith could smell the alcohol on him as he passed by.

Angela was facing Max. "Is that why you sent the checks?" she said. "You felt guilty about my mother not being able to get a job?"

Max shook his head. "Bella could have gotten a job easily and"—he looked around the table—"some of the rest of you with real talent could have or did. Bella wanted steady work to be there for you, Angela. I was the conduit for the child support money. That's all. I wanted to add to it and did sometimes, but your mother was very proud. She wasn't about to take handouts, even from me. Just what she thought was right from your father."

Angela was flushed, although Faith had noticed she hadn't finished even one glass of champagne. The young woman looked very angry. "So who is he? Is he here at this table?" She smacked it with her hand.

"Such drama," Alexis said, drawing the words out. "Honestly, Max, I was mad for a while. I thought if you had given me the part I should have played, it would have led to a row of Tonys on the mantel. So, I got a row of Emmys instead—it was a more than decent sitcom role, Mr. Ames—and a shitload of money. Like Adrian, it was a lucky break for me the show closed. Probably for James, too. So please blow out your candles, eat some cake, and bring this production to an end. My flight leaves at one tomorrow and it can't be soon enough." She turned to Angela, "And, honey, no one cares who slept with your mother."

Faith thought Angela was going to deck Alexis. She leaned across Phil Baker and said, "Don't you ever say anything about my mother again! In fact, don't say anything to me at all!"

As she finished the sentence, the lights went out. Eve let out a small scream before they came on almost immediately.

"Please no one be concerned," Ian said. "We have an ample generator that starts automatically."

Faith had left matches on the service cart in the hall, got them, and started lighting the tapers in the candelabras on the sideboard. She doubted anyone noticed. Despite Ian's reassurance, she wanted to be sure there was some reliable light in the room.

"Angela asked you a question, Max," Betty said. "Is he here? Is her father one of your guests?"

"That's for him to say," Max answered.

Betty directed her next comments across the table at her former husband. "You always had an eye for her, Phil," she said. "Her daughter looks much like Bella. Both beautiful women, and beautiful women were always your thing, weren't they? It's you, isn't it? And Jack knew. You'd see him whenever you were in town, and I never figured you for friends. Jack—unlike you—was a decent person."

"You think you're so smart," Phil lashed out. "You have no idea what the guy was like."

"But you *are* Angela's father?" Tony said. "I always thought you were the likely candidate. Jack told me Bella was in love with you and thought you'd leave Betty. Then when Betty left you, she must have thought you'd do the right thing and marry her. The baby would already have been born. But that isn't you, is it? Max found out and made you pay up?"

"I'm sure Mrs. Fairchild can drum up Baggies for some DNA samples," Eve said. "I've got plenty of Q-tips. Okay by you, Phil? We all want to know."

Angela was visibly shrinking away from the man next to her. Max, Faith realized, had deliberately placed them next to each other. Had he also said something to Betty, or Tony? To goad Phil? After Angela's arrival last night had he planned for this revelation to provide closure for the girl? But it was a horrible way to find out.

Faith wanted to go over and get Angela out of there. Leave herself. This was not what she had bargained for. All these ugly secrets exposed, each more damning than the next. But she couldn't. There was still a possible killer at large—or so Max claimed. Had he sent the casket to himself? Was it all staged?

"I couldn't let you find out, Betty," Phil pleaded. "I loved you. I've always loved you. It was a slip."

"And the slip is sitting next to you," Betty said acidly. "I'm sorry, Angela. Your mother was a lovely person, but I'm afraid you lost big time when it came to a father."

For a moment, Betty seemed lost in thought and no one else said anything. She started to speak again, slowly—her words were dripping with hatred. "You pushed him, didn't you, Phil? He didn't fall or jump. You wanted him out of the way before coming here. You knew Bella had just died and Max was the only one left with the truth." Her horror-stricken face was duplicated on some around the table.

"I never even saw him!" Phil screamed. "Why would I get rid of him? Yeah, the money had been bleeding me dry for years, but she's an adult now. It was almost all done."

"Such devotion," Tony Ames murmured.

"Look, Angela," Max said. "I can't tell you to forget all this, but now you know why your mother had the money come through me. She never wanted to see Phil again, but she also wanted to make sure he paid. I'd know if he didn't. Alexis is right. Let's call it a night? Have a little cake and all turn in?"

It was hard to read Angela's face—disgust, disappointment, anger. Faith saw traces of all these and something else. Relief? "I wanted to know," she said. "It's why I came. I'm just sorry it's not you. This man here means nothing. He's a stranger and I intend to keep it that way. I was his slip, that's all."

Travis Trent had been quiet all evening. Faith had the impression that he was not a very talkative person. Someone who could produce the right patter when needed but otherwise an observer. He rose partly from his chair. "Phil, if I find out you had anything to do with Jack Gold's death—and I am making it my business to find out—I'll kill you myself."

He sat back down. "Now Max is right. Time to wind things up."

That was Faith's cue. She and Ian quickly cleared the plates and she went out to the kitchen for the fruit and the fruit coulis. When she got back, Ian was putting candles on one of the devil's food cakes. Max saw them and said, "No candles and let's ditch the song, too. I've had about as much birthday as I can take. Pour more drinks and let Mrs. Fairchild serve dessert."

It was Faith's impression that several people had left to freshen up during the main course of the meal, but Chip had still not returned. She took orders and sliced the cakes. She'd expected no one would be hungry, but after the startling revelations the *Heaven or Hell* guests were ravenous. The cupcakes and fruit were disappearing, too. Even Alexis took some.

When Faith served Max, he whispered to her, "Find Chip. He's loaded and apt to do something stupid like fall down the stairs."

Adrian had gotten up. He was walking toward the window to

look at the storm and overhearing said, "I passed him in the hall a while ago and he was none too steady. I think he was going into your library, Max, to sober up."

"Not likely. But he does know where I keep the booze in there. Start in the library, Mrs. Fairchild."

Faith had seen enough dead bodies to recognize one immediately, and Charles Frost was dead. He had taken off his jacket and was slumped over Max's large desk in his shirtsleeves, one arm hanging down from the chair, the other tucked below the desk. All the lights were on, and as she went over to check his pulse, she noticed something odd on the desktop: a snake hook. She knew what it was because Ben's friend Josh went through a pet snake phase and Ben agreed to feed the corn snake when Josh's family was on vacation. Faith didn't want Ben doing it alone, although the snake was harmless, and went with him. The experience fortunately did not have to be repeated, as Josh's mother convinced him a dog would be more fun. "No more mice," she'd told Faith. "I couldn't take it anymore. Cleaning up after a puppy is a joy."

Did Max have a heptarium? She looked on the other side of the desk. There was a small crate, the top open and a screen unhinged. She'd have to go get Max and call the police.

The door opened and James Nelson stepped into the room, closing it behind him. "With everything happening tonight, I thought I should follow you and see if I could help with Chip. Dear God! What's happened? Is he . . ."

"Yes." The word stuck in Faith's throat and she couldn't get another out. Something had happened here. Something unnatural.

"That's a snake hook," James said, moving toward the body, "which means there must be a snake." He walked behind Chip. "His hand is in the drawer." He pulled out a handkerchief and opened the drawer wide. There was a small slender snake curled up in the far corner.

"Well, what do you know! A coral snake. There's an old rhyme: Red and black, friend of Jack. Red and yellow can kill a fellow."

The snake had bright red and yellow bands.

James pushed the drawer back to the original position. "The problem with these creatures is that the head and tail look the same. It can be fatal if you get the wrong end. If he had been given an antivenom immediately he might be alive. The bite causes rapid paralysis and respiratory failure."

Faith had been listening to the natural history lesson, frozen in place. She unfroze. "There's a landline in the kitchen to call the police. I'll go tell Max."

As they left she used her apron to remove the key from inside the door and lock the room from outside.

So it had been cousin Chip in the end. He would have known how to deliver the coffin, casting suspicion on any number of people. He hadn't expected to be a guest, but he'd have been able to slip into the house and library almost anytime tonight. If he hadn't made his fatal mistake, the snake would be waiting for Max. Since Ian was leaving on vacation, Faith remembered, no one would come to Max's aid in time. Faith knew from Ben that poisonous and nonpoisonous snakes could be purchased easily online. He'd wanted a pet when Josh got his and showed her the sites. She'd been appalled.

Nelson headed for the kitchen and Faith back to the dining room. It was over, but she felt wretched.

She watched to see that James found the kitchen and then the lights went out.

And stayed out.

The candles shone brightly and unlike the last time Faith entered the room, the atmosphere had cleared and it merely seemed that people were tired. Ian was pouring more wine for some of them. She went up to Max. "Could you come into the kitchen and show me where the flashlights are so the guests can find their way upstairs?" She assumed that all their cell phones were in their rooms, so they couldn't use those.

In the kitchen she told him about Chip and that James had come in after her.

"My cousin was last on my list, except Angela. I invited him in the end because I wanted someone who I thought had some family feeling for me. Well, he did," he said bitterly. "His mother and he quickly went through the Frost money. I'd offered to buy the house a number of times. Just before she died, my aunt agreed but with the stipulation that when I died the house would go back to Chip—'a real Frost' I think she said. Over the years he hit up some distant cousins for money, took a job or two, and finally started to borrow from me against his expectations. I guess at this point he wanted the lump sum—what was left—from the sale of the property. Even subtracting what he owed me, it would have been a considerable amount. I want to hope his motivation was desperation. And not pure animosity."

James Nelson came in the back door, drenched. "I went to see why the generator wasn't going on. The landline is dead, and I'm not getting any cell signal even out in the open field. We need to get the police as soon as possible, although they might have a problem getting up the drive."

"Ian made sure it was treated and the gate can be operated manually if the power goes off."

"Take my van, James," Faith said. "It has four-wheel drive, and I'll write out directions to the Weston police in case the GPS doesn't work. They're the closest. Or maybe Ian should go. He must know where the station is."

No," Max said abruptly. "I need him here. There are flashlights in the pantry, Faith. Bring them in and I'll tell everyone that Chip has met with an accident. No need for details now. If they don't want to go to their rooms, I'll light the fire in the winter parlor and people can sit there."

As Faith handed James her keys, he said grimly, "I'm ninety-nine point one percent sure that someone tampered with the generator. I've been trying to think who was in the room when Ian told me where it was and it's almost everyone."

Before the police arrived, Max told Faith and Ian he had changed his mind. "They're not stupid. They'll know something's up." He ushered everyone into the parlor and told them that a rare snake Chip intended to give Max as a birthday present had tragically bitten the giver—"Chip knew of my plans to add a heptarium in the conservatory." He forestalled any speculation by advising everyone to get some sleep. When it was apparent no one wanted to be alone in the dark guestrooms, Ian lit a fire in the fireplace and Faith offered coffee or other drinks. The two of them left the room and Ian said, "I'll clear the dining room table."

"The police will want everything left as is," Faith said.

"As you would best know," he said, and the admiring note in his voice surprised her.

The local police arrived, soon followed by the state police. Faith's friend and sometime partner Detective Lieutenant John Dunne had retired, but Faith recognized one of his colleagues. Although it was supposed an accidental death, the library was treated as a crime scene. The coroner had been held up by the storm, but the police brought bright lights, and Faith showed them the small breakfast room where they could take statements. Ian took one of them out to the generator in the hope they could get it working. Power was out in all the neighboring towns.

By four in the morning, having ruled the death accidental, the police had packed up and left, expressing condolences to Max on the death of his cousin. All were free to leave, and since they were still unable to phone, Ian asked one of the local police to get in touch with the car service and have them send a van, not individual cars, as soon as they were able. He advised the guests to change, pack, and grab some sleep.

"I'll do that on the plane," Eve said. "I don't want to close my eyes for a minute in this place."

Faith had been keeping an eye on Angela all night. The girl was obviously both mentally and physically exhausted. She took her into the housekeeper's room and then went to get her books from the office and bag from the upstairs guestroom. Angela changed and lay down on the bed. She was asleep instantly.

The guests, Max, and Ian had spent the night in the parlor by the fire, but Faith had put her down coat on and stayed in the kitchen. Restless, she tried to tidy things up but decided to leave everything after a few attempts. Seized with a sense of foreboding, she did accomplish one task . . .

Power was restored at seven. As soon as Faith heard the hum of the refrigerator, she got up from the chair where she had been drowsing and got to work on breakfast for those who might want some. The van arrived at ten and drove off in the brilliant sunshine. The storm had passed and the only noise was a steady drip from the melting ice on the trees and roof of the house.

Max entered the kitchen, having seen his guests off, and Faith quelled her impulse to hug him. Chat's words came back—"Max Dane is not a nice man." And what he had done with *Heaven or Hell* was not nice. Still the weekend, and days leading up to it, had revealed another side. The side shown in his shattered face. "Angela is moving into the apartment I keep in the city and will start Columbia Law in the fall. She got a scholarship and at first didn't want me to pay—just like Bella—but I pointed out she'd be depriving another student, and she gave in. I'm hoping she'll want to stay in touch with me."

"I think she will," Faith said. "How about some coffee? Breakfast?"

"Just coffee, thank you." He sat at the counter, staring out the windows at the beautiful winter scene unfolding, snow sparkling.

She set a full cup down in front of him and went back to putting things away. She'd used some toby jugs for cream and the coulis. Ian came in, dressed in a handsome topcoat and pulling a large Louis Vuitton travel bag.

"I had hoped, no assumed, you'd put your trip off for a while," Max said.

"No, I'm afraid not. I won't be putting anything off now, Max." His hand went into his pocket and he pulled out a gun, aiming it at Max. "Poor Chip. He thought the snake was harmless and a joke. I slipped him some cash when I gave it to him with my instructions. I was sure the fool was so trashed he'd muff it and get bitten. If not, I made sure the generator wouldn't work and I'd have been able to get the pet to do its work."

Max stood up. "Ian! What—"

"No, enough talking. I've been listening to you for too many years." Ian had put his other hand up, gesturing that Max stop. "And now, your casket is in the icehouse ready and waiting. Unfortunately, Mrs. Fairchild will have to join you. As they say in detective novels, she knows too much. Did you tell her I was your principal beneficiary? Maybe not. You're so very private. I certainly didn't know that the man you referred to as 'cuz' was such a close blood relative until the other day in the summer parlor. Bit of a shock. Meant he had to go—could have been a problem if he contested."

"Ian," Max screamed. "I can't believe this!"

It was as if Max hadn't said a word. Ian showed no emotion whatsoever. "They built those icehouses well back in the day; your screams will be unheard." His eyes continued to be fixed on Max even as he addressed Faith. "Mrs. Fairchild, I'm afraid in the course of the job you became enamored of your boss. The guilt at cheating on your husband, a man of the cloth, was so great that murder-suicide was the result. Max, thought by many to be an insane recluse, took you to where he had placed the coffin. The one, incidentally, it will be found, Max, you ordered yourself. The receipt is on your desk upstairs now with instructions for delivery."

Ian was grinning. "The casket. So brilliant. I knew you would fall for it, Max. And my suggestion that Mrs. Fairchild, because of her reputation as a sleuth, do the catering. I knew she would not pose a problem for me, and I was right. You fell for that, too. You were in control. Calling the shots as always. It was always about you."

Happy that Ian was so loquacious, Faith backed up against the cupboard where she'd been putting the toby jugs. She slipped her arm behind her back. Ian was still focused on Max, who looked as if he was about to faint. After his last exclamation he hadn't opened his mouth, set in a tight line.

Faith opened the drawer and took out the gun. The one fit for a woman.

She aimed it at Ian who, noticing her at last, began to laugh uproariously. "Oh, good try, but of course I removed the bullets!"

"And I put them back." An impulse last night in the dark. She'd easily found them in one of the jugs. She pulled the trigger and the first shot went wild. The second hit him squarely on target—his kneecap. He fell to the floor screaming, and Faith grabbed a decorative but heavy copper saucepan, striking him firmly on the head.

It hadn't been any of the invited guests after all. It was Mrs. Fairchild in the kitchen with a revolver. And Ian was Mr. Boddy.

CHAPTER 11

Aleford might be sentimental about Valentine's Day in private, but when a public meeting was scheduled on the date, people were expected to leave their wine and roses and show up. Since this was a Planning Board meeting, there was no hesitation. Rumors about the change in the developer's proposal had been rife, and when Bradley Peters presented his completely altered plan for an assisted living and affordable housing facility the room actually broke into applause. Faith looked at her husband. It had been his idea—he thought. Blake Sommersby was whispering something in Tom's ear. Congratulations, no doubt.

Patsy Avery had told Faith why Blake had moved out to Aleford. Ms. Sommersby decided the clock was ticking too fast and was pregnant. Knowing Patsy and Will, she decided Aleford would be a fine place to raise a child. The pregnancy explained why she had refused coffee and opted for mint tea, Faith realized. Tonight Patsy revealed that Blake's significant other had recently proposed. He'd decided he very much wanted to be a dad and raise a family after all. Patsy was giving Blake a combined wedding/baby shower soon. And no, Patsy, a fine cook, was doing it all herself. Faith was not to take one step into the Averys' kitchen, but be a guest.

After the scene in Rowan House's kitchen, the police arrived swiftly for the second time in twenty-four hours. When Tom got back from Loon that night, Faith had had to give him an account of the weekend—word had already spread. She left a number of things out—the casket for instance—but enough was revealed that Tom once again begged his wife to avoid the kinds of perilous situations she seemed all too eager to seek out. "What would I do without you?" he repeated over and over again. While the three days had shaken her from the kind of doldrums she'd been experiencing, Faith found herself promising no more such gigs. And meant it. This one had been murderous on too many levels.

Pix and Faith were in the back of the room as usual and had been talking softly. "Samantha got a cute valentine from Zach. Like the ones kids put in the valentine box at school," Pix said. Faith remembered how much fun it had been to open the little cards. "I'm a Sucker for You" and "You Auto Be My Valentine."

"They seem good together," Faith said.

"I think so. And she loves the new job." Samantha had been headhunted at the recommendation of her former firm, accepting a position with a Boston-based philanthropic foundation. "She says giving away money instead of making it for people is what she should have been doing from the start."

Marian Cho was taking comments and questions. Even Millicent could find nothing to object to and said so. Faith let her mind drift.

Since that Sunday, Max hadn't wasted any time putting a number of things in motion besides law school for Angela. Rowan House was on the market under its former name, Frostcliffe—the contents, except for his books and theatrical memorabilia, were to be sold at auction for the benefit of the North Benet Street School, where Max's father had trained.

Max Dane was living in Manhattan and had gone back to work on none other than a revival of *Heaven or Hell*. One that would be significantly different as an off-Broadway production with a revised script by the famous British author Fiona Foster-Fordham, several new songs—lyrics by Betty Sinclair, the music introducing a new young composer she had discovered. Tony Ames was choreographing a few new numbers but keeping the opening and finale. Max had offered Alexis and Eve parts, but both had refused. Kristin Chenoweth had gotten wind of the project and it had always been her dream to be in a Max Dane production. Fiona—Adrian—was tailoring the script for her. Her involvement might mean Broadway after all. Max wanted James Nelson to direct, but was firmly told no. James liked his life just the way it was, but would be happy to look at early run-throughs and offer an opinion. Max had the drawings for Jack Gold's set and wanted to duplicate them—as well as Bella's costume designs.

When he heard that a performer at Manhattan's famed Café Carlyle had to cancel because of illness, Max pulled strings to get Travis the job. It turned out that fans had not forgotten Travis Trent, especially those of a certain age, well-heeled regulars at the café. Travis was already fielding offers from the Algonquin and other cabaret locations after the Carlyle job had ended. No more Atlantic City boardinghouse. At the moment, until he found an apartment, Max was putting him up in the hotel itself.

Travis was feeling mellow and very happy. He'd been playing a variety of love songs for Valentine's Day and taking requests. The venue was an intimate one, and the audience seemed in love with each other—and him.

A woman entered and walked straight to a front table.

"Play our song, Trav. Play it for me." It was Eve. He got up and led her to the piano. Sitting close they sang it together.

"Heaven or Hell
Who can tell?
Below or above
What the devil is love?"

AUTHOR'S NOTE

I'm sitting at my desk with a stack of *Playbill*s next to me. Although Max Dane's musicals are offstage in this book, Broadway has been in my mind throughout. Living in northern New Jersey, not far from Manhattan, meant growing up with theater in my family. My parents had friends who were professionals and went to Broadway and off-Broadway performances often. When we were old enough, we did too.

I wish I had the *Playbill* from the very first production I saw: Gertrude Lawrence, the famous British actress, in Rodgers and Hammerstein's *The King and I,* a matinee in 1952. The musical, which opened in 1951, had taken Broadway by storm. Rex Harrison turned down the role of the king, and Yul Brynner, who would forever be associated with it, was cast. I was quite a little girl but remember the two of them whirling about the stage to "Shall We Dance," Lawrence's hoop-skirted silk gown shimmering brightly in the spotlight. The other memory that is still so clear all these years later is of the vibrant colors—the costumes and the sets. The songs must have made an impression as well, but so many were hits that I can't be sure whether I am recalling the original experience or the repetitions. Sadly, Gertrude Lawrence died of cancer unexpectedly in September 1952 and Deborah Kerr played Anna in the film. As a first stage memory, nothing could ever equal Lawrence's elegant, vibrant figure in Brynner's arms.

My mother, Alice, and her sister Ruth loved musicals. We used to tease my aunt because she wore out the record of *Carousel,* playing it so much she had to buy a new one. We grew up knowing the lyrics to all the classic musicals. Looking over at my *Playbills* there's Robert Preston and Barbara Cook in *The Music Man*, Joel Grey in *Stop the World—I Want to Get Off* (directed by Anthony Newley), Nancy Kwan in *Flower Drum Song,* and many more. We would take our chances on a Saturday morning, going from Broadway box office to box office—we couldn't go wrong!

Starting when my cousin John and I were twelve, our mothers allowed us to go into the city on our own. While musicals were all well and good, we thought of ourselves as "serious" theatergoers. Richard Burton's *Hamlet*—I still get shivers. Albee's *Tiny Alice* with John Gielgud and Irene Worth, *The Deputy* with Emlyn Williams and a very young Jeremy Brett! Colleen Dewhurst as Miss Amelia Evans in Carson McCullers's *The Ballad of the Sad Café*. Just now looking at that *Playbill,* I notice that the artist Leonard Baskin did the cover. And inside those covers, besides reading about the play and the cast, it is and was almost as much fun to look at the ads—"Does She or Doesn't She?," "Give her L'Aimant . . . before someone else does," and listings for restaurants long gone. We always ate at one of the Automats—the best macaroni and cheese ever created or the baked beans in the little green pot.

One of our family's closest friends was the director, actor, and playwright Jack Sydow. When he was the assistant director for *Once Upon a Mattress* in 1959, he not only gave my younger sister, Anne, and me front-row matinee seats but also took us backstage afterward to meet Carol Burnett, then at the start of her illustrious career. At one point during the show, when the ladies quite literally in waiting appeared onstage, Anne had whispered to me,

"How can those ladies be pregnant without husbands?" We were so close that Burnett heard. Ushered into her dressing room later by Jack, she was laughing about it, the distinctive laugh that would become so famous. "Oh, I know who you are!" she said. It has remained a family joke for years.

Jack provided me with the amazing opportunity to be a part of a Broadway show when he directed Arthur Miller's *The Crucible* with Denholm Elliott and Farley Granger in 1964. Jack wanted to use the actual hymns as they would have been sung for certain scenes and asked me to do the research. I used the Rose Memorial Library at Drew University in Madison, New Jersey, which has an extensive collection of theological volumes and manuscripts, including an original Bay Psalm Book. I'm looking at the *Playbill* now: page eleven, "Musical Research by Katherine Page." I was there for opening night—meeting the actors afterward—and saw it several more times in New York, and then once when it went to Philadelphia. I thought Farley Granger was the handsomest man I'd ever met and wept for him as John Proctor again and again. When the run was over, Jack gave me his director's copy of the play marked with his notes.

Jack is also the one who told my parents, after trekking out to Livingston, New Jersey, to see me as Emily in my high school junior class's production of Thornton Wilder's *Our Town*: "She was marvelous—and she should never play anything else!" I haven't.

Broadway has had its ups and downs, especially when television arrived in every household; but there's always been something like a *Wicked* or *Hamilton* to tighten any flickering lights. So many of the names I've mentioned here in this Author's Note—what I always refer to as stepping from behind the curtain—won't be familiar to many readers, but the productions will be, enduring as they are. There is nothing like live theater. Community productions, summer playhouses, a play reading group in a living room.

Go see a show!

P.S. Those of you who are film buffs may recognize several that informed the writing of this book: *The Wrong Box* (1966), *Sleuth* (1972 version), *Deathtrap* (1982), *Clue* (1985), and especially *Murder by Death* (1976). These also explain why Max Dane and Michael Caine became one in my imagination.

Have Faith in Your Kitchen

by Faith Sibley Fairchild
with Katherine Hall Page

Fallen Angel Cocktail

(Adapted from London's Savoy Hotel Bar)

4 ounces dry gin

1/2 ounce fresh lime juice

1/2 ounce white crème de menthe

1 dash Angostura bitters

Shake the ingredients in a cocktail shaker with ice and strain into a chilled cocktail glass. Garnish with a twist of lime or sprig of mint.

Put on a flapper headband or top hat and enjoy!

Serves 2.

Deviled Eggs

6 hard-boiled eggs, peeled

1/4 cup mayonnaise (Preferably Hellmann's or Duke's)

1/2 teaspoon Dijon mustard

Salt

Freshly ground black pepper

Paprika, smoked or plain, or Old Bay Seasoning (optional)

Halve the eggs lengthwise and scoop out the yolks. Mix with 1/4 cup mayonnaise, mustard, a pinch of salt and dash of pepper for the traditional version. Combine and add more mayo if you like a softer filling. Pipe back into the shell or use a teaspoon to fill. Sprinkle with paprika, smoked or plain, or Old Bay.

Enjoy altering this basic recipe to whatever appeals to your taste buds. Some of the things to consider adding to the yolk/mayo mixture—either stirred in or on top when stuffed back—are: capers, crumbled crisp bacon, tiny shrimp, crab, deviled ham (deviled Deviled Eggs!), chopped chives, flavored mustards, wasabi, curry powder, chutney, and of course caviar!

Platters of deviled eggs are the first items to disappear at a party or a picnic. They are not difficult to make, but somehow we don't make them for ourselves and they are always regarded as a treat. Variations of stuffed hard-boiled eggs go back to ancient Rome. Medieval cookbooks offered recipes that included adding raisins with sweet spices like cloves and cinnamon to the yolks. Why the dish is called "deviled" eggs likely refers to the process of "deviling," a culinary term first mentioned in Great Britain in the late eighteenth century for foods that were highly seasoned or prepared with hot ingredients.

During the 1940s mayonnaise became de rigueur for real Deviled Eggs in the United States, but our Fannie Farmer, ahead of the culinary curve in so many ways, mentions mayo to bind the yolks in the 1896 version of the *Boston Cooking-School Cookbook.*

Himmel und Erde *(Heaven and Earth)*

2 1/2 pounds Russet potatoes, peeled
  and cubed

3 apples, roughly 1 1/2 pounds,
  peeled, cored, and cubed

3 tablespoons unsalted butter

1 tablespoon honey

Squeeze of lemon juice

1 teaspoon salt

1/4 teaspoon freshly ground black
  pepper

Place the potatoes in a large saucepan and cover with cold water. Bring to a boil and then turn the heat down to a simmer and cook for 10 minutes more.

Add the apples and continue to simmer until the potatoes are done (check with a sharp fork) and the apples soft.

Drain, reserving a little of the water. Put back on the heat and stir briefly to dry.

Add the butter and mash. Faith relies on her old-fashioned potato masher. Add the honey, lemon, salt, and pepper and stir vigorously for a fluffy result. If the mixture is too dry, add a bit of the water.

You may also serve the dish with crumbled crisp bacon and fried or caramelized onions on top. Granny Smiths or other tart apples give *Himmel und Erde* a nice sharpness, but any apples are fine. Nutmeg and thyme also give it a different sort of flavor as a change from the basic recipe. Garlic too.

Serves 4–6.

My friend Andrew Palmer, who is a wonderful cook, suggested this dish when I was asking for foods with some mention of heaven or hell in the name. A traditional German farm dish, it is a find. We've been having it as a side dish with pork, roasted chicken, and sausages. Cabbage in various forms has been a fine additional side.

Lobster Pasta Fra Diavolo

Two 1 1/2 pound lobsters

1 medium yellow onion, diced

3 cloves of garlic, minced

4 tablespoons olive oil

1 (28-ounce) can peeled tomatoes
   (San Marzano, if possible)

1 tablespoon tomato paste

1/4 cup dry white wine

1 teaspoon salt

1 teaspoon red pepper flakes

1 (16-ounce) package fresh or dry
   linguine

Steam the lobsters using your favorite method. You may also substitute shrimp, peeled and deveined, for lobster. When the lobster is done, remove the claw, knuckle, and tail meat. Use the body and all the shells to make stock if you wish. Devein the tails and cut all the meat into bite-size pieces, reserving the claws to decorate the top of the finished dish.

Sautee the onion and garlic in the olive oil until soft. Crush the tomatoes in a bowl (an old-fashioned potato masher is perfect) and add to the onions and garlic along with the tomato paste, wine, salt, and pepper flakes.

Simmer for 15 to 20 minutes, stirring frequently as the sauce thickens. While the sauce is simmering boil the water for the pasta. Cook the pasta according to the package directions, usually 8 to 10 minutes. Reserve a cup of the sauce. Drain the pasta and add it to the rest of the sauce, coating the linguine thoroughly. Add the lobster pieces and stir.

Transfer the pasta onto a large heated platter and decorate with the claws, pouring the cup of sauce on top. You may further add some chopped Italian parsley as well, but Faith is a purist and likes to see only lobster.

Serves 4–6 amply.

It is unclear where Fra Diavolo, "brother devil" style, originated, but most sources place it in New York's Little Italy on or before the 1930s. Some insist that it was brought over here from Naples. Whatever the truth, it is a blessing!

Angel Food Cake

9 large eggs

1 1/4 cups cake flour

1 1/2 cups granulated sugar

1/8 teaspoon salt

1 teaspoon cream of tartar

1 teaspoon vanilla extract

1/2 teaspoon almond extract

If necessary, move an oven rack to the lowest position. Preheat the oven to 325 degrees Fahrenheit.

Separate the eggs, being sure not to get any of the yolks in the whites, reserving the yolks for another use. Set the whites aside for a half hour while you sift the flour, sugar, and salt four times in a separate bowl.

Beat the egg whites until they form very stiff peaks. Add the cream of tartar and the vanilla and almond extracts when the peaks are close to stiff.

Slowly fold the sifted dry ingredients into the whites, about an eighth of a cup at a time.

Pour the batter into an ungreased tube pan, preferably the kind with a removable bottom.

Bake for 50 to 60 minutes until the top is golden brown.

Invert the cake (Faith does this on top of a full bottle of wine) and let cool for at least an hour. It's still a good idea afterward to run a thin spatula around the edge.

A fruit compote or fruit sauce, especially a berry one, goes well with the cake. You may also use the yolks to make a custard sauce as well. And this cake is heavenly with just ice cream!

Serves a party!

Now, what else to do with the yolks? You can make hollandaise, mayonnaise, or béarnaise sauces. But you have just made a cake, so you might just save them (two days covered in the fridge) and add some to an omelet, frittata, especially a pasta one, or make a very rich spaghetti carbonara.

ABOUT THE AUTHOR

KATHERINE HALL PAGE is the author of twenty-three previous Faith Fairchild mysteries, the first of which received the Agatha Award for best first mystery. *The Body in the Snowdrift* was honored with the Agatha Award for best novel of 2006. Page also won an Agatha for her short story "The Would-Be Widower." The recipient of the Malice Domestic Award for Lifetime Achievement, she has been nominated for the Edgar, the Mary Higgins Clark, the Maine Literary, and the Macavity Awards. She lives in Massachusetts and Maine with her husband.